Praise for Lia Farrell

TWO DOGS LIE SLEEPING

"Another fantastic whodunnit from Lia Farrell. This series is now one of my firm favourites and I'm really excited to see where she takes the series next."
—Cozy Mystery Book Reviews

"The story is told from several points of view—Mae's, July's, Ben's, and others—and each point of view adds greatly to the story. Not only do the different viewpoints bring more information to light, but more characters are developed and the reader is drawn into the lives of a number of them. And through it all, there are a number of dogs who add even more charm to a delightful cozy mystery. This is the second in the Mae December Mystery series and I have read the first as well. The books stand alone just fine, but my choice would be to read them in order so that the growth in some of the personal relationships can be fully savored. Mystery readers can't go wrong if they take a trip to Rosedale, TN, to meet Mae December and the entire cast of *Two Dogs Lie Sleeping*."
—Cyclamen, Long and Short Reviews

"A mix of drama with some comedic moments (well, there are dogs; and a four-year-old), *Two Dogs Lie Sleeping* is an enjoyable read. You really want to know how Mae and Ben get along; if Dory will move up in the police and if Mae's sister will—at last—get over Tom Ferris and make peace with her husband."
—I Love a Mystery Reviews

"The dog days of summer have never been quite like this. From its opening with a single gunshot on a sultry August evening to its satisfying conclusion, Lia Farrell's tale of greed and murder explores a compelling range of human (and the odd canine) relationships with an intriguing cast of characters and an imaginative plot. Fast paced, multilayered, and thoroughly enjoyable."
—Kathleen Hills, author of *The Kingdom Where Nobody Dies*

ONE DOG TOO MANY

"The author has worked carefully on the setting so that I really did feel as if I were a part of this rural town and I could picture the scenes as well as the people. Character interactions and the descriptions of daily life definitely ring true, and the characters seem to be very real. Fans of the cozy mystery will certainly enjoy adding Mae December to their list of charming detectives."
—Long and Short Reviews

"A lively tale with plenty of twists, turns, and unexpected situations to satisfy the most ardent cozy mystery lover. The story is told in several voices, including Mae, Sheriff Ben, and Detective Wayne, with Mae's best friend Tammy piping in occasionally, giving the tale several viewpoints of the mystery. Farrell's additional cast of characters are fun folks to get to know, and the setting of the Tennessee countryside is charming. Animal lovers will enjoy the interaction with Mae's kennel customers, and fans of whodunits will love figuring out the intriguing plot as the story moves along …. A fine introduction to what promises to be an exciting series to follow."
—Sharon Galligar Chance, Fresh Fiction

"The story is a combination of police procedural, rocky

romance (at least two of them), and a stroll through the world of dogs. Even for readers who don't find canines especially appealing, this novel—written by a mother/daughter pair—still has its charm. The plot is fairly straightforward, the major protagonists are believable, and the perpetrator's motives are quite understandable."
—John A. Broussard, I Love a Mystery

"A tidy little mystery peppered with likeable characters, interesting back stories, and lots of canine lore. *One Dog Too Many* is an entertaining book to read on a lazy day."
—Mary Marks, *The New York Journal of Books*

5 Thumbs Up: "What a great start to a series. This debut novel contains exactly all the right ingredients needed to make a perfect cozy mystery.... Through a crisp writing style the authors bring their characters not only to life, but has them serving sweet iced tea to the reader as they progress through this book, and in this way it I found it very easy to connect with them and establish a relationship; even their gossip made me feel included in their everyday lives."
—Cate Agosta, Cate's Book Nut Hut

"With an equal mix of charm and intrigue, Lia Farrell has created a twisty tale of murder and wagging tails."
—Jane Cleland, author of The Josie Prescott Antiques Mysteries

"Dog lovers and cozy mystery fans alike will be charmed by this first book in an exciting new series featuring Tennessee dog breeder Mae December. *One Dog Too Many* gets off to a fast start as the Lia Farrell writing team pulls the reader into a dog-gone good tale of murder set in the beauty of the Middle Tennessee countryside."
—Marie Moore, author of the Sidney Marsh Mysteries

THREE DOG DAY

THREE DOG DAY

DAY

A MAE DECEMBER MYSTERY

LIA FARRELL

CAMEL
PRESS

Seattle, WA

Camel Press
PO Box 70515
Seattle, WA 98127

For more information go to: www.Camelpress.com
www.liafarrell.net

Cover design by Sabrina Sun

Three Dog Day
Copyright © 2015 by Lia Farrell

ISBN: 978-1-60381-971-8 (Trade Paper)
ISBN: 978-1-60381-972-5 (eBook)

Library of Congress Control Number: 2014951811

Printed in the United States of America

For Truly Scrumptious, Doozy, Bandit, Lucky Boy and Riley; sweet dogs who went on home this year. We will miss you. And for Millie Roo; we're glad you stayed right here.

Also by the Author:

One Dog Too Many

Two Dogs Lie Sleeping

Acknowledgments

—

W<small>E WANT TO</small> personally acknowledge and thank the many people who made this book possible. First among them is Carol Jacobsen, Professor of Art and Women's studies at the University of Michigan. She is an award winning social documentary filmmaker and the Director of the Michigan Women's Justice and Clemency Project. Her Project works to free women prisoners who were convicted of murder but who acted in self-defense against abusers and did not receive due process or fair trials; and to conduct public education and advocacy for justice, human rights and humane alternatives to incarceration for women. The fictional Abused Women's Commutation Project in *Three Dog Day* is loosely based on the important real life work they do.

We would also like to thank Detective Lieutenant Robert Pfannes of the Ann Arbor Police Department for his consultation on the interrogation of suspects and the use of evidence in interviews. We wish to thank Daniel Degnan, MSW, for his help in adding authenticity to the descriptions of the Huron Women's Prison in Ypsilanti. He is the social worker for a woman in the facility who killed a police officer. Lastly, we would like to thank Joe Elenbaas for his information on weapons and knives that have been used in all our books.

Our apologies to the Potawatomi tribe members who reside in Hannahville, Michigan. Unlike the poor people we depicted in this story, the Hannahville Indian Community is a rapidly growing entity with a vibrant social, economic, and cultural existence. They are a federally recognized tribe with a casino, an 18-hole championship golf course, an island resort, schools and modern homes.

We would like to thank our publication team: Dawn Dowdle our literary agent (Blue Ridge Literary), Catherine Treadgold, Publisher and Editor-in-Chief, and Jennifer McCord, Associate Publisher and Executive Editor as well as Sabrina Sun, graphic artist for Camel Press. We continue to be grateful for all their help and to Sabrina for her wonderful cover designs.

Last, but certainly not least, we want to acknowledge Will Schikorra, who single-handedly made our website. He also keeps it up to date and helps enormously with computer issues from day to day.

Prologue

———

January 2nd

H E LOOKED DOWN at the knife, shaking in his left hand. His forearms and hands were red with Web's blood. He set the knife on the ground and took a deep breath. *Got to be smart about this.* Trying not to look at the dead man's face, he pulled Web's denim jacket off the body and went through the pockets. No wallet. He laid the jacket on the ground and rolled Web onto it, face down. He quickly found Web's wallet in the back pocket of his brown corduroy pants. He stuffed it in his jacket pocket; he would get rid of the wallet after hiding the body.

The cold wind carried the sounds of barking and howling across the field. He would have to hurry. Someone could show up anytime now. He ran to the back of Web's truck and dropped the tailgate. There were some rags and tools in the truck bed, including a shovel. A bottle of water lay in the front seat. Pouring it on himself, he washed off as much of the sticky blood as he could, then went back and got the knife. After wiping the handle down, he poured the rest of the water over the blade and wrapped the knife in the rag. Getting caught was not an option. His whole future lay in the balance.

The top few inches of ground were frozen hard. Despite the January chill, sweat dripped off his forehead as he worked. Soon he had a hole big enough to bury the rag-wrapped knife. He stomped the ground, packing it down hard. With any luck, the forecasted snowstorm would come and blanket this field. He put the shovel in the back of the truck and flipped Web's body back over, dragging him by his feet until he was close to the truck. Crouching down, he put an arm under Web's knees and the other arm under his neck. With a grunt of effort, he heaved him up and into the truck bed.

He smelled blood. Spots danced in front of his eyes and his mouth filled with excess saliva. He slammed the tailgate shut. Swallowing hard, he picked up Web's jacket and climbed into the truck, where Web's keys dangled in the ignition. He turned the key and the old truck roared to life. After driving across the field to the edge of the bluff, he turned so the back end faced the river. The bank was steep here. He put the truck in park but left it running when he got out, leaving just enough room to walk behind the truck and open the tailgate one last time. Pulling Web's limp body to the edge, he hurled it down toward the dark, fast-moving river below. He heard the splash and closed his eyes for a second. *I'm sorry, Web. But you shouldn't have come after me with that knife.*

The river arced in a horseshoe shape around the broad, flat field. It was starting to snow, and the light was fading from the winter sky. If he could put the truck over the bluff on the other side of the field, it would be upstream from the body. Web's body should float farther and faster than the heavy truck. He drove to the other corner of the bend in the river and nosed the truck right up to the bluff, then put the shifter in neutral and opened the window all the way before climbing out.

His heart was pounding and there was a ringing in his ears. The adrenaline reaction was making him tremble all over, but he had to do this. He pushed with all his remaining strength against the rear bumper. The truck eased forward slowly, then picked up speed as the front end went down, crashing through trees. He leaped back and the truck rolled down into the river. He turned and ran through the gathering dusk and heard the slap and whoosh as the vehicle went in. The water would rush in through the open window and the old truck would submerge quickly.

There weren't any lights on yet at the distant house. The snowflakes cooled his cheeks and the cold burned his lungs. He was almost back to his own truck. He deepened his breathing, trying to slow his thudding heartbeat. The wallet could go in the incinerator at the lab tomorrow. He had always been smart—smarter than anyone he knew. If he went home, cleaned up, and kept his mouth shut, no one else would ever know what he'd done this day.

Chapter One

——

January 3rd
Mae December

Mae December, thirty years old and, to her mother's dismay, still single, delayed the release of her dogs for a few minutes. She looked out the window toward the barn, amazed to see it was snowing. The Middle Tennessee area was much more likely to get freezing rain than snow, but this morning a blizzard of white blanketed the yard. She released the dogs from the laundry room, pulled on her barn jacket, and let the dogs out. Titan, her male Welsh corgi, sniffed the snow and began to run around barking in excitement, his short legs churning up the fresh snowfall.

Thoreau, the creaky old Rottweiler Mae had inherited when her former fiancé Noah was killed in a tragic automobile accident, stepped stolidly out into the white world. The Tater, her blond corgi puppy, joined Titan, plowing a pathway through the three inches of snow with her little chest. Snow reached the tops of her short legs. Tallulah, her black pug, gave Mae a sideways look that plainly said, "Are you out of your mind, woman?" The pug sat on the top step looking down in a disgruntled manner at the white stuff. Mae nudged her out into the world with the toe of her boot.

After taking care of chores in the barn and feeding her two boarding dogs, Mae ran back to the house. Mae owned a boarding kennel and also bred designer puppies that were half corgi and half pug. She called them porgis and had been successful selling them across the country. Tallulah, the pug who had been the original mother of the porgi litters, was now retired. The small, snow-hating dog had already peed and dashed back into the house. The Rottweiler was also waiting on the stoop when Mae returned from checking on her boarders. She let them in and cast her eyes over her shoulder at the two happy corgis, who showed no sign of wanting to come inside. She would leave them to romp for a while, since they seemed delighted with the rare covering of white fluffy stuff on the grass.

Mae's kitchen phone rang almost as soon as she hung up her barn jacket. It was her neighbor, Annie Butler.

"Good Morning, Annie."

"Hi, Mae. I have a big favor to ask. Jason and I went into Nashville to see one of our friends play at The Bluebird last night. The roads got bad and we decided to stay overnight at his house. Anyway, we're headed back this morning, but I was wondering, could you drop by our place and let the dogs out? There's a key under the mat by the back door."

"Sure, no problem. I'm sure Baby isn't going to want to go out in this storm, but Bear will." Baby was a porgi. The Butlers had purchased Baby from Mae almost a year ago. Bear was the Butler's high-energy black Lab, a rescue dog.

"I was just going to take Titan for a walk. He's crazed with excitement about the snow. I'll take Bear too. She always needs exercise."

"Thanks a lot, Mae. See you soon."

Mae looked outside at the swirling white world and the outdoor thermometer, which read thirty degrees. Calling Tater into the house, she grabbed her gloves and barn jacket, pulled on her boots, clipped a leash on Titan's collar and walked out to the car. Driving down the street with Titan as co-pilot in the front seat, she noticed the snowflakes were becoming thicker. The sky was totally white. When she got to the Butlers, both Baby and Bear were delighted to see her. She let the dogs out, while she refilled their food and water bowls. Baby dashed back into the house when Mae called. The little porgi was shivering. Like her mother, Tallulah, she did not enjoy the cold. She loaded the Butlers' young black Lab, Bear, into the rear cargo area of her Explorer.

"Hey dogs," she told them cheerfully, "we're going for a walk."

By the time they got to her favorite hiking trail along the river, the wind was rising, but Mae thought she and the dogs would warm up soon from walking. The trail ran high above the smoothly flowing river. A tree had fallen, creating a rippling cascade of white foaming bubbles in the dark amber water. Hiking through the high oak and beech forest, Mae remembered how it looked in the spring when the hill was a cascade of trillium, anemones, violets and may apples—a tapestry of pale colors falling sharply down the green ravine.

The wind rose and Mae started walking faster. The dogs kept pace with her. They were having fun darting into the woods to bark at the falling snow before she pulled them back. Her arms were getting tired from pulling on their leashes, so she decided to unhook them.

About twenty minutes later, Mae arrived at the highest point of the trail where a rough staircase, put in by the park service, descended down to river level. The snow was falling so heavily, it was like being inside a Christmas snow globe. She called the dogs. Usually Titan would bark when she called, even if he didn't come right away.

"Bear. Titan, come," Mae yelled, louder now. There was no sign of them and no barking either. She began hiking back down the trail to determine where the dogs had diverged from the main track. As she hurried along, Mae was unhappy to see that the snow had completely covered the main path. Her footprints were filling in already, but twenty minutes later, she still hadn't seen or heard the dogs.

A little farther on, she spotted a spur off the main track going deeper into the woods, away from the river. It was filling in fast, but there were faint indentations in the snow. Mae jogged down the spur. In another fifteen minutes, she saw them, a large dark shadow and a smaller reddish one, darting ahead into the woods. *Little monsters.*

"Titan, Bear, come here." They barked, racing ahead of her. Mae picked up her pace and turned deeper into the forest, trying to catch up with the runaways. Tall white pines predominated over oak and beech in this part of the woods, their soft forest-green needles encrusted with snow.

A few minutes later, Mae stopped, having nearly run into a tree. Blackberry canes and tall teasels stood among the pines. She'd gotten off the trail. The wind howled, blowing the snow into drifting white swirls. Mae turned in a complete circle, but nothing looked familiar. The dogs were nowhere in sight and she couldn't hear them.

Moving forward slowly, with thorns catching on her jeans, she tried to get her bearings. Heavy cloud cover and swirling snow eclipsed the sun. Mae reached into her jacket pocket and pulled out a thin flashlight. Holding it ahead of her and pushing forward through heavy brush, she came out into an open field and saw a building looming up out of the storm. Somehow, she had walked off the field and into a residential area. She sighed in relief.

Her feet hit gravel under about four inches of snow and she walked to the side of the structure. It was a garage with vinyl siding, and to her relief, both dogs were standing by a side door. Taking a deep breath, Mae clipped the dogs' leashes back on. They jumped to lick her face, excited, breathing clouds of mist in the air. The side door was open. Thinking she would just get warmed up for a minute, she ducked inside. The dogs followed, barking.

"Quiet," she said and downed them on the concrete floor. The building was larger than she thought at first, a long open space. There were no windows and it was very dark. Mae felt the wall for a switch and flicked the lights on. She reached in her pocket for her cellphone. It wasn't there. She could see it in her mind's eye, lying on the front passenger seat in the car. *Crap.*

"Hello," Mae called out hesitantly in the dark cavernous space. "Is anyone here?"

No one answered, but at the sound of her voice the dogs barreled out of their "down, stay" and jumped up against her. Bear practically knocked her off-balance. Mae righted herself; her whole body was cold, right through to the bones. She wasn't going to be able to get any warmer in the unheated building. The large garage seemed menacing. *I need to get out of here and find my car.* She hurried with the dogs to the side door, nearly tripping over a large pile of copper pipes. They weren't wrapped in any kind of packaging. Mae flipped off the light and emerged into the storm. The wind howled; the dogs jumped with excitement.

There had to be a driveway leading to the garage, and beyond that, a road. If she got to a road, she could figure out where she was. However, after several fruitless minutes walking in each direction for thirty paces and then returning, she realized there was only a gravelly square with the garage in the middle. There was no driveway and no house she could see. *Why would someone build a garage in the middle of nowhere?*

She knelt down by the dogs. "Bear, home," she said. "Titan, go home." The dogs stared at her and she repeated the command, louder. "Home." Mae loosened her grip on the leashes and slowly Titan started walking toward the forest, away from the garage. The valiant little corgi, with snow up to his shoulders and short legs churning, was breaking a trail with his belly.

Could he really get her home? Bear stared up at Mae. She clearly had no idea what the "Home" command meant.

"Go on, Bear. Good boy, Titan."

Over an hour later, after hearing many repeated commands for "Home" and lots of verbal encouragement, the dogs led her out of the forest into a low, brushy bog. Beyond it, Mae saw a gravel road she recognized. She was several miles away from her car, but she knew the way from here. Overwhelmed with gratitude, she knelt down and hugged the excited dogs.

"Good boy, Titan. Good girl, Bear." Mae found herself in tears of cold and confusion. She got to her feet and started walking on legs that felt heavy and stiff. She dug for a tissue in her pocket and wiped her nose. She felt an ache in her throat and lungs. Another half hour of hard walking in what had become a serious white-out and Mae stood beside her car. She loaded the dogs, started the engine and looked at her cellphone. It was out of charge. *Figures.*

Fifteen minutes later, she walked into her house, having dropped the exhausted young Bear off at the Butlers. Mae poured herself a hot coffee, grabbed a towel and dried Titan's fur. Corgi ears were supposed to stand up straight, but his were drooping with fatigue. She rocked him in her arms. He was asleep in seconds, not even stirring when she laid him in his bed. Still feeling chilled, Mae got a blanket and curled up on the couch. Thoreau came up and sat beside the sofa. His large solid presence was always a comfort.

"I'm so glad I still have you, old sweetie," she said. The big Rottweiler licked her hand. Cold and exhausted, she fell asleep. About an hour later, the house phone rang. Mae sat up and grabbed the phone. "Hello."

"Hi, Mae, it's Ben. Are you okay?"

"Yes, sure, honey. I'm fine."

"You sound funny."

Ben was Mae's handsome boyfriend and the sheriff of Rose County. They had been a couple for nearly a year. They met when Mae turned in a report that her neighbor, Ruby Mead Allison, was missing. Shortly thereafter, Mae stumbled on Ruby's dead body and found herself a suspect in a murder case. It had been a rocky start. Once Ruby Mead Allison's killer had been identified, they were hit by another complication when Ben found out he had a son by his former fiancée, Katie. But they had gotten past all that and now were quite happily in love.

"I'm okay now, but I got lost in the snowstorm today. I'm finally starting to warm up."

"I'm glad you're all right. You should take a hot bath if you're still chilled. Listen, Mae, I don't mean to cut you off, but I wanted you to know that I won't be able to come over until late tonight, if at all. We've got cars in ditches all over the county."

As Sheriff of Rose County, Mae's boyfriend had a lot of responsibilities. And many people in Middle Tennessee were not used to driving in wintry conditions. Still, Mae was disappointed that Ben would be late.

"At least the kids are still out on Christmas break," she said. "The last thing you need to deal with is school buses on these roads."

"You're right, Mae. They were supposed to go back tomorrow, but it looks like they'll get at least one more day off. Maybe two. I've gotta go. Hopefully I'll see you late tonight."

"Be careful out there," she told him. *I don't want to lose you like I lost Noah.*

"I will. Bye."

Chapter Two

—

January 5th
Dory Clarkson

IT HAD BEEN two days since the big snowstorm, and things were mostly back to normal in Rosedale, Tennessee. Miss Dory Clarkson, Sheriff Ben Bradley's glamorous office manager of a certain age, had arrived at the office early. She was reading the "How to Become a Deputy" section of the Tennessee Sheriff's Manual. Her perfectly polished French manicure gleamed, showing up nicely on her coffee-colored fingers as she flipped quickly through the pages. The temperature in the sheriff's office was a little lower than optimum. Dory reached for the blue suit coat hanging on the back of her chair and put it on.

She felt around in the pocket and pulled out her lipstick and a mirrored compact. After applying another layer, she pursed her lips and looked briefly at her unlined bronze complexion and new shorter hair style. *You've still got it, kiddo.* The office phone rang and she answered in a distracted tone, saying, "Sheriff's office." Stupid phone was a nuisance, disrupting her studies.

"About damn time somebody answered the phone. Who is this?" The man sounded furious, at the end of his rope.

"This is Miss Dory Clarkson. I'm the office manager. What can I help you with?" Dory used her most soothing voice, trying to defuse the man's frustration. It was awfully early in the morning for this level of drama.

"I'm Logan Yancey. Don't know if you know who I am, but I'm building that multi-million dollar new subdivision up on the ridge, north of town. It's called Pine Lodge Estates."

"Yes, Mr. Yancey. Do you wish to report a crime?"

"I certainly do," he said. "I've had about one hundred thousand dollars' worth of high-end building materials hijacked off my site. The bastards took three fireplace inserts and all the copper piping for four houses in addition to two pallets of Carrera marble for the entryways. I expect you to get someone out here today to investigate."

"Certainly, sir," Dory said.

Sheriff Ben Bradley opened the front door to the office and came in with a blast of cold air. Dory touched her finger to her lips, and he grabbed the door quickly before it could slam behind him. Dory flipped the phone on speaker so Ben could hear the conversation.

"What time can I expect someone here?"

"I'll write up an incident report right now and talk to the sheriff ASAP. What's your phone number please?" He gave it to her and she jotted it down. "Thank you, Mr. Yancey. We'll get back to you right away, sir." Dory rolled her eyes at the sheriff.

"Who was that?" Ben asked, after she ended the call, "and how did he get you to do all that 'yes sir' stuff? You don't give me that level of respect."

"That was Mr. Logan Yancey. He's the builder of that new luxury development called Pine Lodge Estates. He had some building materials ripped off to the tune of about one hundred K. Could you call him back and get the details? I need to get back to my studying." Dory handed Ben the phone number.

"Thought you were supposed to be *working* here," Ben said. He rubbed the back of his neck and narrowed his eyes, but Dory caught a glimpse of a twinkle in his eye.

"Women, as you know, Sheriff, are capable of doing two things at once." She gave him a pointed stare. The sheriff raised his arms in surrender and walked down the hall to his office. Dory called after him, saying, "And if you'd hired another staff person to help handle the office duties like you *promised*, we'd have enough help around here."

Only a few minutes later, the phone rang again. Trying not to reveal her exasperation, Dory said, "Rose County Sheriff's office."

"Can I speak to the sheriff?" the adolescent male voice squeaked.

"He's on the line with someone else right now. I'll give him a message. Do you wish to make a complaint or report a crime?"

There was a long pause and at that moment Dory turned her attention away from the deputy manual and came to complete attention. A young person rarely called the office, and if they did, they usually hung up almost immediately, giggling. Dory was on alert and concerned.

"What's your name, honey?"

"It's Ray, but I, well I don't want to tell you my last name."

"That's fine, son. Are you all right? Do you need an officer?"

"No. I clean dog cages after school for a breeder. He says he's a breeder, but I think this place would be called a puppy mill. The mother dogs can't even turn around in the cages and if I don't come over there, they don't always get water and food. I can't come every day. I'm only in ninth grade." His voice cracked again.

"I'll have to do some checking with the sheriff or one of his deputies, but I'm afraid puppy mills aren't illegal. However, what you're describing may be animal cruelty and that's against the law. Give me the name and address of the property owner, please."

"The guy I work for is named Jerrod Clifton. The address is fifteen hundred, North Branch. Rosedale Township." His voice was so quiet it was almost a whisper.

"Thank you, Ray. I'll get on it."

They said goodbye just as George Phelps, their portly freckled deputy with reddish hair, walked into the office, yawning. Dory pounced on him immediately. As he walked past her desk, she stood up, put her hand on his arm and smiled up at him flirtatiously. Looking up at him was difficult; after all, she was exactly his height—five feet, five inches. She bent her knees slightly and poured on the charm.

"George, honey, could you help me out for an hour or so?"

"Um, what do you need, Miss Dory? I'm kind of busy right now. I have stuff to do on the computer."

Dory just refrained from rolling her eyes. The laziest person in the office, George used his computer mostly for playing online games. She had discovered this one day when she was snooping through his "Favorite" sites. After that, she felt it was important to monitor his work to ensure that his mind was on his job. She paused in chagrin, realizing she wasn't exactly on the job at the moment herself.

"I just need you to get the phones for a while, sweetie. I'm taking my deputy exam soon and I need to study. I'll use the conference room, so I'll be here if you need me. Please, George?"

George gave her a hapless stare and without waiting for his assent—which Dory considered a foregone conclusion—she left the room quickly, her leopard-patterned stiletto heels clicking. George sighed and sat down at Dory's desk. The phone rang again, almost immediately.

"Sheriff's office," she heard George say dolefully as she entered the conference room and closed the door.

EARLY THAT AFTERNOON—after the sheriff had evicted George from her desk, sent him out on a routine call, and returned her to the phones—Dory turned on her computer and Googled the Tennessee statutes for the definition of a commercial breeder. It read:

> Any person who possesses or maintains twenty or more adult female dogs for the purpose of the sale of their offspring as companion animals.

She wished she had asked Ray how many animals were in the kennel. She was still troubled by his cracking voice. "Poor kid," she said quietly to herself, "he just wants to do the right thing and I can't even help him. Some deputy I'm going to be."

She did some more reading, finding the basic standards for animal care. The American Society for the Prevention of Cruelty to Animals (ASPCA) could order a raid, using animal cruelty statutes, but probably needed more information than an anonymous tip from some boy in the throes of a voice change. She walked down the hall to Sheriff Ben Bradley's office and knocked on his half-open door.

"Yes," he answered, looking up from the papers on his desk.

"I got a call this morning asking us to look into a puppy mill. The person who called said there was neglect and possible cruelty going on. The property belongs to a Mr. Jerrod Clifton. Should I call the ASPCA and report it?"

"Definitely," he said. "Please call before you leave today. If Mae December found out somebody in Rose County was being cruel to dogs at a puppy mill, she would never get off my case. In fact, you should probably ask her what she knows about standards for breeders. Hey, Dory," Ben looked at her with eyebrows raised, "I've been thinking about you. I know you're going to take the deputy exam soon, but would you want to do the investigating on this one? I could make you the investigator in charge of the puppy mill case if you'd like that."

"Really?" Dory ran around to Ben's side of the desk and grabbed her boss in a tight hug. "Thank you, thank you!"

"Don't thank me yet. If the ASPCA does a raid, I'll expect you to go to the site and assist. You'll have to write up a report. And check to see if this Jerrod Clifton guy who owns the puppy mill property is in the system, will you?" A corner of his mouth rose in a lopsided grin.

Miss Dory Clarkson floated out the door on a cushion of air. Back at her desk, she called the ASPCA and spoke with the director of the Nashville office, a Mr. Lawrence Gunderson. He said he would dispatch an agent to check out the facility immediately. He would let her know if they raided the facility. Dory intended to go with them.

ON HER WAY home that evening, Dory thought back over the months since the successful closing of the Tom Ferris case last August. That was when the idea first occurred to her to become a deputy. Her subtle questioning of Evangeline Bontemps about Tom Ferris' Last Will and Testament and the night she went to the biker bar with Detective Wayne Nichols had been eye-opening. She had always excelled at ferreting out background data, but learning how to establish rapport with people for the purpose of eliciting information was intoxicating. When Sheriff Bradley thanked her on TV in the press conference, she knew her days as the office manager for the Rosedale County Sheriff's Department were numbered. A sense of satisfaction came over her every time she remembered her boss' words thanking her for her contribution to the "solve."

The journey from office manager to deputy, however, was proving challenging. There were both physical and knowledge tests she had to pass. Now, half a year later, she had been working out in a gym for months. The standards were surprisingly high. The candidate needed a high school diploma. That wasn't a problem. The person had to be fingerprinted by the Tennessee Bureau of Investigation. She had taken care of that part and her fingerprints did not turn up any criminal record. She was relieved. There had been that one time in high school when she'd found that perfect lipstick and had been just the teensiest bit short of money ....

The required session with a psychologist had been a breeze. Its purpose was to certify that she was mentally fit for the duties of a deputy. She had enjoyed chatting with the man and passed with flying colors. In fact, he told her she was almost "too well adjusted" to enjoy chasing criminals. Her medical exam was also a breeze. "You're going to live to a hundred," the doctor told her. The drug screen urinalysis showed no trace of drugs, as she knew it wouldn't. Dory hated what drugs did to people and never used them.

The problem was the two-phase test of physical ability and agility. There was a broad jump, sit-ups, push-ups, chin-ups, and a dummy drag. Then there was a mile-long run. Dory had hired a personal trainer, Alex Compton, a good-looking young black guy who worked diligently with her for months. He was encouraging, although he frowned whenever she had to stop to catch her breath. Passing the physical challenge was going to be tough.

When she saw the chart stating the physical requirements, Dory learned that the age for women only went up to age fifty-nine. Miss Dory was just a tad bit over the age limit. To her irritation, she found that males could take the test up to the age of sixty-nine. After a quiet, confidential chat with Evangeline Bontemps, her dear friend and attorney, she raised the issue with the sheriff, biding her time until Ben was in a good mood—after a night he spent with his girlfriend, Mae December. She showed him the chart that specified upper age limits for both men and women.

"See, Sheriff, this just isn't right," Dory said. "Look at this table here. Old guys can take these tests up to the age of almost seventy, but fit women of a certain age have been excluded. Ms. Bontemps says its discrimination." Sheriff Bradley sighed.

"Dory, I'm impressed with your commitment to becoming a deputy, but I'm not willing to enter a lawsuit over this." He shook his head. "We might even win, eventually, but it would cost a bundle and it could take years. You could be dead by the time we won the case."

"Can't you have your auntie, the judge, help with this?" she asked. "We don't need to change the rules for everybody, just for me."

The sheriff shook his head. "How old are you anyway, Dory?"

"I know your mama raised you better than that, Sheriff," she told him. "Asking a woman's age is off limits." Lowering her eyes so he wouldn't notice her evasion, she said, "I'm eligible, just wanted to get your reaction."

In fact, Dory was above the listed age, but when she completed the online application for the deputy test, to her surprise it didn't ask her age.

They probably knew asking was discrimination, Dory thought. She called Evangeline to tell her the good news.

"Of course, they could ask your age when you check in for the test," Evangeline said cautiously.

"With my youthful good looks?" Dory asked. "I doubt it. Luckily women of color don't age as fast as white women do."

"It's odd, isn't it?" Evangeline mused. "There's still so much prejudice against black skin, yet it ages better and stays youthful-looking longer. I just hope they don't ask you for your driver's license."

"Me too," Dory whispered. All the months of effort would be wasted if she didn't get a chance to take that exam.

WHEN DORY GOT home, she called Mae—Ben Bradley's girlfriend as well as the daughter of Suzanne December, one of Dory's oldest friends. Dory quickly acquainted Mae with the details of what young Ray had reported.

"A puppy mill! In Rose county? It just makes my blood boil. I have no idea why they aren't against the law. That's nothing like what I do, breeding one or two litters a year. My females only have three or four litters before I retire them. Those poor females have litter after litter until they die."

"I know. It's awful. I'm going to do something about it. Ben appointed me as an investigator and told me I was in charge of the case."

"Will you be able to assist the ASPCA when they raid the place?" Mae asked.

"That's the plan," Dory answered with determination.

Chapter Three

———

January 5th
Mae December

IN ALL THE seventeen years that Mae December had known
her best friend Tammy Rodgers, she had never seen her like
this. Even when she was a thirteen-year-old with braces and
no figure to speak of, Tammy was a well groomed, high-energy
morning person. Mae had returned from the barn after doing
her kennel chores to find Tammy sound asleep on her sofa.

Mae stood in the kitchen, quietly helping herself to coffee
as she studied her friend, who lay sprawled on the living
room sofa. Tammy was wearing ratty sweats. Sweats! And no
makeup. With disheveled hair. She was also snoring.

"Tammy, wake up," Mae said, touching Tammy's shoulder.

Tammy sat up with a sudden snort, staring at Mae.

"What's that awful smell?"

"That is not an awful smell. I might not be a gourmet cook,
but I scrambled some perfectly fresh eggs a little while ago and
made toast," Mae answered. "Would you like coffee or tea?"

"I don't feel good." Tammy's forehead glistened with sweat
and she had dark circles under her large brown eyes.

"I'm not going to lie, you don't look good." Mae shook her head. "I don't think I've ever seen you so un-glamorous. Where did you get those sweats?"

Tammy looked down at the oversized stained pants with a frown of disgust. "These are Patrick's. All my pants are too tight in the waist. I don't understand it—I've actually lost weight—but it's like my proportions are all off."

Something was definitely wrong with Mae's dear friend, who suddenly bolted from the room and ran down the hall. She heard the bathroom door slam. The unmistakable sounds of retching followed soon after. A few minutes later, Tammy emerged. She shucked off her sweatshirt.

"I'm going to throw this disgusting thing in your washer. Can I borrow a shirt? I must have the flu or something."

Looking at her friend standing there in sweatpants and a bra, Mae could have counted her ribs, but there was a tiny swell to her abdomen. And her bra was barely getting the job done.

"You do look thinner, except in the chest."

Tammy nodded. "I know. Usually I can barely muster up a B-cup. These are not my normal boobs. They're sore, too." She sighed and walked into the laundry room. She came back out in her bra and panties "Can I just go upstairs and find something of yours to wear? I decided to wash those gross pants, too."

"Help yourself," Mae told her, with a smile, "and while you're up there, I have an early pregnancy test you can use. It's under the sink in my bathroom."

Tammy stopped dead in her tracks, whirled around and stared furiously at Mae, her eyebrows rising high under her silver-blonde bangs.

"No, it can't be." She gave a vehement shake of her head. "We've been very careful." She plunked down on the bottom step. "If I'm pregnant, I'm going to kill Patrick."

"Well, you should probably pee on the stick first," Mae pointed out cheerfully. "I'm going to bet it'll be positive, but you might as well find out."

Tammy rose without another word. After shooting Mae a slit-eyed glare, she stalked upstairs. Mae went into the kitchen for another cup of coffee. Ten minutes later, Tammy was back, wearing a pair of Mae's ancient Levis and a brown sweater. The jeans were rolled up, and the sweater was too long on her petite frame, but at least she had found Mae's lipstick and brushed her hair.

"You look almost human. Feel better?"

Tammy held the stick in her hand. She showed Mae the plus sign on the end. The two women looked at each other in silence.

"I guess I better call Patrick and let him know." Tammy sighed.

"Here, put that stick down." Mae put a napkin out on the kitchen counter. Tammy put the stick on it and washed her hands.

"Your phone's on the coffee table. I'll give you two some privacy. I'm going to take little Tater outside."

Tammy stood there, shoulders slumped.

"Cheer up, honey. It's hardly the end of the world. You love Patrick, he loves you and you're thirty, with your own business. It's not exactly a disaster. In fact, I think your mom will be thrilled."

"I know," Tammy muttered, "but this pregnancy thing is a real game changer."

"It is that. Are we going to need to plan a wedding?" Mae asked, not sure if her determinedly single friend wanted marriage, even now.

"I have to think about it, Mae. You know I've always felt I was destined to be single."

"Right, but with lots and *lots* of boyfriends." Mae rolled her eyes. "Since you and Patrick got together, though, he's been the only one. I'm thinking a Valentine's Day wedding would be nice."

No answer from her friend, who turned away from the

window and headed toward the living room, cellphone in hand.

"Congratulations, Tammy. You're going to be an awesome mom, you know."

Her friend threw a tiny smile over her shoulder. "Thanks Mae-Mae. I hope you're right."

BEN WALKED INTO her kitchen after eight that night. Mae was standing at the sink, rinsing off silverware before putting it in the dishwasher. Tater, her corgi puppy, was sleeping right behind Mae's feet. Seeing a moving reflection in the window, Mae stepped backward and trod on the curled-up pup. Tater yipped in protest.

"Sorry, Tatie." Ben scooped the little dog up and planted a kiss on Mae's cheek. "Looks like I startled your mama."

"I didn't hear you come in," Mae told him. She shut the water off, dried her hands on the dishtowel and stood on tiptoe to give Ben a big kiss on the mouth. "I should have known she'd be right behind me. Tatie follows me around like she's my satellite. Unless there's a man nearby. Then the little hussy ignores me completely."

Ben laughed, looking down at the strawberry blonde corgi nestled into his chest. "So she acts like this with all the men in your kitchen, Miss December? I thought I was the only one. You two girls are gonna break my heart."

Mae shook her head. "She's the heartbreaker, not me. She *does* love you best, but she'll flirt with Daddy or Patrick if they're around. Put her in her crate, please. It's time for her to go to bed for the night."

Ben walked across the kitchen and ensconced the Tater in her crate. While he latched the door, Mae enjoyed the view of his cute backside.

"Speaking of Patrick," she said. "I have big news." Mae grabbed the open bottle of Cabernet off her counter and snagged two wineglasses with her other hand. "C'mon in the living room and I'll fill you in."

Mae and Ben settled in on the couch, sitting close together. Ben poured wine into both glasses while she told him all about her morning with Tammy.

"Tammy already told Patrick, of course, but don't tell anyone she's pregnant yet, okay? She may not be ready for the whole world to know."

Ben agreed, and then told her about the call Dory had gotten that day, reporting possible animal cruelty at a puppy mill in the township.

"Would you like to help Dory with the investigation?" he asked, putting an arm around Mae's shoulders and pulling her in closer to his side.

Mae smiled up at him. "Of course, if Dory wants my help, I'd love to. She called me a little while ago to tell me about the report." She tilted her head and gave him a thoughtful look. "I think you actually just asked me to get involved in your work, didn't you? That's a first."

Ben nodded. "I know. I usually don't want you getting in the middle of cases. But this shouldn't be dangerous. I suggested that Dory call you. Actually, puppy mills aren't against the law, and you *are* the dog expert. I appointed Dory as the investigator in charge, so I'll check with her tomorrow. I'm betting she'll welcome your help."

"She told me. When the ASPCA raids the place, Dory's planning to be there. I hope I can tag along. Puppy mills just infuriate me."

They stayed up for another hour, discussing Tammy, Patrick, the pregnancy and the potential investigation into the puppy mill. Mae was warm, sleepy and happy as could be. The wall Ben had been keeping between her and his work was coming down. She felt closer to him than ever before.

Chapter Four

—

January 6th
Sheriff Ben Bradley

SHERIFF BEN BRADLEY and Deputy Rob Fuller were on site at Logan Yancey's Pine Lodge Estates development. The wind was fierce, nearing gale-force in its intensity. Mr. Yancey, the developer of the project, was already red and getting redder. He was pacing, making jabbing motions at the empty areas where the stolen building materials once stood. He kept running his hands through his wavy hair that stood up in tufts. The volume of his monologue—liberally salted with expletives—continued to rise. The lawmen had gone to the construction site to obtain the builder's statement.

Snow still blanketed the ground from the rare blizzard. The wind held a sharp bite, and the sun was yet to make an appearance. The sheriff looked over at his deputy, Rob Fuller, who was watching the angry builder with obvious fascination. *Probably waiting for this guy's head to blow right off his shoulders.*

"Mr. Yancey," Ben interrupted, "do you have paperwork on all the missing materials? Or a site manager who has those records?"

The builder exhaled forcefully and came to a halt, glaring at the sheriff. "Paperwork? I don't handle paperwork." He stared at the clipboard in Deputy Fuller's hands. "I do *real* work, not paperwork. Kind of old school that way."

Ben fought back a smile. He and Rob made brief eye contact. "Sir, are you saying you don't have any records from suppliers to substantiate your claim of theft?"

Logan Yancey virtually vibrated with rage. He leaned forward, standing nose-to-nose with the sheriff. Ben didn't back down.

"I'm not *claiming* anything! The materials were right here yesterday and now they're gone. What the hell are you going to do about this crime, Sheriff? Instead of questioning me, you need to be catching whoever stole my materials."

Spittle flew from the man's lips, landing on Ben's cheek. He wiped it away with the back of his hand and confronted the agitated man, close enough to smell onions on his breath.

"You need to get yourself under control, Mr. Yancey," the sheriff said in a low voice. "I don't want to have to call an ambulance for you." When the builder opened his mouth to respond, Ben held up his hand. "You've made your report. As soon as you supply proof of the materials that you allege were stolen, we'll start looking into the matter."

Logan Yancey gave a quick, irritated nod. He strode away without another word, climbing up the steps of the trailer he used as an on-site office. The door slammed behind him.

"And you're welcome," Ben muttered under his breath. "C'mon, Rob, let's get in the car. I don't know about you, but my feet are frozen."

Ben drove slowly down the steep hill, appreciating the view that spread out below him. The black tree branches were tipped with snow, and each rock and fence post stood out in sharp contrast to the white background. A mile or so farther along, he slowed even more, then pulled onto the shoulder and put the car in park.

"What're you doing, boss?" Deputy Fuller looked up from the clipboard in his lap where he had been jotting down notes. Rob's nose was red, and the lenses of his silver-framed glasses were fogged from the warmth of the car. His short, golden-brown hair was disheveled from the stiff breeze up on the ridge. "Do I need to get out?"

"No, I'm just going to take a photo with my phone and ask Mae to paint a picture of this scene. I have to tread lightly, though. Mae only paints what she wants to." Ben opened the door and quickly took four different shots of the striking scene before climbing back in the warm patrol car.

"I thought Miss December ran a kennel and bred dogs. Is she an artist, too?"

Rob's innate interest in the people around him was a trait that boded well for his future as a detective, Ben thought. He put the car in gear and started down the hill. "She's a painter—a really good one," he answered. "Have you ever seen any of Malone's paintings?"

The young deputy nodded. "In that gallery in Rosedale. I went in there with a girl I used to date. Is that what her paintings look like?"

"Exactly." The sheriff smiled. "In fact, Mae's full name is Maeve Malone December. Malone is her brush name, the one she signs her paintings with. I bought one of her paintings from that gallery before we ever met."

AFTER LUNCH, BEN sat down at his desk in his office. His door stood open and Ben could hear the phone ringing at Dory's desk. What he didn't hear was anyone answering it. He sighed, got up, and walked down the hall.

"Dory," he called. "George? Anybody here?"

Silence. The conference room door was closed. He opened it and saw his office manager. Her feet, stylish in red heels, up on the table. She was poring over the deputy's manual in her lap and didn't even look up.

"Ms. Clarkson, I *do* hope I'm not disturbing you," Ben growled. She snapped her feet on the floor and gave him a winning smile, head tilted to one side.

"Not at all, Sheriff. I'm just studying. For my exam you know."

"Phones aren't troubling you in here?"

"Phones? I put George on phones before I came in here. Why?"

"Deputy Phelps is AWOL, so you need to get back to your desk."

Dory frowned. She stood up and walked toward her station. "I'll find the slacker." She stopped walking, glanced at her watch, and turned back to the sheriff.

"Sheriff, I wanted to tell you that I checked in with the ASPCA. Two agents went out to the Clifton property yesterday to take a look at the conditions for the dogs. Unfortunately, no one was at home and the barn where the dogs are kept was padlocked. They left a 'Notice to Call' on the front door. If the owner doesn't get in touch with the ASPCA in the next couple of days, they will schedule a raid, because of how cold it has been and the risk these conditions pose for the dogs. I asked Mr. Gunderson, the director, to inform me when they're going to raid the property so I could meet them there. Oh, and Cameron Gomez asked to meet with you. She'll be here soon."

"When Deputy Gomez gets here, send her on back. When George materializes, tell him I said he's on phones until you take your exam. As soon as he takes over, you can go home and study. And if you need any help with the puppy mill investigation, Mae is available to assist you."

She raised her eyebrows. "And you're okay with that? My, my, how times have changed. I'll call her later. Thank you, Sheriff Bradley." Dory nodded graciously. "Deputy Phelps can't elude me for long." She turned and stalked off in search of the errant George.

* * *

SHORTLY THEREAFTER, BEN heard a tap at his door and looked up. It was his newest hire, twenty-six-year-old Cameron Gomez. She had been working in the office for several months and was a refreshing contrast to the lackadaisical George. So far she had kept a low profile, and Ben wondered why she wanted to meet with him.

"Come in, Cam." One of Officer Gomez's first acts had been to ask Ben to call her Cam.

After giving his hand a firm shake, she stood in front of his desk with her shoulders back like a curvaceous little soldier. Her brown eyes crinkled at the corners, and her lips curled into a big smile. Ben was in love with Mae, of course, but he appreciated a beautiful woman nonetheless.

"Please have a seat," Ben said. "I know you asked for this meeting, but I wanted to talk to you, too. As you're aware, we're short-handed. Detective Nichols has requested a leave of absence and Deputy Fuller is moving into a new role—assuming he passes the detective exam. And then there's Dory's deputy exam that's taking her away from the front desk." Ben suppressed a sigh.

The fluorescent overhead light flickered, then steadied. Cam looked up and Ben saw something that her uniform collar normally covered. It was a bad scar, puckering the smooth honey-colored skin of her throat.

"I was wondering if you might be able to take a turn on the phones until Dory takes her exam."

"Yes, sir. Happy to, sir."

"You don't need to call me 'sir' all the time, Cam. You should know by now that we're usually pretty informal around here—not like Captain Paula's operation in Nashville." Ben had recruited Deputy Gomez from Captain Paula's shop. "Now, what did you want to talk to me about?"

Cam shifted in her chair. "I'm trying to figure out the chain of command, everyone's role at the office." She paused.

Ben bit his lip, nodding his encouragement. He could tell where this was going.

"So, other than you, is Miss Dory in charge?"

"That certainly didn't take you very long. It took me a couple years to wrap my head around it, but yes. Eudora Clarkson is my second in command. She's been running this place ever since I was a kid, probably before you were born. If you need help, go to her first."

"And Deputy Phelps and Deputy Fuller are my superiors, right?"

Ben stood up, walked around to his office door and closed it. "Technically, yes. George Phelps has been here a long time too. Not as long as Dory." He sat back down. "Is he on phones right now?" Cam nodded. "He doesn't aspire to be anything but a deputy, and doesn't seem anxious to advance his career, although there are times when he is a big help. Rob, on the other hand, is a real go-getter. Does that clear things up?"

"I think I've got it, except for CSI. We haven't had a major case since I started and I realized last night I don't know what crime lab we use."

"Good question. Hadley Johns and Emma Peters are the lab techs. Our lab is in the building, but you have to use the other entrance to get there—from the rear parking lot. And Dr. Estes is our medical examiner. He works for Rose County as well as the Mont Blanc Police Station. Hopefully you won't be meeting him right away, since that would mean we had a murder to solve. Until recently it had been a decade since we'd had a murder in Rose County. This past year we've already had two cases."

Her brown eyes widened. "So the sheriff's office doesn't have a major crimes unit?"

"That's correct. We're a one-stop crime shop around here, but you'll get the hang of it." He looked at his watch. "Sorry to cut this short, but I've got lots of paperwork to get to. Please check with Dory, if you don't mind, and tell her you'll be sharing phone duty with George until she gets this deputy exam out of the way."

"Thank you, Sheriff. And thanks again for hiring me." She gave him a shy smile and slipped quietly from the room.

Chapter Five

———

January 7th
Sheriff Ben Bradley

WHEN BEN ARRIVED at the office early in the morning, he was pleased to see that Dory was already at her desk. He immediately asked her to assemble everyone for a staff meeting so he could hand out assignments for the current cases. Ben was still standing by Dory's desk when young Rob Fuller, sheriff's deputy, drove into the office parking lot. He climbed out of his car carrying a white paper donut box and grinning from ear to ear.

"George," Ben called, as Rob headed toward the door, "Come on out here. You too, Cam. I believe our brand spanking new detective, Mr. Rob Fuller, has arrived."

When Rob walked through the office door moments later, all of them gave him a standing ovation. He raised both hands overhead in Vs of victory.

"Let's get this meeting started," Ben told everyone after the congratulations died down. They walked to the conference room and took their seats. "Our major case at the moment is the loss of construction materials for a development of million dollar homes. Mr. Logan Yancey, the developer, reported the theft. Since then I've checked with Chief Granger over at Mont Blanc and found that several contractors in the area have lost materials, in particular copper piping. I talked to Wayne at home last night. He called one of his CIs, a guy he called Jacko. According to Jacko, there's a copper theft ring operating in the area. Yancey's stolen materials included copper piping. Rob, you'll be lead on this one. George will be second."

"Did Detective Nichols give you any contact information for this Jacko?" Rob asked, poised to write down the information.

"Sure did. He lives in one of the old run-down apartment complexes on Charlotte Pike in Nashville. Dory has the address and phone number."

"Could you pass those donuts, please, Sheriff?" George asked. Ben handed the box to Dory, who was seated between them.

Dory ostentatiously withdrew a small plastic baggie of celery and carrot sticks from her purse, helped herself to a few, and pushed the white donut box down the line to George. She eagle-eyed George as he pulled three donuts from the box. When Rob pulled out two of her former favorites, blueberry, Dory could stand it no longer.

"You keep eating like that, Rob, and your belly's going to be bigger than George's." She gave him a disapproving stare.

"Jeez, Dory, do you have to start in on me so early in the morning?" Rob asked.

"If you keep eating donuts at that rate, your gut will get so big you won't be able to find your own man business," Dory said. Rob colored and everyone else cracked up.

"Okay, enough with the comedy. Let's get back to work," Ben said. There were a few more snickers, but Ben kept a straight face and the mood grew serious again. "Do you have the paperwork from Mr. Yancey yet, for his stolen building materials?" he asked Rob.

"His wife emailed the receipts to me this morning. She

apologized for how 'difficult' he can be, nice lady."

"Difficult is one way to put it. When I left the office yesterday, I drove through a new subdivision near Mr. Yancey's project, and I think I might have spotted at least some of Yancey's missing materials. Look at this," the sheriff said, pulling out his phone. He enlarged one corner of the image on his camera. "See? There at the bottom of the hill. What does that look like to you, Detective?" Ben pointed to several bulky snow-topped cubes covered with tarps.

Rob Fuller looked down at the picture and back at his boss. The corner of his mouth quirked up on one side and he nodded.

"Someone hid those stolen materials in plain sight," Rob said. "I'll check out who owns that property."

"It might not be all of Yancey's missing materials, but it's probably the pallets of marble flooring," Ben said.

"Sheriff, where is Detective Nichols this morning?" Dory asked. "I thought he'd be here."

"He's working at home today," Ben told her.

Having worked with the man now for several years, Ben knew that Detective Wayne Nichols often came in late to the office, unless there was a major crime to investigate. Since he often worked nights in bars and on the streets meeting with confidential informants, and was so good at nailing the perpetrators, everyone gave him the benefit of the doubt when he didn't show for routine staff meetings.

The sheriff continued handing out assignments for other lower level thefts, checking on the drunk tank, DUIs, spouse abuse complaints, and an assortment of other matters. As the meeting was coming to a close, Ben said, "I wanted all of you to know that Dory got a tip on a puppy mill from an anonymous whistle blower. She called the ASPCA because there may be animal cruelty involved. The property belongs to a guy named Jerrod Clifton. Dory, did you find anything in the system on him?"

"Couple of speeding tickets. The guy has a heavy foot, but that was all."

"Okay. I've appointed Dory as the investigator for this case."

"Congratulations, Miss Dory," Cam said in her soft voice. Dory beamed.

BEN HAD A lunch appointment at noon to meet Patrick West, Tammy's boyfriend, at Nadine's, a little dive on the outskirts of Rosedale. He was guessing that Patrick wanted to discuss the baby, or possibly Ben's own experience being a single dad. Ben had a son named Matthew. He had learned of his son's existence when he was four years old and Katie, Matthew's mother and Ben's former fiancé, moved back to Rosedale and informed him that he was a father. Although Ben's initial reaction had been far from positive, less than a year later, he couldn't imagine life without his little boy.

Wondering how Patrick had reacted to the news of his own impending fatherhood, Ben walked into the restaurant. The full-figured, redheaded proprietor gave him a big smile.

"Hello, Sheriff Bradley, how're you doing today, hon?"

"Just fine, Miss Nadine. How 'bout yourself? What's cooking?"

"Well, I just devilled up some eggs to go along with the sugar bacon we got in. Randy's making some hot chicken back there right now, and we've got biscuits and gravy, of course."

Ben spotted Patrick West, Noah's younger brother, who waved at him from a booth near the window in the rear of the crowded dining room. "There's my friend. Good to see you, ma'am. I'll try not to order one of each."

Nadine chuckled. "Go sit down, Sheriff. Shelby will be by with some coffee in a minute."

Ben made his way past the counter and between the tables, exchanging greetings and complaints about the unusually cold weather with several of Nadine's other customers. He sat down across from Patrick. "Been here long?" he asked.

"I got here five minutes ago," Patrick said. Lean, tall, and dark-haired, he wore his familiar wide smile. He strongly resembled his big brother, Noah, who had been engaged to Mae before a traffic accident claimed his life. "Haven't even seen a waitress yet. This place is packed."

"Well, I'm glad you wanted to meet here." Ben looked around the dingy, crowded space. "I love the food, but Mae won't come here. Says she goes up a size just thinking about it."

"I know. Tammy won't eat here either. Speaking of going up a size ...." He paused while Shelby poured a coffee for each of them and quickly took their orders. As soon as the waitress was gone he looked at Ben and said, "I just got some big news the other day. Tammy's pregnant."

"Whoa. Congratulations, right?" Patrick was smiling, so Ben figured this was good news.

"Yep. We're getting married, so congratulations are definitely in order. And I'd like to ask you to be my best man."

"I'd be honored. Listen, Patrick, I don't mean to pry, but I don't know what you do for a living. And you know kids are expensive, right?" Ben laughed. "At least mine is."

Patrick looked down at the table for a second, then back up at Ben. "Mae never told you, I guess." He gave a little sigh. "I'm in graduate school, getting my MFA in creative writing. But that doesn't explain where my money comes from, does it?" His cheeks reddened and he frowned slightly.

Ben was intrigued. "No, it doesn't, but you don't have to tell me if you don't want to."

"My grandparents set up a trust fund," Patrick said in a quiet voice. "In the beginning, Noah and I both had one, but the money in Noah's trust came to me after he died. My mother's family has oil money—tobacco on my father's side. That meant Noah could pursue his songwriting dreams while he was alive, and now I can stay in school as long as I want and then write. And I can support a wife and child."

Ben could tell that Patrick was uncomfortable discussing

finances and quickly changed the subject. "Well, are you going to want a blowout bachelor party, or something more low key?"

The two men discussed ideas for the bachelor party while eating their delicious, high-fat meals. They had both ordered deep-fried chicken, mashed potatoes and gravy, fluffy dinner rolls, and collard greens with iced tea and sweet potato pie. Finishing the last bite, Ben suddenly realized how long he'd been away from the office.

"I've got to get back to work, Patrick," he told his young friend. "But thanks again for asking me to be your best man— and for raising my cholesterol levels."

He drove back to the office, mulling over Patrick's life-changing news. *Maybe it's time for me to start looking for a ring for Mae.* His phone rang and he saw Mae's face on the screen.

Chapter Six

January 7th
Mae December

IT WAS A cold, clear morning. Mae's dogs hadn't barked, so she slept in until almost nine. After getting dressed, taking care of her own four dogs and having some coffee, she checked on her boarders in the barn. Her aunt and uncle had left their pair of Boston terriers with her and gone to Florida to escape the cold. The condo they had rented didn't allow pets, so Domino and Maggie Pie, their adorable black and white terriers, would be staying with Mae until the weather warmed up and her relatives came home. They were eight-year-old littermates who had never been separated. Domino, the male, didn't stir when Mae walked into the barn. He was curled up next to his sister Maggie Pie, who opened her large black eyes and gave a half-hearted wag of her stumpy tail before going back to sleep. Mae checked their water dishes. She would feed them later, since Aunt Jean never fed them before three in the afternoon.

Lulu was another story. The Louisiana leopard hound, also known as a Catahoula, had checked in yesterday. Her owner, a local sportsman, had trained her to be a retriever. Large and spotted with a short coat, she was typical of her breed in being very high energy—a field dog, not a house pet. She leaped to her feet when Mae came to her kennel, assuming an alert and intelligent expression. She seemed poised for action and not particularly interested in the food Mae put in her dish.

"Hello, Lulu." Mae gave her a considering look. "I need some exercise today and I bet you wouldn't mind a walk."

At the word "walk," the big dog jumped up and put her paws on the wire mesh of her kennel cage. She stared at Mae and gave a small growling whine that seemed to indicate her approval.

"Okay, let me go take care of a few things first and then we'll head out." Lulu's long, spotted tail swooped from side to side.

Mae went back to her historic farmhouse, which was at last completely renovated after three-plus years of work. She returned some emails and cleaned up her kitchen, then took a quick shower. She dried her willful thick blonde hair and ponytailed it, then applied some lotion and lip balm and got dressed. Going downstairs, she got her cellphone and purse and put on warm hiking boots. She found her hat and gloves and put her barn jacket on over her sweatshirt and jeans. She grabbed a protein bar for her breakfast and went back to the barn to get Lulu.

Her friend and hair-stylist Kim was an avid hiker and had recently told Mae about a nature preserve with some challenging trails. The trail she had told her about ran along the north side of the Little Harpeth River. Mae thought this would be a good day to check it out. Lulu's owner, Ray Crowell, had told her that Lulu was a "highly trained" field dog who didn't need a leash, but Mae brought a stout one anyway. Since this would be a new trail for her, she didn't want to worry about Lulu running off. Her recent experience with getting lost in a snowstorm was *very* fresh in her mind, so she buttoned her fully charged phone into the pocket of her jacket before she even started her car.

Mae looked in her rearview mirror as she was buckling her seatbelt and laughed at the look of excited impatience in Lulu's eyes. The young hound was whining again, and moving back and forth in the cargo area of Mae's SUV.

"Sit, Lulu." Mae said in a loud, firm voice.

Lulu sat, and they were on their way. Kim had texted directions to Mae's phone, and she knew it would be a drive of almost half an hour. The outside temperature display on her dashboard read twenty-nine degrees, but the sun was out and everything sparkled. Mae cranked up her radio and enjoyed the ride, alternating between a country station and a Motown and classic soul station she'd recently discovered, singing along at the top of her lungs.

She found the nature preserve parking area with no problem. The gravel lot was deserted. *Good thing I've got a big dog with me.* Lulu wouldn't harm anyone, but she had a look of deceptive ferocity, due to her large size and wild markings. She clipped the heavy duty leash onto Lulu's collar and found the marker for the blue trail, which Kim had said was her favorite. The big dog surged ahead, sniffing and pausing to pee every few yards. They stayed on the path, following the blue arrows every time there was a fork in the trail, and ended up down near the bank of the Little Harpeth River. The sun was beginning to warm the air, and Mae took off her gloves and paused to put them in her pocket with the cellphone. Lulu tugged hard on the leash suddenly and seemed to be headed right to the edge of the dark, fast-moving water.

Mae pulled back on the leash, shouting "Lulu, no!" but she was no match for the strength and determination of the eighty pound dog. Mae stumbled and grabbed a tree to steady herself. The leash slipped out of her grip and Lulu jumped down onto a rock ledge, sniffing at something at the very edge of the water. The hound sat down, threw her head back and howled. Mae got a clear view of what Lulu had been sniffing, let out a scream and jumped down to grab Lulu's leash.

A man lay face down, with one arm trailing in the water. His flannel shirt and brown corduroy pants were wet and covered with debris from the river. His face was turned away, but the skin on his neck and the hand on the side nearest her was a horrible shade of pale blue and dotted with mud. Mae pulled Lulu back and knotted the leash over a branch, then went back to kneel on the rocky ledge by the water. She tentatively touched the man's hand. It was cold and stiff, like a partially defrosted steak. Mae gagged, tasting coffee and the protein bar she'd had earlier.

Standing back up, she swallowed convulsively and shook her head. Mae took several deep breaths. There was nothing she could do for this poor man. No ambulance could save him. *I don't need to call 911, I need Ben.* She went over to Lulu, who had stopped howling and was emitting a low, steady moan.

"It's all right, Lulu." Mae retrieved the leash and patted her on the smooth dome of her head. She and the big dog clambered up the bank. They were almost back to the trail when Lulu took off, pulling hard on the leash. Mae slipped on the icy mud and put her left hand down to break her fall. She heard something snap and felt a sharp pang in her wrist. For a minute she lay there, smelling the wet leaves right under her nose. Lulu sat down beside her head and licked Mae's cheek. She heard a low whimpering sound and realized it wasn't the dog. Forcing herself to look at her wrist, she was horrified to see her hand bent at an unnatural angle. *Oh, God, it's broken.*

Mae rolled to her right side and used her uninjured hand to push herself to her feet. She walked slowly and carefully the last few steps to the trail and dropped the handle of Lulu's leash. Her owner claimed that Lulu didn't need it anyway.

"Sit, Lulu. Stay." She pulled her phone out of her pocket and entered Ben's number with her thumb, cradling her bent hand against her chest and standing where she could see the body. The sun was still bright, but she couldn't feel any of its warmth. The water rippled past, and the man's arm floated. Tugged by the current, it was the only part of him that still seemed alive.

"Hey, beautiful. I was just thinking about you," Ben responded on the second ring.

"Ben, I found a man, by the river." Her words rushed out in a voice that was pitched much higher than normal. "I think he must have drowned."

"Hold on. Are you sure he's dead? I can call an ambulance."

She took a shaky breath. "Yes, he's very cold. And his skin looks sort of … blue. But I might need an ambulance." She fought back a wave of pain and nausea. "I think my wrist is broken."

"What? Why didn't you say so?" Ben's voice got louder in her ear. "Where are you right now? Are you still beside the body?"

"I'm a little ways off. I can see him from here, but I pulled Lulu away and climbed back up to the trail after I made sure he was dead. That's when I hurt my wrist."

"Who's Lulu?"

"She's a new boarder that came to the kennel yesterday. I was walking her near the river at that nature preserve off North Branch Road."

"Okay. You and Lulu stay right where you are. I'm on my way, and I'll have an ambulance and Dr. Estes, our Medical Examiner, meet us there."

"Why do you need Dr. Estes?" Mae asked.

"We need to be sure it was a natural death."

"Oh," Mae replied softly. She cleared her throat. "Will you be able to take Lulu back to my house and stay there tonight if they decide to admit me?"

"As soon as Dr. Estes is done, I'll give Lulu a ride, and then I'll meet you at the ER. Hang on, Mae. I'll be there as soon as I can."

Mae put the phone back in her pocket, then lowered herself to the ground and leaned against Lulu. She looked at her hand again. Hanging against her chest, it looked as limp and lifeless as the dead man. She quickly closed her eyes. Strangely enough, her injured wrist was the only place on her body that felt warm. Mae shivered and put her good arm around Lulu. Together, she and the big dog waited for Ben.

Chapter Seven

―――

January 8th
Dory Clarkson

THE SHERIFF'S OFFICE had swung into high gear after Ben informed the staff that Mae had found a dead body in the Little Harpeth River and then broken her wrist. After seeing Mae into the ambulance Ben said that it had taken him and Dr. Estes only minutes to determine that the man, as yet unidentified, had been stabbed to death. They now had a murder, and Sheriff Bradley wanted his team working 24/7. Their second major case, the copper theft ring, also required investigation.

Ben asked Dory to release the medical examiner's photographs of the anonymous drowning victim they called John Doe to the Nashville police post. Sheriff Bradley told her he was reluctant to post photographs of a dead man in the media or online, feeling that it raised anxiety in the community. A competent police artist could draw the man as though he were alive, however, and the drawing could potentially be used to identify the victim.

Nashville Police Captain Paula Crawley agreed to have her

police artist do a drawing of the man's face and to post it in the incident room in Nashville. The stabbing victim had several tattoos, and these were photographed and posted, along with the drawing of his face. Ben had originally charged their new detective, Rob Fuller, with the copper pipe theft case, but said he wanted him to accompany him to the morgue where John Doe had been taken that morning. He assigned George and Cam to tracking down their victim using public arrest records, background checks, registering with all missing person databases, and calling local hospitals. Obviously their victim wasn't in the hospital, but his attacker might well have sought medical care for knife wounds.

On top of everything else that was happening, it was the day of the ASPCA puppy mill raid. Although Dory offered to stay at the office in case her assistance was needed, Ben told her to go with Mr. Gunderson to investigate the Clifton property.

"I'll have Cam take phones," Ben said.

"Did they keep Mae overnight at the hospital or send her home?" Dory took a close look at the sheriff, who was puffy-eyed and wearing a wrinkled shirt.

"I took her home around eleven and stayed with her, but neither of us got much sleep." He shook his head. "She doesn't react well to pain medication, and they just splinted her wrist for now. They're waiting for the swelling to go down to see if she needs surgery."

"I was hoping she could go with me today, but I guess not." Dory was struck by a sudden thought. "Do you think finding a murdered man in the river close to the Clifton property and a puppy mill on the grounds means there's a connection?"

"It's circumstantial, but I'm suspicious." He looked at Dory, squinting his blue eyes in a small frown. "That's why I want you on site."

She smiled at her young boss.

* * *

MISS DORY CLARKSON, wearing tight jeans, boots and a fitted wool jacket with a faux fur collar, met a small crew of ASPCA employees and volunteers at the property of Jerrod Clifton early that morning. Mr. Clifton had not responded to either the Sheriff's citations or the notices from the ASPCA. However, the severe weather coupled with the report by the teenager named Ray that Clifton had been gone for over a week, gave the ASPCA the right to intervene.

The crew walked through icy patches of grass, ducking their heads against the wind until they reached the double doors of a padlocked barn. A large sign on the building read, "Pit Bull Puppies for Sale. Good bloodlines." The lead ASPCA investigator, a man named Larry Gunderson, had a pair of bolt cutters in his hand.

"Are you Miss Dory?" A hand tugged at her sleeve.

"What is it?" She looked down.

"It's me, Ray Fenton. I'm the one who called you about the dogs." The short skinny kid had scruffy brown hair, light hazel eyes, and a bruise on his right cheek. He was unremarkable physically, but Dory knew this boy had the right stuff. "When you left me the message that the raid was going to be today, I thought I should come. The dogs know me. The mother dogs are used to me handling their puppies. I didn't want anybody to get bit."

"Glad to meet you at last, Ray," Dory said, smiling. She turned toward the ASPCA crew and called, "Mr. Gunderson, could you wait a moment?"

The large, square-jawed man turned toward them. He had a five o'clock shadow already, even though it was only eight in the morning.

"Mr. Gunderson, I'm Dory Clarkson, an investigator from the sheriff's office." She said the word "investigator" with a touch of pride. "I'm the one who filed the report. This here's Ray Fenton. He's the one who alerted the sheriff's office to the problems at this facility. He's volunteered to help today. He says he can get the puppies out of their cages without anyone being bitten."

"Thank you, Ray. We'll get the puppies out first. Let me introduce you to my assistant, Allison Ware. You two can work together." Gunderson looked back toward the driveway where Dory saw a white panel van with a large parabolic mic on the top of it. A reporter was getting out of the car.

"Those damn reporters are here. They better not get in the way," Gunderson said.

Mr. Gunderson snapped the padlock on the barn and swung the barn door to the side. The large man and slight teenager walked in. Dory followed. Stopping outside the dark open doorway, she stood alone in the icy barnyard for a moment. She could hear the fearful and enraged barking of frightened animals—a chorus of desperation from being confined for so long. Soon these dogs would be in clean cages at the ASPCA facility. They would be bathed, fed, and examined by the volunteer vets. It was going to be a good day. She had to follow every step of this operation she had mentally labeled, "Save the baby pits." After that, she owed Sheriff Ben Bradley a comprehensive report. Dory walked quickly into the darkened barn.

One of the staff members turned on the lights. Another was backing up the big truck, through the gate toward the barn door. The beeping of the truck, signaling people standing nearby to get out of the way, sounded loud and clear in the cold air. When the truck's engine was turned off, staffers brought cages and long poles with circular wire hoops at the ends into the barn. If an adult dog made a break for it, they would encircle the dog's neck and hold the dog until it could be crated. The smell of the place was making Dory's eyes water.

Dory could see Ray handing puppy after puppy to a young woman who put them into a labeled crate. The two young people were working together well. When the mother dog was alone in the cage, Ray grabbed her collar with authority and led her out, speaking to her quietly.

In a surprisingly short time, all the mother dogs and puppies were crated and in the ASPCA truck. Gunderson and Ray approached the adult male dogs, which were in a back room in the barn. The ASPCA Investigators stood near the crates, discussing how to remove the dogs.

"Hey Allie," Mr. Gunderson called and the young woman who had helped remove the puppies came over. "Did you remember to bring the kibble?"

"Yes, sir," she said and brought over a sack of dog food.

"Let Ray here feed them," he said.

"Here you go, Bubba." Roy tossed dog food to him and the other male dogs. When the dogs quieted down, Ray opened the door to Bubba's cage and Mr. Gunderson expertly captured his neck with a ring on the end of the long pole. The dog went meekly into the cage one of the agents had brought over.

"Mr. Gunderson," Dory called. "Can I speak to you for a moment?"

"Yes, of course." His voice was pleasant enough, but his face was tight with disgust and anger. "I hate these puppy mills. There's barely enough room for these mother dogs to stand up. A lot of these places keep the females in cages for years. They never get out. They are bred, give birth, nurse their offspring and are bred again, sometimes for years before they can't reproduce anymore. And then they're put down."

"What's going to happen to the puppies and the mother dogs now?"

"The usual routine, I suppose," he said. "Although we're a little short of space in the ASPCA facility. We'll have to advertise on TV for some help from our fostering community. A lot of them won't take pit bulls. And my wife has drawn the line. She says we don't have room for another dog." He sighed.

"I know someone who might be able to help," Dory said, smiling for the first time since she entered the cold, filthy barn.

"Her name's Mae December. She's a local breeder and I talked to her already about this case. She said that she could take care of some of the puppies and would work on finding good homes for them. Unfortunately she broke her wrist yesterday. I know she'll help if she can, though." Dory took one of Mae's business cards out of her jacket pocket and handed it to Mr. Gunderson, who glanced briefly at the card before pulling out his wallet and tucking it inside.

"December? I've heard of her. She's got a good reputation. If she'll foster some of the pups, it'll be a big help. Sorry, Ms. Clarkson, I have to get that last dog." Gunderson opened the cage and swiped the long pole with a neck ring toward the largest male. The dog ducked, pushed past the cage door and darted out free. He rapidly disappeared into the tree line.

"Damn it," Mr. Gunderson said. "Can I have some help here? The big male is loose."

They fanned out from the barn, calling to the dog. Dory followed what she thought was his trail, although the snow was mostly gone now and it was hard to see tracks on the frozen ground. After about fifteen minutes of yelling, calling and salting the ground with treats, the team came upon the dog Ray called Big Daddy. The male pit bull was back out in the open field, digging eagerly into the ground, piling dirt up behind him.

Mr. Gunderson warily approached with the neck pole, but Big Daddy was intent on his digging. Dirt and snow were flying behind him. Gunderson waited, watching the powerful dog. When he stopped digging and lifted his muzzle up, Gunderson quickly got the loop around the dog's neck. The male fought hard, growling and nearly standing on his back legs in his desperation to be free. As everyone else returned to the barn, Dory and Ray stayed a few minutes longer. Looking down into the hole the dog had been digging, Dory noticed something that caught the light.

"Ray, could you come here a moment, please?"

Together he and Dory moved aside some more dirt, slowly unearthing a rag soaked in what looked like dried blood and a vicious looking hunting knife.

"You don't need to look at this stuff, Ray. Just stay here and don't let anyone touch anything. A dead body was found in the river behind this property yesterday. Please don't tell anyone. This material might be evidence. I'm calling the sheriff."

Allison Ware walked over and asked her what was going on. Dory told her they had found a rag and a hunting knife that looked to be covered in blood. The young girl trotted off in the direction of the reporter and camera crew, and Dory made her call to alert Sheriff Bradley. Moments later, a young woman with dark hair and striking features, wearing what Dory thought was a little too much makeup, hurried over. A man with a video camera and another guy with sound equipment were right behind the brunette.

"Carrie Allen, Channel Three News." She stuck her hand out and Dory shook it.

"Dory Clarkson. I'm an investigator for the Rose County Sheriff's Office."

The reporter glanced at the skinny cameraman behind her, and he turned the video camera on. The shorter, balding soundman handed Carrie a microphone. She held it up and said, "We're on site today with Investigator Dory Clarkson from the Rose County Sheriff's Office. She has been assisting the ASPCA investigating reports of animal cruelty, but something else has been uncovered." Carrie Allen stuck the microphone in Dory's face.

Dory spoke directly into the microphone, feeling like a movie star. "I found a knife that was wrapped in a bloody rag and buried over there. One of the dogs actually dug it up."

"Can you comment on whether that blood is from a person or an animal?" Carrie Allen's brown eyes gleamed, and she leaned closer to Dory.

"I don't know what or who the blood came from," she

answered. "But I do know that the sheriff's girlfriend found a ...."

Dory clamped her mouth shut at a sudden flashback of her boss during a murder investigation last spring, saying, "No one but myself or Detective Nichols is to talk to the press." *Oh, shit. What have I done?*

"I can't tell you anything else," Dory blurted. "The sheriff's on his way here. This interview is over."

"That's it then. Come on," Carrie told her crew. She flounced to the news van without looking at Dory again, the two men in her wake. Dory watched the van pull away with some relief. At least her boss hadn't shown up while she was being interviewed. She was grateful for that small blessing.

When Ben arrived later with Detective Rob and Deputy George, they had lab tech Emma Peters with them. They took pictures, then bagged the rag and the weapon. Everything would be taken back to the lab for processing.

"There's an awful lot of blood on the rag." Ben looked from Emma to Dory. "First thing we need to do is find out if it's human or animal blood. Maybe it was somebody killing a dog." He grimaced. "Or maybe we got lucky and this is the murder weapon for our John Doe from the river. If he fought off the attacker, we might get fingerprints. If he's in the system, we might get an identification. Good work finding this, Dory."

Investigator Clarkson gave him an uneasy smile, but didn't respond. Hopefully that interview would never be aired.

Chapter Eight

January 9th
Sheriff Ben Bradley

DETECTIVE ROB FULLER'S complexion had taken on a pale greenish hue, and Ben didn't think it was due to the lighting in the morgue. Knowing it was much easier to get a full report from Dr. Estes on his own turf, Ben had gone to the morgue with Rob to garner any helpful details for their new murder case. He hoped Rob wasn't going to throw up or pass out, but it wasn't looking good. Dr. Estes was reading aloud from his report.

"Do you need to go outside?" Ben whispered, touching Rob's shoulder.

"Am I *interrupting* you two gentlemen?" Dr. Estes asked, peering intently over the top of his bifocals. He was aware that he did not have Ben's complete attention. The man was proud and touchy; he hated any sign of disrespect.

Rob blinked and took a deep breath. "No, sir, not at all, sir. I've never been in a morgue before. I apologize." He looked at his boss and whispered. "What should I do so I don't get sick?"

Dr. Estes looked disgusted, "As you well know, Sheriff, I have no time for neophytes. You will leave." Dr. Estes inclined his head toward Rob and glanced at the door.

Ben gave the ME a reproving stare, which Dr. Estes ignored.

"Can we have a moment please, Dr. Estes?" The sheriff turned to Rob and said, "Get a paper towel from the dispenser over there, wet it with cold water and put it on the back of your neck." Rob walked to the other corner, away from the body on the slab. Ben turned back to Dr. Estes. "Please continue."

Dr. Estes lowered his eyes to his report and began a lengthy discourse concerning the stab wounds and the condition of the body of their as yet unidentified victim—a white male in his mid-forties.

"He was in good health, but his teeth were bad. He was five feet, eleven inches in height and slightly overweight at one hundred and ninety-two pounds. No significant scars on his body. And he has had no dental work done except for one cavity that was filled probably twenty years ago. Doubt we'll be able to ID him that way. With these floaters fished from rivers, it's tough to get a precise time of death."

"Could you make an educated guess, Doctor?" Ben asked.

"Guess? *Guess?* You know better than that, Sheriff. I never guess." There was a brief pause and narrowed eyes. "However, I can *estimate* that the man has been dead for a week to ten days. Today is the ninth, and he was found on the seventh. So somewhere between January first and January sixth, I'd say."

Rob Fuller walked back to stand beside Ben. His color had improved. "I'm okay," he whispered.

"I'll send you a copy of the written report by email," Dr. Estes said, "but I can tell from these wounds that his attacker was at least six feet tall and left handed." He pointed to one particularly deep gash in the victim's chest. Rob glanced at it, clapped his hand over his mouth and rushed out the door. Dr. Estes rolled his eyes. "That young man is not welcome in my laboratory again," he said coldly. "As I was saying, the cuts were made with a five to seven inch blade, possibly ceramic. It was very sharp."

Ben took out his phone and showed the ME the picture he had taken of the knife Dory found the day of the puppy mill raid. "Could this knife have made those wounds, Dr. Estes?" he asked.

The ME glanced at the photo. "Yes, if the size of the blade matches up. I can't tell the blade size from your photo, so there's no way to be sure."

"Our lab is still running tests on the knife, but I can have them send you the measurements today."

"That would be helpful." Dr. Estes continued with his report. "He has defensive wounds on his hands and some bruising, as you can see here. This was a fight, not an ambush."

"Thank you, Dr. Estes. I apologize for my colleague. Please get your report to me as soon as you can and we'll try to get him ID'd."

Rob was waiting outside the patrol car when Ben left the building. "Feeling better, Detective?"

"Yes, I'm better now. Sorry, boss." His complexion had gone back to its normal, somewhat pasty white hue.

"That's all right. I felt sick too, the first time I went to the morgue. It gets easier. Dr. Estes can be a crotchety old pill. But he's the real deal. Very thorough. You better not go back to his lab until you're totally under control. Try taking some Dramamine first next time."

"Do you think the bloody rag and knife that Dory found during the ASPCA raid belonged to the killer?"

"Certainly could have. That Clifton property is pretty extensive, almost forty acres, and the Little Harpeth River runs through the back of it. Once the report comes back from the lab, we'll know for sure. If the knife Dory found was used to kill the guy, it's a lucky find. There could be DNA evidence from both the victim and the perp on it."

Rob was driving back to the office when Ben said, "At least

solving this case is going to be easy, compared to either of our last two murder cases. John Doe was thrown into the river from somewhere near Jerrod Clifton's property and Clifton's not around. He's obviously the killer. All we have to do is ID the victim, locate Clifton, and we can sew this thing right up. I'll have Dory get a BOLO out on his vehicle." Ben quickly texted Dory with the request, then called Emma to tell her to send the knife measurements to Dr. Estes.

Detective Fuller was quiet for a few minutes and then said, "What about our other big case—the copper pipe theft investigation?"

"Did you find Wayne's contact, Jacko, yet?" When Rob shook his head, Ben said, "I'd like you to go back to finding Jacko, at least until we get the fingerprints and DNA typing back from the lab for our John Doe." Rob pulled into his parking spot and put the car in park. He opened the door and chilly air rushed in.

Rob got out of the car, slamming the door and looking over at Ben. "I'll get going on it, boss."

The sheriff was pleasantly surprised to see Dory at her desk. He grinned at her, saying, "Why, Miss Clarkson, nice to see you at work, for a change." Dory didn't give him the satisfaction of rising to the bait, but merely gazed skyward.

"Dr. Estes thinks the man whose body Mae found near the river probably died recently. He must have been thrown in the river near or on Jerrod Clifton's property, and there was no sign of Clifton. Once we run him down, this one's going to be a piece of cake. Nice work on finding the rag and the knife by the way. Did you get that BOLO out on Clifton's vehicle?"

"Did I get the BOLO out? *Did I get the BOLO out?* You know better, Sheriff," Dory frowned.

"Okay, Miss Touchy, I was just checking. Thanks, Dory."

Dr. Estes' report showed up in Ben's email inbox about an hour later. It was disappointing. He stated that he'd found no definitive way to ID the victim from the manner of his death or his physical condition. Nor could he give Ben a tighter time frame on the date of death. The date range was listed as between January first and January sixth. The measurements Emma sent him of the knife appeared to match the wounds on their John Doe, but he couldn't give a definitive answer as to whether it was the murder weapon. Ben clenched his teeth. In most cases, the ME was able to give them a time of death within a few hours. That big time window was going to make this a lot harder. As a start, he'd have Deputy George look up hunting knives and compare them to the photo of the knife Dory found. He went in search of George.

Surprisingly, George was at his desk. The deputy quickly hit a key on his computer but not before Ben caught a glimpse of the game of solitaire he'd been playing.

"Damn it, George, I've told you before, I won't have you playing computer games when you're on the clock. And we have a murder to investigate. Why the hell aren't you looking for our John Doe?"

"Sorry, boss," George said, in a lugubrious tone. "Cam said she'd focus on identifying the victim and I could take care of what I was working on before."

"That's not work, so just cut it out. If it happens again I'm writing you up, understand?" George nodded, a blush staining his freckled cheeks. "I have a job for you," Ben went on. "See if you can identify the exact model of the knife Dory found. My guess is that it's a hunting knife. Dr. Estes says the blade that made the wounds on our John Doe was between five and seven inches long and may have been ceramic. That should narrow it down. Once we have the model number, I want you to get information about sales of those knives in the past year. If need be, go to the stores for the information, and if they aren't cooperative, tell 'em you're working a murder case."

"I'll get started right now." George looked down and began assiduously typing on his desktop computer. After making sure George was truly looking up nearby sporting goods stores, Ben went down the hall to see what Cam had found. So far, she told him, she had drawn a blank.

George knocked on his door about an hour later.

"The knife Dory found is a Boker six inch. I found two stores that carry that type of hunting knife in the area. They're required by law to keep information on gun sales, but not on knives. They have a list of names of gun owners in the Rosedale area with addresses. I thought I'd start with a hunting supply store called Meeker's—it's out in the township near the Clifton property. I'll see what they have on Mr. Jerrod Clifton and anybody else who's a gun owner in that general locale. The store owner said that people who buy hunting rifles often buy knives like this for field-dressing deer."

"Good work, George. You and Deputy Gomez can head out there. Grab lunch on the way. Mr. Meeker will be much more accommodating to an attractive female deputy."

"I bet," George smiled but then his mouth drooped and he bit his lip. "My wife won't be too happy about me having lunch with Deputy Gomez, though."

Ben put his hand over his mouth to hide his amusement. Mrs. Phelps would be giving George a lot of credit if she thought he could ever get close to, let alone seduce, the lovely Cameron Gomez.

"Tell the Missus I ordered you to go to lunch with Deputy Gomez. In fact, I might make Cam your new partner," Ben said, lips twitching. "If your wife has an issue, she can take it up with me."

"Okay, boss."

"And when you and Cam are done with that, swing by the Clifton property and see if Jerrod's back yet. Put a citation on his door ordering him to appear at the office. It's mostly farms in that area, but talk to the nearest neighbors on both sides to see if they saw any unusual activity around Clifton's place since the first of the year."

Detective Fuller appeared in Ben's doorway a few minutes

later. "I tracked down Jacko Jones. His girlfriend answered the phone at his apartment." Rob had a piece of paper in his hand. He glanced down at it, then back at his boss. "Delightful woman. She said, and I quote, 'That sorry piece of shit hasn't been home in three days. Check the worst bar in town and he'll be under it.' I guess that means Bar-None." Rob apparently knew the local bars well. Bar-None was a watering hole for the serious imbiber.

"You can take this one by yourself, Rob. But if you go in uniform, that place will empty right out. Just go home first and put on some old clothes before you head over there."

"Yeah, probably need something I can burn afterward. I'll let you know what I find." He gave Ben a quick salute, turned on his heel and was gone.

Rob called back several hours later. He had tracked down Jacko and persuaded him to drink some coffee. Once he had sobered up, Jacko admitted to being aware of a copper theft ring operating in the vicinity of Rosedale.

"He offered to give me details about some people he thinks are involved, but he wanted money and for us not to look too closely into whatever role he 'might' have had in the operation. What do you think, boss?"

"Okay," Ben said, "money's probably the only way to get the information out of him. But try to limit the damages, will you? And tell him I'll let him go this time. He's probably not smart enough to run an operation like large-scale copper theft. But maybe he can help us nail some of the lower echelon and they can point us to the ringleaders."

"All right. I'll see how much of a discount I can get on the price of Jacko's information."

Chapter Nine

—

January 9th
Detective Wayne Nichols

AFTER SUCCESSFULLY CLOSING the Tom Ferris murder case at the end of the previous summer, Wayne Nichols, chief detective in the Rosedale Sheriff's Office, had asked Sheriff Ben Bradley for a leave of absence. Ben said he needed time to consider Wayne's request. In most cases, a leave was granted only for illness or injury in the line of duty. Wayne had been grazed by a bullet during the Ferris case, but since then had made a complete recovery.

When Ben asked why he wanted the leave, Wayne told the sheriff—and John Granger, the police chief from Mont Blanc—that he needed the leave to pursue a "fugitive from justice." It was a partial truth; his foster mother, Jocelyn, had killed her husband Aarne, and to Wayne's knowledge she had never turned herself in for the crime. He intended to bring her to justice, he told them. In fact, there was a lot more to the story, for he had never dealt with his remorse over leaving Jocelyn behind when he fled.

It wasn't going to be easy—what he knew he had to do.

After decades of keeping his past deeply buried, he had finally told his girlfriend, Lucy Ingram, an ER physician, about his early life in foster care with an abusive family. He admitted to running away from the place at seventeen, afraid he might one day attack, or even kill, the foster father who violently abused his foster mother. His little brother, Kurt, had begged him not to go. Wayne had promised him that he would return one day.

"I went back there three years after I first left," he told Lucy, seeing in his mind's eye the dingy ranch house on the gravel road, the only childhood home he could remember. He and Lucy were in bed at her house. Lucy wore a soft T-shirt and was sitting up, her arms around her knees, her long brown hair reaching her shoulders. Wayne lay beside her, naked except for a St. Anthony's medal on a chain around his neck. He touched the medal from time to time as he told her the story. Since recovering from the gunshot wound he received at the end of the summer, he had been working out, eating right and trying to improve his health. His hair was more salt than pepper and his body had many scars, but his belly was flat now and he felt better than he had in years.

"It was getting dark by the time I found the place. Jocelyn's husband Aarne's truck was parked in the yard. I opened the screen door and called my foster mother's name. She screamed. She didn't recognize me in the dark."

Emotions wracked him—the guilt he felt about leaving his foster mother with no protection from her abusive husband and the sorrow that swamped him when Jocelyn told him his little brother Kurt was dead.

"Where do you think Jocelyn could be now, Wayne?" Lucy asked him, a frown creasing her forehead.

"I don't know," he said. "I never heard from her again."

"How old would she be?" Lucy asked, her voice low and gentle.

"I think she would be in her mid-seventies, if she's even still alive," Wayne said. His tone was bleak.

"Didn't you ever try to find her?"

"No. For a long time, I just pushed the whole thing down deep inside. Years would pass without me ever thinking about it, but the Tom Ferris case made me realize something." He took a deep, shaky breath. "I have unfinished business with Jocelyn Outinen. Both Aarne and my little brother, Kurt, are dead. I hate to think of Kurt in an unmarked grave."

"That's why you asked for the leave of absence, I assume," Lucy said.

"Yes, but the sheriff and Captain John Granger both have to approve the leave. Granger lost a detective in Mont Blanc to retirement in the fall, so I was filling in there. I raised the issue again with Sheriff Bradley recently. He said he would look into it. Whenever I wasn't busy on an active case, Ben said I could use the office and resources available to the police to try to find my foster mother. I haven't had much progress so far. I'm meeting tomorrow with Mark Schneider, Captain Paula's computer whiz kid. I'm hoping together we can locate her."

"If anyone can, it's you," Lucy said. She lay down and put her arm across Wayne's chest. He was stirred by her scent and closeness, wanting to share every second of the searing night he unearthed his brother's body, buried in sand toward the back of their property, but there were still things he couldn't talk about.

He flashed back, standing in the dark, putting an arm around his foster mother, feeling her violent quivering.

"I stabbed him like the pig he was," Jocelyn said. Her breathing was noisy; she was baring her teeth like an enraged animal.

Wayne and Jocelyn walked out to the driveway and opened the door to Aarne's pickup. His body fell out on the gravel. Wayne tried to get Jocelyn to go to the authorities, saying her sentence would be short since she'd killed Aarne in self-defense, but he couldn't convince her.

Now, almost forty years later, he was unable to escape

the past any longer. He had to locate Jocelyn, ask for her forgiveness, give his brother a final resting place, and pay for his own crime. Against every rule of police procedure, the gun used to kill his little brother was hidden in Wayne's apartment. He had never turned in the evidence or reported the murders, afraid that the gun would lead the police to charge Jocelyn with his foster brother's killing.

While waiting for his leave to be approved, Wayne had continued to perform his regular duties at the office. However, whenever he was caught up, he used personal contacts, letters and databases both civilian and criminal in what so far had proved a fruitless search for Jocelyn Outinen.

Because Jocelyn was his foster mother, he began by investigating whether she received a subsidy from the Department of Children's Services for support of her foster children. Their records showed that the payments had stopped decades ago. There was only a single note in the file. It read "Family moved. No forwarding address."

He had searched extensively for Jocelyn's social security number. She was Native American, had probably been born at home and many Indians did not have social security numbers. Confusion existed over names, ages, and family relationships because of the intricate sociological structure of Native American tribes. Proof-of-age problems were so intractable that special tolerance was provided for most Indian claims. Despite his efforts, he found nothing.

Wayne moved on to the National Missing and Unidentified Person's System. Called NamUS, it was a huge database maintained by the U.S. Department of Justice. To his surprise, someone had reported Jocelyn missing a few months after Aarne's murder. After contacting the Justice system, he learned two reports had come in with an address in Hannahville, a Potawatomi reservation town in Michigan's Upper Peninsula. Wayne knew Jocelyn Outinen was a member of the Potawatomi tribe. He could still recall some words from that lovely language.

"Wayne, can you stay over tonight?" Lucy's voice called him back to the present.

He replied with regret, "No, I'd better get up and go."

"Too bad. I don't have a shift until eleven tomorrow," she said. Her eyes were teasing, sparkling with amusement.

He smiled down at her and ruffled her hair. "I've got that meeting in Nashville early." Moonlight shone through a crack in the bedroom drapes. Seeing the swell of her breasts under the sheets, he pulled the blanket down gently and touched his lips to hers. She placed her arms around his neck as she softly kissed him back.

IT WAS COLD the morning of January ninth on Wayne's drive to the Nashville police headquarters. An icy rain was falling and mist lay on the fields between Rosedale and the big city. Winter had already begun in the Middle South and Wayne felt the pressure of time passing. The older he got, the quicker the days seemed to fly by. He checked his cellphone and found a text from Ben, one that he hadn't seen yesterday. The sheriff had called him on his way to the scene to tell Wayne about Mae finding a body in the Little Harpeth River, an apparent drowning. This text said John Doe died from stab wounds. A murder.

"Damn it," Wayne said aloud, thinking he should just withdraw his request for a leave, now that the sheriff's office would be investigating another murder.

Mark Schneider was waiting for him at the entrance to the Nashville police post. He was a skinny, nerdy looking youngster with spiky black hair and black-rimmed glasses. He reminded Wayne of a punk version of Clark Kent, only without the muscles. Three silver studs stuck out of his left ear, and as he turned to lead Detective Nichols down to his work area, Wayne saw a dragon's head tattoo rising up on the back of Mark's neck from under his T-shirt.

"I finally got something for you," Mark said over his shoulder as he ran down the stairs. Wayne's breathing quickened. At last, something was going to break.

They entered Mark's lair, stuffed with computer equipment. It was in the basement of the building. The cellar of the police post had been built at great public expense because Tennessee's thin layer of topsoil lay only inches above enormous granite and sandstone deposits that went down hundreds of feet. The result was a basement that was cool and soundproof, a perfect environment for the many humming, whirring computers that required protection from heat and humidity.

"Come in and sit here," Mark said, quickly moving a stack of printouts to the floor.

Wayne drummed his fingers on the computer desk. He was anxious to hear any news Mark might have. "What did you find?" he asked, bypassing the polite greetings that usually grease the social wheels in the south.

"Hang on, where did I put it?" Mark asked himself as he scrounged through piles of paper. "Right, got it. You found Jocelyn's marriage license and gave it to me a while ago. Using that, the State of Michigan Native American database and a skip tracing site, I linked her married name up to the name she's serving time under. Her name now is Joci Kemerovo. She's Potawatomi."

"So, she's alive then," Wayne said, exhaling in relief. "And she's in prison?"

"Serving time in Michigan. Murder in the second degree, but she got life. Here's the file."

Wayne grabbed it like a drowning man seizing a life preserver. He clapped the kid on his shoulder. "Good work. Where did you say she was incarcerated?"

"Huron Valley. It's in Ypsilanti, Michigan. There's a note in the file saying that they suspected her of murdering her son, Kurt, but his murder was ultimately listed as killed by a person or persons unknown."

Wayne shook his head, troubled. Jocelyn had not killed his

little brother. Her husband Aarne had done it. But he finally had a starting point. "Thank you, Mark."

"NBT," Mark said. At Wayne's confused expression he translated, saying, "No Big Thing." He grinned at the detective's reaction.

BY THE TIME Wayne walked out to his truck to return to Rosedale, a sense of hope was beginning to creep back in. His foster mother, Jocelyn Outinen, whose maiden or tribal name was Joci Kemerovo, had turned herself in to the authorities after killing her husband. He wondered how long she lived with guilt before she went to the white man's law. Most killings on Indian land were considered reservation business and were dealt with by the tribal councils or tribal police. But Aarne Outinen was white and had not been killed on the rez. Killing a white man was white man's business. If Jocelyn had gone to the tribal elders to confess, they would have taken her to the police.

Jocelyn had been in prison for decades. He gave a long sigh of relief. Tomorrow he could begin working on his new goal—getting Jocelyn freed. It was a good beginning, but the atonement for his own crime might not be so easy. He mentally revisited the statute he knew by heart.

Aiding, abetting, accomplice and accessory charges allege that you intentionally helped someone commit a crime. That help can come before, during or after the crime. Examples include covering up for a loved one who you know committed a crime.

Even without checking the statute again, Wayne knew he was guilty. He had helped Jocelyn Outinen cover up a murder. How could he possibly get the deceased Arne Outinen convicted of killing his brother and set Jocelyn free without turning the cold case evidence over to the police? That evidence would send Wayne straight to prison. His phone buzzed and he saw the number of the sheriff's office.

"Nichols," he said.

"Wayne, it's Ben. Nothing has come up in Cam's search of the databases or from Captain Paula's staff to ID our vic. Any ideas?"

"I got to thinking about that blood-stained rag and knife Dory found the day of the ASPCA raid. Anything that links the material to the victim?"

"Not yet. The knife had been wiped; no prints showed up. The DNA analysis will take longer. However, since the body was found near the back of Clifton's property, my guess is that Dory's find is likely to be the murder weapon."

"What about Clifton? Has he turned up?"

"No, he's still in the wind."

"Do you need my help with this one, Ben?" Wayne asked, hoping on some level that the discovery of a new murder victim would require his services and prevent his ill-boding odyssey. "I finally got a breakthrough, thanks to Mark Schneider, and located my foster mother. She's in prison at Huron Valley in Michigan. I'm seeing Evangeline Bontemps tomorrow to figure out how to proceed. I thought I'd use some of my personal time, unless you need me."

"You might as well work on your private stuff at least until we get an ID for our John Doe. I'll keep you in the loop and if we need help, I'll ask, but this one looks like a slam dunk. Rob needs a case or two to cut his teeth on."

"Okay. Call if you change your mind."

Chapter Ten

January 9th
Mae December

"MAE'S PLACE. How can I help you?" Mae heard her mother answer the business phone when it rang in her kitchen. "Just a moment," Mama said, and brought the phone to Mae, who was lying on the living-room sofa. She had hoped for a call from Ben with an ID for their John Doe, the poor dead man she had found in the river, but looking at the screen, she saw that the phone number was from an unknown caller.

"Is this Miss December?" A man's voice asked.

"This is she."

"This is Larry Gunderson calling from the ASPCA. I got your name from Dory Clarkson with the Sheriff's office. She said you might be available to foster some puppies from a place we raided. They're pit bull pups, so we're having a little trouble finding homes for them. Do you think you could take two or three until we can place them?"

"Was this a dog-fighting operation, Mr. Gunderson?"

"We didn't find any evidence of that, just a puppy mill that was crowded and dirty. There was definitely animal neglect, probably cruelty, but no dog-fighting as far as we could tell."

"Good. I'd hesitate to take puppies if they were bred to fight—for the safety of my own dogs." She did a quick calculation in her head. "I'm only boarding three dogs right now, so I can take three of your puppies. Have they been immunized?"

She heard Gunderson sigh with relief. "Thank you so much, Miss December. We're working on immunizing the puppies now. Got some kids in from the vet school giving them physical exams and shots. They'll be ready to go in a few hours. Could you come by and get them today?"

Mae made arrangements to pick up two females and one male in mid-afternoon. Mr. Gunderson thanked her once more before she ended the call. She handed the phone back to Mama, who was narrowing her dark eyes at Mae.

"What?"

"You know what! I'm here to help you, because of your broken wrist, and you just agreed to foster three puppies." She gave a quick shake of her sleek, dark head. "How are you planning on even getting there to pick them up, let alone taking care of all these dogs with one good hand?"

Mae smiled at her agitated parent. "I guess it's lucky I'm right-handed, Mama. I can drive myself over there if I have to."

"Not on pain pills, you can't!" she exclaimed.

"I'm just taking some ibuprofen," Mae reassured her. "The other stuff made me feel sick, so I stopped taking it. And since they were able to cast my wrist after the swelling went down, it feels a lot better, really."

"Well I'm driving you over there anyway," Suzanne declared. "I need to run a few errands, but I'll be back in time."

TAMMY ROLLED IN an hour later, looking much better than the last time Mae saw her. They had talked briefly when Mae called her best friend about breaking her wrist and finding a drowning victim in the river, but she didn't want to discuss anything serious with Tammy today. She looked to be in a wonderful mood, and she had pulled herself together. Her short, silver-blonde hair was clean and fluffy. She wore a gray sweater dress and high, black boots. Her dark eyes sparkled almost as much as the large diamond that adorned the ring on her left hand.

"Ow, that thing just blinded me." Mae laughed. "I'm going to have to find my dark glasses if you're going to wear that in here."

Tammy smirked at her. "I don't know what you're talking about. I can barely *see* this tiny little stone." She waved her left hand in front of Mae's face and the large, emerald-cut diamond flashed in the light of Mae's kitchen window. "How's your wrist? Are you feeling better?"

"Yes, I am. I don't have to have surgery, thank goodness." She tilted her head. "And speaking of feeling better, you look a lot perkier than you did the other day. I take it Patrick proposed, and you said yes."

"Well, it wasn't really a traditional proposal," Tammy said, smiling down at her engagement ring. "I couldn't reach him the other day, so I finally sent a picture to his phone—the pregnancy kit stick with a plus sign."

"You didn't! I can't believe that's how you broke the news." Mae shook her head. "C'mon, let's go sit down in the living room and you can tell me the rest of the story."

MAE SHARED THE news with her mother on the drive over to the ASPCA office in Nashville. Apparently Patrick, after seeing the picture on his phone, had been quick to react. He had proposed by sending Tammy a selfie. In it, he was down on one knee, holding a handmade sign that said:

The only way I could be happier about you having our baby is if you would PLEASE marry me! What do you say? If yes, meet me at Estate Jewelry on Main St. in an hour.

Tammy had showed Mae the picture on her phone, and told her all about the selection of the ring—a one and a half carat diamond in an antique setting that just happened to fit her perfectly. She had bubbled over about the small ceremony she'd like to have and wanting to do it soon, before her belly got too much bigger. She was determined that her wedding photos show her in the best light possible.

Mae decided not to tell her mother that she had offered to host the ceremony and reception at her house on Valentine's Day. Tammy had been thrilled at the idea. All of her best friend's reservations about getting married seemed to have melted away like last week's snow. Mae had never seen Tammy so happy, and she was determined to give her two friends a wonderful wedding. She thought briefly about Noah, her former fiancé, who had died in a car accident. Noah had been Patrick's big brother. He would have loved to be the best man at Patrick and Tammy's wedding. She swallowed a lump in her throat.

PULLING INTO THE parking lot behind the ASPCA building after her thirty-minute drive, Suzanne parked Mae's Explorer as close to the door as she could get. The snow might be gone, but it was a brisk thirty-two degree day with a biting wind. They didn't want the puppies to get chilled. Mae and Suzanne went into the one story brick building that smelled of dog food and disinfectant in equal measure. The sounds of whining and barking were muffled but inescapable in the small reception area, where a young girl with a stud in her nostril and her hair dyed cherry red sat behind a metal desk. She wore earbuds that were plugged into her cellphone and appeared to be watching a movie on her iPad while her own musical selections played in the background.

At the desk, Mae cleared her throat loudly. The girl looked up with a start, quickly pulling out her earbuds. "Sorry," she said. "I didn't hear you come in. Can I help you?"

"I'm Mae December," Mae said. "I told Mr. Gunderson that I'd take three of the pit bull puppies to foster. He said to come this afternoon to pick them up."

The girl frowned. "Is Mae December like, your real name?"

Mae gave her a bright, insincere smile. She had been asked this question far too often in her life. "Sure is. This is my mother, Suzanne. What's your name?"

"I'm Francie."

"All right, Francie, I need you to check and make sure those three pups are ready to go, and help me get them into my vehicle. If there's any paperwork I need to fill out, I'll start on that while you check on those puppies."

Francie sighed and rose to her feet. She rustled around in a file cabinet behind her desk, finally pulling some papers out that she stuck in a clipboard and handed to Mae.

"I don't have a pen. Just fill those out."

"I have a pen in my purse," Suzanne informed the sullen girl.

And that is more than enough of your teenage 'tude. "Could you let Mr. Gunderson know that I'm here?" Mae asked.

Francie opened her mouth to give her a tart reply then must have thought better of it. Instead she nodded and went through the glass doors behind her desk. Mae hoped she'd return with someone who would be a little more helpful. She made brief eye contact with her mother, who shook her head. Sitting in one of the old waiting room chairs, Mae took the pen that Mama had fished out of her purse and began to fill out the required paperwork. It was her first time fostering and she was worried she might fall in love with the puppies before they went to new 'forever' homes. She shook her head and reminded herself sternly of the four dogs she already owned.

Several minutes later, Francie returned, carrying a white short-haired puppy with a black eye patch and another one that was pure white. A stocky gray-haired man with a square jawline walked behind her with the third puppy, a black and tan. He nodded at Mae and Suzanne.

"I'm Larry Gunderson, Miss December, Ma'am." He smiled at Mae's mother. "If you've finished filling out the forms we can get these rascals loaded up."

"How old do you estimate they are?" Mae asked.

"My guess is about eleven weeks. Did you leave your car running? I wouldn't want these little guys to get sick on you."

"I'll go start the car and let it warm up a little," Suzanne told him. "Their coats are so short, I don't want them to freeze."

"They're so cute." Francie smiled down at the puppies she held.

I guess she's sweeter to animals than people. Suzanne hurried out to the parking lot then came running back inside. "Brrr, I'm already chilled. I cranked the heat up, Mae."

"Thanks, Mama."

"Do you want me to carry one of them?" Mae asked Francie. The girl gave a slight nod and handed one of the puppies to Mae. A female, she was tiny and lightweight, with a dark spot covering one ear that masked one of her eyes.

"She's my favorite," the girl said.

The puppy looked from Francie back up at Mae.

Mae smiled. "The other little female is so shiny she looks like a pearl. Maybe that's what I'll call her. I need to figure out names for the other two."

Francie and Mr. Gunderson followed Mae out to her Explorer. Suzanne opened the hatch and they put all three pups into the nest of blankets in a crate in the back. Snuggled together, they were adorable.

Mr. Gunderson told her the type of food the puppies were used to and Mae said they'd pick some up on her way home. She shook hands with Mr. Gunderson and thanked him for the good work he was doing in the community. Mae climbed into the passenger seat. Her mother closed the hatch, got into the driver's seat, and pulled out of the parking lot. Francie gave them a little wave.

On the way back to her house, Mae thought about names for the baby pit bulls. The male, she decided, would be called Guinness, since he was black and tan and Guinness was a dark beer with tan foam. She would call the puppy with the eye patch "True", since she so fully embodied the breed standard for pit bulls.

Chapter Eleven

January 10th
Dory Clarkson

THE DATE DORY was scheduled to take the deputy test—
January tenth—dawned cold and windy. She had offered
to delay it because of the murder case, but Ben told her to go
ahead. It had been three days since Mae found the body, but
until they got an ID on their John Doe, the staff was focused on
that task. Deputies George Phelps and Cam Gomez would be
tied to the office checking missing person's reports, hospitals,
and the information from nearby police posts in an attempt
to pin down their victim's identity. Detective Rob Fuller was
busy tracking down the copper pipe leads that Jacko, Detective
Wayne Nichols' confidential informant, had provided, freeing
Dory to take the test.

The ground was still patched with melting snow and the
skies were an intense, vibrant blue. Dory took a shower, blew
her hair dry, and put on a long-sleeved flannel shirt and jeans.
She tied the laces of her low boots tightly. In the mirror, she
saw a woman who looked very different from the fashion plate
she usually styled herself to be. No jewelry and no makeup. But

she was pleased with her appearance. She looked like a serious 'don't mess with me' black woman. She smiled a tiny cat smile at herself in the mirror.

She drove to the local community college and made her way to a large auditorium. In the back of the building were three tables manned by officers. Dory gave her name and received a name tag.

"Do you need my driver's license?" she asked, figuring if she was going to be tossed out, it might as well be now. Miss Dory was just a tad over the age limit for a woman to become a deputy in Tennessee. Her friend Evangeline, who was an attorney, had assured her that the difference in cut-off age between men and women to qualify was inherently discriminatory.

"If you pass the test, they can't legally disqualify you based on age alone," Evangeline had told her. "You've worked really hard with that fine looking young trainer of yours. You need to at least try to pass."

"What's your name?" an absurdly young man asked her.

"Eudora Clarkson," she said, reaching to pull her identification from her purse.

"Already got it," the young man said, looking at the computer. "You preregistered. Just let me take a quick look. Okay, I see it here. If you have trouble hearing the instructions, you can sit toward the front."

Dory gave him a look that would have felled a tree. "I can hear just fine, young man." A sense of relief filled her. She was in.

Walking up to the front of the stage, the registration clerk made an announcement.

"Everyone, I need to do a roll call. This is a two-hour timed test with no breaks. If you need to use the facilities, do it now. I'll give you five minutes. We lock the auditorium while the test is proctored."

Dory quickly visited the ladies' room, heaving a sigh of

relief that the person at the check-in desk hadn't asked for her driver's license.

Back in the auditorium, she waited impatiently while all the candidates' names were called and everyone was seated. As the proctor passed out test booklets, Dory took a deep breath. *What were you thinking, Dory Clarkson? This stuff is hard and you're no spring chicken.* She took a deep breath and lowered her shoulders, confidence coming back.

"Old, hell. They got no idea what I'm capable of," she whispered. The man seated next to her gave her a grin.

"I can believe it," he whispered back, chuckling.

At the end of the two-hour examination, Dory turned in her booklet and was told that she would receive her scores online. A young girl gave her a business card with a private URL, a user name, and a password on it. The information would be confidential.

"Just put this in your browser and your name and score will come up. It'll take about a week. If you're ready to take the physical challenge, I can take you out back to the track."

As the seven men and Dory walked on the remnants of snow behind the school, she reviewed her responses to the questions on the content test in her head. She was pretty confident she had done well. *Hell, if George can do it, I certainly can*, she told herself, although she was slightly daunted by remembering that George had passed the tests while in his twenties. *But I'm smarter than George even on a bad day.*

They reached an oval track. At the base of the bleachers stood a guy in a track suit, who started calling out names. Looking at the young men who were stretching and warming up, Dory felt ancient. The man called the candidates up one by one. When he called out, "Eudora Clarkson," she thought she was going to faint. She managed to walk across the field and was given a list of exercises to perform.

"This test requires a broad jump, sit-ups, push-ups, chin-ups, a dummy drag and a one mile run." His voice boomed out. "We're going to do the tests in reverse order. Each of you will do the one mile run first. We're going to time you, but it's not about how much time it takes, it's about your heart rate and blood pressure when you're done. Ready? I'll shoot the gun to start."

Dory heard a cap gun pop, and all seven applicants started running around the oval track. Heart pounding and breathing hard, she finished dead last. A student nurse took her blood pressure, placed Dory's finger in a little pouch to measure her oxygen level, and listened to her heart.

"You're on the border," she whispered. "Are you sure you want to do this?"

"I've got a job waiting for me if I pass," Dory said, her eyes pleading with the young woman.

"This one passes," she called out and Dory gave the girl a quick squeeze on the arm, feeling a surge of pleasure.

"Okay, everybody, now we do the dummy drag. We do this because often you have to be able to carry or drag a wounded person to an ambulance. The dummy weighs seventy-five pounds. You're going to drag it the length of the football field."

Everyone grabbed their dummy and lined up. Dory remembered the night her ex-husband, Elmer, had suffered a minor heart attack. She had practically carried him to the ambulance, praying he was going to make it. She finished last, but the men were starting to nudge each other, smiling. One even cheered her on.

The next test was sit-ups, followed by push-ups. Dory had worked for months on these with her trainer and it paid off. She was breathing hard when she finished, but she passed.

"Almost done," the student nurse told her kindly. "Just the chin-ups now and you'll be qualified."

The chin-ups looked daunting. The bars were quite high in the air and Dory couldn't quite reach them. The others quickly finished their chin-ups and left the field, slapping each other on the back, swaggering. She watched them go with an envious heart. The instructor looked at his watch.

"I'll get you a step stool," the nurse said, but the military style instructor shook his head.

"Ms. Clarkson, you've got to reach the bar on your own and do the ten chin-ups."

After jumping in the air repeatedly for what seemed like a hundred times, Dory gave up. No matter how hard she tried, she couldn't reach the stupid bar; it was a good two and a half feet above her head.

"I thought the purpose of this test was to find out if the candidate was strong enough to do chin-ups. I can do it. This isn't supposed to be a test of how high a person can jump."

"Sorry, ma'am. You can retake in three months." He was already turning away.

"Damn it," Dory called after him. "There were no height restrictions for the test. You're discriminating against me because of my height!"

"Try to imagine how little I care," the man called back over his shoulder. Tears came into Dory's eyes. Her stomach hurt and her pride was black and blue.

On her way home, Dory texted Wayne. "Passed content test and all but chin-ups on physical. Bar too high. Couldn't reach it."

Wayne texted back, "I'll go with you next time."

Then she called her boss and gave him the news.

"Don't worry about it," Ben said, after a brief pause. "You can be an investigator until you pass the deputy test, Dory."

"Thank you, Sheriff. That means a lot."

AFTER GETTING HOME, changing clothes and indulging in a hot bath, Dory got tired of wallowing in self-pity and called her friend Evangeline.

"Hey, what are you doing for dinner?" she asked.

"Girl, I have comfort food. Lots. Come on over. My husband's playing poker with his buddies."

Over cheesy scalloped potatoes and ham, green beans and warm rolls, enhanced by several glasses of Pinot Grigio, Dory began to feel better.

"Detective Nichols said he would go with me the next time I try the physical challenge for the deputy test, but I'm wondering if I should just give up. What do you think, Evangeline?"

"Dory, do you think it's possible you're so set on doing this because you live alone and don't have a man in your life?" Her friend touched her arm. "Maybe you just need someone to talk things over with, day to day. Someone to help you figure out what to do."

"No way. I'm of the opinion that men are too much trouble."

"Mine isn't," she said with a serene smile. "It's all in the way you train them. How long since you've had a lover, my friend?"

"Three in the last four years and not one was as good as a hot bath, a glass of wine, and a good book," Dory sighed.

"That must've been the men's fault. I imagine you know what you're doing in that department." Evangeline chuckled.

"They do call me the Panther," Dory said, batting her eyelashes at her friend, who giggled.

"My husband has some single friends who would give anything to date you," Evangeline told her. The women laughed over food and drink until nearly midnight.

Finally Dory said, "Thank you, my friend, you helped a lot, but I can't give up this deputy thing, I'll retake the test when they offer it again. In the meantime, did I tell you that Sheriff Ben appointed me as an investigator and gave me the case of the puppy mill?"

"Wonderful! Investigators make more money than deputies and they don't have to wear those clunky uniforms and those dreadful shoes. As an investigator, depending on what sites you have to check out, you can even wear stilettoes. Funny how much more information a nicely dressed attractive woman can get out of a man." She grinned.

"Makin' me feel better with every word that's comin' out of your mouth, girl."

The women hugged each other good night.

Chapter Twelve

—

January 10th
Detective Wayne Nichols

DETECTIVE WAYNE NICHOLS needed an attorney's advice about how to get his foster mother, Jocelyn, out of prison. While he knew a number of defense lawyers and prosecuting attorneys from the DA's office, he wanted someone in general practice who could keep quiet about what he was going to say. He had met Evangeline Bontemps at the end of the previous summer when she provided information critical to the solving of the Tom Ferris homicide. Since then, she and Dory had become friends. He was slightly concerned that his secrets might reach Dory, but Ms. Bontemps' reputation for confidentiality was impeccable. Plus, he'd already told Dory part of the story and sworn her to silence. She knew better than to share anything he had told her in confidence.

Evangeline Bontemps' office was a suite in an historic office building in downtown Rosedale. Wayne had been in the building several times while investigating the Ferris case, so he had no trouble finding the well-lit and tastefully decorated office.

"Good Morning, Detective," Evangeline's secretary, Kimberly Reed, greeted him. She was a soft-spoken young woman who wore her dark hair in a braid that hung down her back. "Miss Bontemps is expecting you. She's finishing up a previous appointment and then I'll show you in. Would you like coffee?"

"Thank you," Wayne nodded. Taking his coffee, he sat down in the waiting room and looked at the beautifully framed photographs of the historic downtown area of Rosedale that hung on the wall opposite his chair. Shortly thereafter a man in a dark pin-striped business suit walked out of Evangeline's office, scowling. Evangeline herself came out a few moments later.

"Good Morning, Detective," she greeted him in her low-pitched voice. Evangeline was of Creole descent and hailed from New Orleans. She was slim and dressed in a well-cut plum colored suit. Her hair was very short, which Wayne didn't usually care for on women, but the severe style did nothing to take away from her confident femininity. In fact, it suited her well. "Please come in and have a seat."

Wayne did so, glad that Evangeline closed the door to ensure privacy.

"I'd like to hire you as my attorney, Ms. Bontemps."

"Certainly. What can I help you with, Detective?"

Wayne took a deep breath and began. "There's a woman named Joci Kemerovo who's serving a life sentence at the Women's Huron Valley Correctional prison in Michigan. I knew her as Jocelyn Outinen, my foster mother. She's been in prison for over thirty-five years. She killed her husband in self-defense. He had been abusing her for years. What finally drove her to fight back was finding out that he had killed her other foster son—my young brother, Kurt."

Evangeline settled back in her chair, her warm brown eyes focused on Wayne. "Go on."

"Jocelyn got second degree murder and a life sentence. She's probably in her mid-seventies now."

Evangeline took a deep breath. "How do you know she didn't kill the boy?"

Wayne was impressed that she got to the heart of the problem so quickly. He had been dreading this part. "May I assume that anything I tell you will be held in confidence?"

"You may. This is privileged communication."

"I wasn't a witness to either murder." Wayne went on, "I arrived after the husband died. Jocelyn took me to see where my brother was buried in a shallow grave. I uncovered him. He'd been dead longer than Aarne, killed by multiple gunshot wounds to the chest. Afterwards, Jocelyn showed me the drawer in the house where the gun was kept. I was only twenty then and not in law enforcement. I was afraid if I left the gun there, the police would think Jocelyn killed my brother. I stupidly took the gun with me that day, a thirty-eight special with a six-inch barrel. I have it still." He stared down at his empty hands.

"So the gun will have both Mr. and Mrs. Outinen's fingerprints on it?"

"She said she never touched the weapon. I took it out of the nightstand drawer using a handkerchief. The gun has never been tested, but if a lab were to look at it, I believe it would show only Aarne's fingerprints. Do you have any thoughts?" Wayne asked.

"Getting Mrs. Outinen released on the basis that the killing of her husband was committed in self-defense is possible, although the state of Michigan is known to be loath to release prisoners. Your first step will be to visit her in prison and determine whether she's mentally capable of contributing to her defense. I saw an article in my alumni newsletter about a group of women in Lansing, Michigan who have established the Abused Women's Commutation Project. Their mission is to get cases reopened where women killed their abusive spouses but did not get fair trials. The legal counsel for the project is a woman I know named Enid Lawton. We were in law school together. I could call her and see what she thinks the chances are for Jocelyn."

"I have Jocelyn's file. I'll copy it and send it to you so you can forward it to Ms. Lawton. In addition to setting my foster mother free, I also want to get the record set straight about what really happened to Kurt. I want to have Aarne Outinen on record as his killer." Wayne tried to steady his breathing.

"That's going to be much more difficult. I assume you wish to avoid serving time for failure to report the crime? And that you don't plan to turn over the gun." Evangeline's eyes focused on him like a laser beam.

"Yes." Wayne paused. His heart was beating hard and he could feel a sheen of sweat breaking out on his forehead. "I tried to get Jocelyn to turn herself in after Aarne's murder, but when I couldn't, I helped her escape. I'm guilty of covering up two murders and withholding evidence." Wayne heard his voice wavering and hated himself for it.

"I'm going to need some time to look into this, Detective. Meanwhile, I suggest you leave as soon as possible for Michigan to see Jocelyn. It's an election year, and although the governor is a strict law and order man, this is a hot button women's issue. He won't want it to hit the media. With the correct pressure from Ms. Lawton, he might commute Jocelyn's sentence to time served."

"How long should I plan to be in Michigan?" Wayne asked. "I'm using personal time for this. And I'd like to remain in touch with the office, since we have two major investigations going on."

"A journey into the past won't be quick. This sort of thing takes time." Evangeline's tone was serious. "I'd plan on two days. You need to meet with Jocelyn's doctor to get her health records, the social worker to attest to her mental health, and the deputy warden to find out what kind of a prisoner she's been. I also wonder why Jocelyn took you and Kurt in as foster children. Do you think either of you could be a blood relative of hers?"

Wayne was startled into silence. It had never occurred to him that he and Jocelyn might be related.

"After that, provided I can get you an appointment, you can drive up to Lansing to meet with Ms. Lawton. She'll probably want you to meet with staff members from the Governor's office, and that could take some time to arrange. I'll let you know what I find out." Evangeline rose, reached across her desk and shook Wayne's hand. Her hand was soft and cool in his sweaty palm and when he looked directly into her eyes he saw the pity there. The facts lay between them—a palpable ancient history with the power to send Wayne Nichols to prison. And they both knew it.

WAYNE WENT HOME to pack a suitcase for the trip to Michigan. He called Ben and heard the discouraging news that nothing had turned up on their John Doe. Wayne offered to return to the office, but the sheriff said it wasn't necessary. Until they got an ID, they were stymied. Evangeline called to say that she'd gotten him an appointment with Enid Lawton on January twelfth, the day after tomorrow.

"I'd get on the road as soon as possible, Wayne. It's about an eight-hour drive to Ypsilanti. I checked the weather. It's rough up north, but if you can get there tonight and see Jocelyn tomorrow, you should be able to make the appointment in Lansing on the following day."

"Icy conditions don't bother me," Wayne told her. "I learned to drive on snow and ice, and I don't scare easy."

Wayne felt less confident when he was north of Tennessee. The roads were a nightmare, with multiple semi-trucks overturned on both sides of the freeway. After a long grueling drive, Wayne reached the Marriott in Ypsilanti late that evening. He had phoned for reservations and was shown his room with a minimum of fuss. He ordered from room service—a steak and a glass of red wine. As soon as he finished eating, he fell into bed.

DETECTIVE WAYNE NICHOLS drove his truck into the parking lot at Ypsilanti Huron Women's Correctional Facility the next morning. He parked in the lot and joined a line of people waiting to be admitted. This was the only prison in Michigan that housed women—over two thousand in a facility that had been built to hold a quarter of that number. After identifying himself through a microphone, he waited while the person checked with someone in administration.

The exterior gate slid open. Wayne was now inside the fence, walking up the concrete sidewalk through the flat emptiness of a snowy entrance yard. He strode beneath a long row of cell block windows. The hair on the back of his neck rose. He was being watched. Another electronic lock let Wayne through the door of the administration building and into the presence of a female guard. Wayne gave his name and produced his credentials, including his detective's license.

"Who are you here to see?" the bored guard asked him.

Just in time Wayne remembered the name Jocelyn was imprisoned under. "Joci Kemerovo," he said.

The guard typed her name into a computer and said, "Acute Care Infirmary, second floor. Somebody has to take you up there. Hang on. We have to wand you first."

About twenty minutes later, a tall female guard in a brown uniform appeared, checked with the guard at the front desk, and approached Wayne.

"Follow me," she said. Her voice was deep and her stride almost as long as his. His breathing quickened. His legs seemed stiff, and his knees were almost locking. He licked his lips and swept a hand across his forehead to wipe off the sweat. When something metal fell clanging to the floor in a room off the hallway, he jumped. He dreaded meeting his foster mother after all these years—after all this time he had failed to find her. Or even look for her.

When they entered the Infirmary, Wayne was blasted with the smell of bleach underscored by the rank odor of infection. Jocelyn was lying in the third bed. She was curled in a fetal position, away from him. He would never have recognized her, had it not been for the name on the chart hanging at the end of her bed. She looked impossibly tiny. The coverlet hardly rose over her body. He fought down the terrible urge to flee. But he had come this far. He had to see it through.

"Can you give us some space?" Wayne asked the guard. She nodded and walked to the far corner of the room. He leaned over his foster mother's bed and whispered, "Little mother, can you talk to me?"

Her eyes snapped open. "Wayne, is it you?" Her voice was high and cracked.

"Yes, it's me."

"Help me sit up," she said and held out her hands. Wayne took them in his, seeing the veins through the thin skin and enlarged knuckles, blue from arthritis. He eased her into a sitting position. She was so thin she could have been a concentration camp victim.

"I remember you." Her voice was filled with sorrow. "You told me to go to the white man's law. I got life for killing Aarne. I killed him, but you know that man deserved to die." Her dark eyes glittered.

Wayne drew in a sharp, pained breath at this reminder, stricken with guilt at the knowledge that his advice had led to her present circumstances. He started to tell her that he hadn't known where she was all this time, but there was no point in protesting. He should have tried to locate her decades ago.

"I'm trying to get you out of here, Jocelyn. I'm going to meet with an attorney."

"I've been turned down twice for parole already. You told me that I would only get a short sentence. I've been here for so long." The words came out in a rush of anguish.

Wayne sagged like a rag doll with its stuffing removed. Guilt was a sword in his gut and it took some time for him to muster up enough composure to speak to her again.

"I need to ask you some questions, little mother. When you went to the police and confessed to Aarne's murder, where did you tell them his body was? I buried him near Kurt the day you left. Did they find both bodies?"

"Yes. And they found the knife I killed Aarne with in the house. They could tell Kurt had been killed with a gun. They found the bullets. They asked me a hundred times where the gun was. I never told the law anything. I was afraid they would go after you."

"Oh my God! You should have given me up," Wayne's voice broke. His throat was choked with unshed tears as he said, "Why save my worthless hide?" They looked at each other in silence for a while until Wayne asked, "Little mother, did you even have a trial?"

"No, I confessed and was sentenced. I didn't get a lawyer either."

"What? Damn the bastards." Wayne was lost in thought for some time. Then he asked, "Did you tell anyone about Kurt's death before the day you killed Aarne?"

"Yes, Becky Wilshire. She was my neighbor, you remember. She and her husband owned the farm next to ours. I was sitting under the pine trees near Kurt's grave, crying, when she found me. She said I had to call the police. I told her I would, but I wanted time to say goodbye to my son first."

"Did you kill Aarne that night?"

"Yes." Jocelyn paused, closing her eyes for a moment. She went on in a low voice, one that revealed an undimmed hatred for her abuser. "It was evening when I heard Aarne's truck. He drove in the driveway and yelled for me. As soon as I got close enough, he got out of the car and knocked me down. I screamed that I knew he killed Kurt. He had a knife. He said he was going to cut me. We struggled, he dropped the knife, and I grabbed it. I told him to stop. I held up the knife in my hand, but he just kept coming for me, calling me bad words. Then I stabbed him." Jocelyn's tiny, withered body was shuddering. Wayne sat down on the end of her bed, causing the guard to step forward. He gestured for her to back off and then put an arm around Jocelyn's thin shoulders.

"It's going to be okay," he murmured. She shook her head. Pulling away from him, she lay back on her pillow. "Really, Jocelyn, if you didn't even have an attorney, that could be grounds to toss out your conviction. I'll try to locate Mrs. Wilshire and see if she'll write a letter of support for you. If none of that works, I'll take the gun to the authorities and turn myself in as an accessory."

"What good would that do?" Jocelyn's eyes were closing in fatigue. "My life is almost over now. It's like the first time, Wayne. You've come too late to save me." Her harsh words were softened by a gentle touch on his hand.

Wayne felt as if an arrow had pierced his heart. Stumbling out of the infirmary, he almost bumped into the prison doctor. He forced himself to calm down and take the opportunity to find out about Jocelyn's medical prognosis.

"How long will Jocelyn, I mean Joci, be in the infirmary, doctor?" Wayne asked.

"Are you a family member?" The man gave him a searching look.

Wayne nodded. "She's my foster mother. When I was young, she didn't use her Native American name, so I think of her as Jocelyn. But as far as I know, I'm all the family she has left."

"I'm sorry to tell you that she's not leaving here." The doctor shook his head. "She has aggressive lung cancer, stage four. She starts chemo next week." He touched Wayne's shoulder briefly before walking away.

Wayne Nichols leaned against the cold cement block wall until the guard told him it was time to go. A fierce wind blasted him on the walk to his car, and he almost welcomed the punishing chill as he thought about his next steps. Icy conditions aside, he had to get to Lansing.

Chapter Thirteen

—

January 11th
Mae December

Mae drove herself to meet Tammy at Promises, the bridal and formal dress shop in Rosedale. She was feeling okay, but low on energy. Still, it felt good to get out of the house. Tammy had already picked out four potential wedding gowns with her mom, and said she needed help narrowing them down. Mae could only hope that an awful bridesmaid dress wasn't about to be inflicted upon her. There were several already hanging in her closet.

She called Ben's office and left a phone message. Hopefully he had gotten an ID on the stabbing victim she found in the Little Harpeth River. Until that happened, she knew she would be no help on the case. In fact, she wondered if she could help at all this time. When the victim was her neighbor, Ruby Mead Allison, or her sister's former boyfriend, Tommy Ferris, she'd had lots of ideas for Ben. This person was a complete stranger. Parking in the alley behind the store, she hurried inside. Her car had barely warmed up on the short drive into town on this frosty morning.

Tammy was standing on a raised circular platform in front of the three-way mirror with one hand holding a long, white satin dress against her torso. She looked at Mae's reflection in the mirror and narrowed her eyes.

"It's sticking out farther already," she whispered. "Nothing is hanging right on me."

Mae stood looking at the dress for a moment before saying, "How about showing me the other three you found? Maybe one of those would fit you better."

Tammy dutifully tried on each gown, her expression more discouraged each time she ascended the circular raised platform. At the end she was pouting. While that pout was known to perform miracles of persuasion with men, it had no effect on Mae.

Mae tilted her head as she gave her best friend the onceover, then glanced around the shop. "I'm sorry to say this, Tammy, but perhaps virginal innocence is not the right look for the over thirty and pregnant."

"What did you just say to me?" Tammy's usual soft, breathy voice turned shrill. The shop manager and her assistant looked at each other and moved over to the far side of the store.

Mae bit her lip. Hoping to forestall a Tammy tantrum, she used the sort of soothing tone that usually worked on a nervous puppy.

"You're always telling me I should play up my best features and downplay the parts I'm not as happy with, right?"

"Right." Tammy bit the word off, but seemed to be listening.

"Well, your skin is glowing and your hair looks healthy. As do your tatas," Mae gestured to Tammy's bosom.

Tammy gave a surprised snort of laughter. "But?" she asked.

"Your waistline doesn't need to be emphasized," Mae told her gently. "Did you pick out anything that's a little more flowing?"

"Mae, you know I like my clothes fitted."

"Maybe a color would be better," Mae said, as inspiration struck. "You're getting married on Valentine's Day. What about red or pink?" She walked over to a display of event gowns in pinks, fuchsias, and reds. "Look at this one." Selecting a low-cut, floor length gown in crimson red, she held it up for her friend to see. The store manager inched closer, and Mae smiled at her.

"That would look amazing on you," declared the woman, whose nametag read 'Shop Manager, My name is Karen.' She took the gown from Mae's hands and held it out to Tammy like a peace offering. "It's a size six, which would usually be *way* too big for you." She gave Mae an almost imperceptible wink. "In another month it will fit perfectly. Clarissa," she called to her associate, "would you help Miss Tammy in the fitting room? She'll need the hem pinned up on this red one."

Tammy allowed herself to be spirited away. Mae sank into one of the brocade upholstered slipper chairs and thanked Karen for smoothing the troubled waters.

"Oh, honey, that was nothing—just doing my job. You should see some of the brides that come in here. They just pitch a fit and fall in it! And she really will be a gorgeous sight in that red gown. We have red satin heels here too. What are you wearing for the wedding? I assume you're her maid of honor, the way you talked her down off the ledge just now."

"She's done the same for me many times. We've been friends since sixth grade. I think it's just me standing up with her. It won't be a big wedding."

"Still, you'll want something to go with the red, if that's the one she selects."

Tammy emerged from the fitting room in the dark red dress, wearing a dazzling smile. She ascended the platform and grinned at Mae and Karen.

"You're brilliant, Mae-Mae. I love this dress! It's a whole lot cheaper than any of the wedding dresses, too. Clarissa said I could have it taken in later and shortened to cocktail length to use again. How about you pick out a black cocktail dress to stand up with me? I can carry white roses and you can carry a red bouquet. It'll be perfect."

Mae turned to Karen. "I think we have a winner. Could you show me some black cocktail dresses in a size eight? I'm not going to try anything on with this cast, but Tammy can pick whichever one she wants me to wear."

Tammy's mother, Grace, had been saving money for her daughter's wedding for years. When Tammy called to tell her about the fabulous red dress and how low the price was, she'd insisted on paying for Mae's dress as well. Mae took the phone from Tammy to thank her.

Grace said, "It's my pleasure, sweetheart. Besides, those two dresses combined are nowhere near what I thought I'd be spending. I'm so happy she agreed to marry Patrick. I was starting to think I'd never see her wedding day. Plus, having a baby on the way .... I'm just tickled to death."

"I know, and you're going to be a wonderful grandma. It's very exciting. I'll give the phone back to Tammy. Thanks again, Miss Grace."

As soon as Tammy ended the call, Mae gave her a one-armed hug and said goodbye. "I need to get home and check on the puppies I'm fostering. And I'm going to try and book a band for your reception. We have just a little more than a month to get this put together, you know."

Tammy widened her eyes. "I know, I'll call you later. Thanks so much, Mae-Mae." She misted up. Pregnancy was obviously making her friend more emotional than ever.

Mae called Jill Chapman after she got home. Jill was a friend, as well as a contact from her 'former life.' During her relationship with Noah, she had met lots of people in the music industry, especially after the song he wrote called 'Miss December' became a big hit. Jill was one of her favorites as a person as well as a performer.

"Hi, Mae," Jill answered on the third ring.

"Hey, Jill. How're you doing?"

"Besides it being way too cold outside, I'm just fine."

The two friends chatted about the unusually hard winter this year, and caught up on each other's lives for a while. Finally, Mae got around to the reason for her call, having abided by the southern custom of exchanging pleasantries before getting down to business.

"Jill, you remember my friend Tammy Rodgers, right?"

"Who could forget Miss Tammy? We called her Cupid because the men just fell in love with her all the time."

Mae laughed. "Right. Well, she's finally getting married on Valentine's Day. It's on a Friday this year and the reception is at my house. I was hoping you could bring your band and play for the party if you aren't already booked."

"I know I'm in town that weekend. Let me check with the guys and I'll shoot you a text if we can do it. Good talking to you, sweetie. Bye."

After ending the call, Mae went back to the boarding barn to check on the three foster puppies and her paid boarders—Lulu, Domino, and Maggie Pie. Mae checked the thermometer on the wall. The temperature inside the barn was only forty-eight degrees, but the pit bull puppies were in their usual pile and the Boston terriers were curled up together as well. Lulu seemed fine in her kennel. She checked everyone's water dishes and gave the puppies their second feeding of the day.

They were still having some trouble eating solid food, so Mae added water to their dishes. It rapidly turned the puppy chow to mush. The ASPCA vet estimated the age of the pups at eleven or twelve weeks, so they needed to eat three times a day. They were so funny, shouldering each other away and putting their front feet in the dish. They were making puppy noises too, practicing their tiny growls. After they finished eating, she washed off their faces with the "wet ones" she kept in the barn for just such occasions. Although it was still cold, Mae led them outside for some play time.

The sun was warm beside the barn where she and the puppies could shelter from the wind. The sky was a vivid blue and she held her face up to the light, feeling a little sun-starved as well as fatigued. The puppies ran around, jumping on each other and growling fiercely. She took them back to their pen after about fifteen minutes, loved on Lulu and her aunt and uncle's Boston terriers for a bit, and went into her historic farmhouse to check on her own four dogs and make some lunch. She had bills to pay and lots of planning still to do for Patrick and Tammy's big day.

Mae was working at her desk in the kitchen later when Dory called, wanting to bring a boy named Ray Fenton over to meet her. Dory had mentioned he was the young man who reported the animal cruelty at the puppy mill. She hoped Mae would give him an after school job. Mae told Dory to bring him over around four that day, then dug around in her freezer for some of her apricot-walnut bread—Dory's favorite. She found a loaf and put it on the counter to thaw.

Her cellphone buzzed on the counter. The text was from Jill. "Tough Act can make it on 2-14, will call re details."

Mae was thrilled by the news. The musicians in Jill's band, Tough Act to Follow, were all excellent, and Jill's voice—smooth, but rough around the edges—complemented her band and vice versa. It would be quite a night. Now, to begin the search for a caterer.

When Miss Dory Clarkson walked into Mae's kitchen at just after four that afternoon, she looked fabulous in a purple sweater dress and high-heeled black boots. She gave Mae a quick hug.

"This young man is Mr. Ray Fenton." She presented her slim, teenage companion, who shook Mae's hand.

"It's nice to meet you, Miss December," he said. He seemed shy—when he shook her hand his face colored a bit.

"It's good to meet you too, Ray. You can call me Mae. I understand you've worked with dogs already." He nodded.

Tallulah, her black pug, skidded around the corner and Ray's face lit up.

"Okay if I pet her?" he asked. Mae nodded. He knelt down and held out his hand. The little pug sniffed him and consented to a belly rub. Mae and Dory smiled at each other. Ray was small for a high school boy. He seemed polite and certainly was good with dogs. Mae knew that he had lost his job after the puppy mill was raided, and Dory said he was a good kid. She decided to trust her own and Dory's instincts and give him a chance.

"I can pay you six dollars an hour, if you can come three afternoons a week after school and help me with the dogs. I think you could ride the school bus here, and we'd work out a ride home for you, if you're interested." She gestured at her cast. "As you can see, I could use a hand around here."

"Yes ma'am, thank you ma'am." He got to his feet. "I can start tomorrow, ma'am."

Mae smiled at his squeaky-voiced enthusiasm. "Good. And really, you can call me Mae. Do you have any questions?"

"Miss Dory told me you were keeping three puppies from the raid. Could I see them?"

"Sorry, I don't have time to show you the puppies now, but you can see them tomorrow."

"Do you have a pure white one?" She could hear the hope in his voice.

"Sure do," Mae said.

"Mr. Clifton gave me one of the puppies. I named her Pearl Jam. I sure hope she's here at your place."

"In that case, go ahead and take a quick look," Mae smiled at him. "I bet that's the little girl I've been calling Pearl."

Ray dashed out to the barn and returned with a huge grin on his face. "She's here," he said. "I'm so happy she's okay. Thank you Miss Mae. I probably need to get home and check on my mom if that's okay."

Mae gave Dory a loaf of her apricot-walnut bread to take

home, walked them out to Dory's car, and said goodbye.

"Thank you for doing this, honey," Dory said.

"Thanks for bringing him over. Oh, and by the way—you know we talked about me helping you with the investigation, not just fostering some puppies."

Dory paused, her hand on the door handle of her car. "You're right. You can drive, right? Come into the office tomorrow. You can look at the photos from the raid and help me with this report. I need to substantiate the animal cruelty claims. Or we can run out to the site. Maybe that would be even better."

"I think that would. Around ten?" Mae asked.

Dory nodded. "Sounds good." She climbed into her red Thunderbird and closed the door. As she started the car and rolled her window down partway, she noticed Ray, already in the passenger seat.

"Okay." Mae waved at Dory and her new hire. "See you tomorrow morning, Dory. Ray, I'll see you after school."

She watched Dory's car go down her driveway, turn left and leave the valley before she went back inside. *This should be interesting. I've never had an employee before.* She walked into the kitchen and made herself a cup of hot tea before going back to the wedding plans.

Chapter Fourteen

—

January 12th
Detective Wayne Nichols

Wayne left his hotel in Ypsilanti, and after fighting the wintry roads for almost two hours, he walked into a large brick building near the Capitol in Lansing. He had spoken with Enid Lawton on the phone yesterday and offered to donate to her project. Wayne was eager to meet with her face-to-face. He took the elevator up to the fourth floor and went down the dingy hallway to a door with Enid Lawton, LLC lettered on the glass. A small white card reading "Abused Women's Commutation Project" had been taped below Ms. Lawton's name.

Wayne knocked and a voice said, "Come in." Inside the door to a small room, a young college-age girl sat at a battered old desk made of oak.

"Good morning," he said. "I'm Detective Wayne Nichols. I have an appointment with Counselor Lawton."

"Yes, sir. She called to say she's been delayed in court. She should be here in about half an hour, but she said that if she didn't make it back here in time, you should meet with the governor's office staffer without her—her name is Carol Kyle-Norris. The building where you're going to meet is 201 Townsend Street—the Capitol View Building. It's on the third floor, Room 306. It's just a couple of blocks from here. You can get something to eat at the little grill opposite the vital records office. It's also on the third floor."

"Okay," Wayne said. "What time should I be there?"

"Eleven o'clock," the young girl said. "Don't worry. Ms. Lawton will join you as soon as she can."

Wayne squared his shoulders. He was intimidated by the thought of meeting with a staffer from the governor's office by himself, but he had some ammunition now. Jocelyn said she hadn't been assigned an attorney. If her memory was correct, that could be grounds for her release.

Just as he was about to enter the revolving door of the Capitol View Building, someone tapped his shoulder.

"Are you Detective Nichols?" a woman asked. She was short, ruddy cheeked, and wearing a dark, hooded parka. He recognized her raspy smoker's voice from their phone conversation. She had caught up with him on a sidewalk that ran in front of the large buildings. The wind was blowing hard, swirling sleet pellets around their faces.

"Yes, and you're Enid Lawton."

"I am. And I'm very appreciative of your offer to donate five thousand dollars to our project. That goes a long way on a shoe-string budget like ours. Let's get a sandwich and talk before we go meet with the staffer from the governor's office."

Over stale, plastic-wrapped sandwiches and dispenser machine coffee, Wayne told Ms. Lawton about the years of abuse that Jocelyn endured before she killed Aarne. Enid's dark eyes sparked when he told her Jocelyn hadn't had an attorney.

"In the past, the old boys' network thought a woman, particularly an Indian woman, could be denied due process without any repercussions. That day is over, thank God. And prejudice is waning. Do you know about the process of getting prisoners released, Wayne?"

"No, my work usually involves getting them locked up, not released," he said and made a wry face.

"Right. There are three avenues of approach. The first is to fill out a commutation form. If that's denied, then we request a hearing before the parole board."

"She's already tried asking for parole twice. They turned her down."

"Perhaps with me writing the appeal letter asking them for a parole hearing, they'll agree to hear her case. If that fails, the third option is to get the case re-heard by a judge. The judge can refuse to hear the case, can deny release, or can grant the attorney's request to release the prisoner. I read the case file Evangeline sent me. Jocelyn should have been convicted of manslaughter and served a maximum of six years. Her murder-two life sentence was a travesty. Were you able to determine what kind of a prisoner Jocelyn has been?"

"I met with the social worker at the prison yesterday after I saw Jocelyn. According to her, Jocelyn has been a model prisoner. She taught inmates how to read and write. She learned sign language and translated for the deaf when they watched movies. She served in the kitchen every day."

"Okay, that's good. What about Aarne's family—would they oppose her release?"

"All dead."

"It's usually helpful to have others write letters of support. Is there anyone left we could ask?"

"I learned something from Jocelyn on my visit yesterday. A neighbor woman found Jocelyn crying by Kurt's grave. Her name was Becky Wilshire. I think she would testify to Jocelyn's profound grief when she discovered that her son had been murdered."

"Okay. Try and track her down then. I'm going to hit this with a three pronged approach. First, I'll submit the commutation form. Assuming we'll be denied, I'll also request a hearing by the parole board. They'll need letters from the social worker and the teachers in the educational unit about Jocelyn's signing for the deaf and teaching inmates to read. See if you can get those. I'll also request a letter from the Warden at Huron Valley, providing she's in support of Jocelyn's release. At the same time, I'll start preparing a Habeas writ for the judge to ask for her release on the basis of time served." Enid Lawton glanced at her watch and said it was time to meet with the governor's staffer.

They met briefly with Miss Kyle-Norris. She was a skinny woman in her early thirties with dark reddish hair and bright blue eyes. Wayne introduced himself and then sat back while the two women negotiated a time for Ms. Lawton on the governor's busy calendar. Having the governor pardon Jocelyn would be their last hope if the parole board denied her release again and if the judge wouldn't hear her case. Walking back to Ms. Lawton's office, as the wind thudded against them, Enid told Wayne she would get to work immediately.

"Before I file any briefs, though, you need to find Mrs. Wilshire and see what she remembers."

"I'm on it," Wayne said. "There's one other thing you need to know. Jocelyn has stage four lung cancer. She's going to start chemo soon and they don't expect her to recover."

"I'll use that," the attorney said in a cheerful voice. Seeing his distressed expression, she apologized. "I'm sorry, Wayne. It's just that her cancer might make the judge feel more sympathetic. We can ask for compassionate release."

All the way back to Rosedale, Wayne prayed that Becky Wilshire was still alive—that she would remember the day she found Jocelyn wailing at Kurt's grave and would be willing to testify to what she saw and heard. None of this would happen, however, if he couldn't find the woman or if she was already dead.

Chapter Fifteen

—

January 12th
Sheriff Ben Bradley

DEPUTY GEORGE PHELPS bustled into Ben's office and stopped in front of the sheriff's desk.

"Yes, George, what do you need?" Ben said, looking up.

"It's Dory."

Ben took his eyes from his computer screen. "What about her?"

"She just called."

As a stand-in office manager or even a receptionist, Deputy Phelps left a great deal to be desired. Dory and Mae had left the office an hour or so earlier, headed out to the Clifton property. Ben was apprehensive about sending Mae out there with her wrist in a cast, but she'd said she wanted to see the conditions at the puppy mill for herself.

"You know you can buzz me, right, George? You don't have to walk down here."

His deputy smiled. "I know I can, Sheriff." George patted his ample belly. "Dory said it's good for me to get up from the desk and move around. Helps keep me trim."

"Right." Ben tried not to laugh and failed. "Did Dory say what she needed?"

"Said she and your lady friend apprehended a suspect. They want you to come on out there and arrest him."

Ben leaped to his feet. "Why the hell didn't you say so?"

Deputy Phelps opened his mouth, then clamped it shut. He followed as Ben grabbed his coat and hurried down the hall. Rob Fuller's door was open.

"Rob, C'mon! We're going out to the Clifton property. It sounds like Jerrod showed up."

Detective Fuller put his coffee cup down, stood up, and threw his coat on in one fluid motion. Walking quickly toward the office door, he asked, "Am I driving?"

"Yes, pull up in one of the patrol cars. I'll be right out," the sheriff told him.

"Boss," George spoke up, "what am I supposed to do now?"

Ben shot him a glare. "Call Dory and tell her we're on our way. And you're on phones at least until she gets back. If anyone calls in a complaint, send Deputy Gomez to take care of it. And no computer games!"

ROB HIT THE siren as soon as Ben shut the passenger door and buckled his seatbelt. He drove slightly over the speed limit until they were out of the downtown area of Rosedale and then he floored it. Flying down the narrow, twisting country roads, he gave his boss a daredevil grin.

"Where'd you learn to drive like this? I know it wasn't the police academy."

"Gran Turismo." The young detective's smile grew even wider. "It's a videogame."

Great. "Well, we're getting close. Kill the siren and slow down. I need to call Dory." He hit the speakerphone and called Dory's cell.

"Hi, Ben," Mae answered Dory's phone sounding a little breathless.

"Everything all right there? We're getting close. Is Dory okay?"

Mae giggled. "It isn't Dory you need to worry about. She's fine, but she um, I guess *subdued* would be the word. She *subdued* the suspect and she can't talk on the phone right now. What did you say, Dory?" Ben heard Mae and Dory talking. "Right. She's sitting on his back."

Ben was at a loss for words. He looked helplessly at Rob Fuller, who was shaking with laughter.

"Where is the suspect?" Ben finally asked. "The one she's sitting on, I mean." *May as well keep the comedy rolling.* Rob was laughing so hard, he started to cough.

"We're in the field behind Jerrod Clifton's house," Mae said. "We wanted the suspect to stay in the garage so we could tie him to something, but he's been very uncooperative. He tried to get away and then he sassed Dory, so she tripped him and sat on him. Just drive past the house and the barn and you'll see us out here." He heard a dial tone.

"The garage?" Rob looked at the sheriff. "I didn't think there was a garage at the Clifton's. Not by the house anyway."

"I didn't notice one either."

Rob turned into the long gravel drive that started at a thick tree line and continued into open fields up to the house and barn where Jerrod Clifton had been running his puppy mill. He drove past the house and out into the field, which was rutted and still held traces of snow. Ben could see Mae standing in the distance. Her hair was blowing away from her face like a bright flag tossed in the wind. There was a building even farther beyond her that Ben thought must be the garage.

"Over there. Do you see her?" Ben pointed to the right.

Rob aimed the patrol car toward Mae and rolled to a stop a little ways away. She was standing close to Dory, who was, indeed, sitting on the broad back of what looked to be a full-grown man.

Ben got the cuffs out and he and Rob exited their vehicle.

"How's it going there, Investigator Clarkson?" the sheriff asked. He winked at Mae. Rob was chewing his lower lip in an effort to maintain his composure. Ben knew he could not make eye contact with him or it would be all over.

"It'd be going a whole lot better if you'd cuff this man." Dory gave him a look reminiscent of his ninth grade algebra teacher—an ogress of a woman who'd been known to reduce Varsity football players to tears. "While you were taking your sweet time about it, your girlfriend and I had to apprehend this fool on our own."

Dory rose to her feet, Rob hauled the suspect to a standing position, and Ben put on the cuffs. He was a stocky man with dirty-blond hair and a short beard.

"Jerrod Clifton, you have the right to remain silent," Ben started to Mirandize him.

"I'm not Jerrod!" the man burst out. "I tried to tell these crazy women, but they wouldn't listen. They cornered me out in the garage and then the old one called your office. I tried to get away and then she pulled some judo move on me. I'm gonna lodge a complaint for police brutality."

"Don't make me laugh," Detective Rob Fuller said. "You're a big guy. Nobody will believe that Dory Clarkson, who isn't even an officer of the law, brutalized you. With the help of a woman in a cast! And if you're not Jerrod, who are you?"

"I'm Jerrod's brother, Mike. My ID's in my car over yonder. I was looking for Jerrod out by the garage back there. He wasn't in the house or the barn. Then these skirts showed up and chased me out here. She tripped me and threw me on my face in the field." He glared at Dory, who had started toward him at the word "skirts."

"Stand down, Investigator Clarkson." Ben turned to his scrappy investigator and his lovely girlfriend, both of whom were giving him guilty looks. "Is that true? And why were you all the way out in that garage anyway? That's way outside the scope of the animal cruelty investigation."

The two women glanced at each other and then started to speak at the same time.

"One at a time, please," Ben said, looking at Mae. His head was starting to pound.

"We were done looking around the house and getting ready to go when we noticed a car parked behind the barn," Mae began after another glance at her accomplice. "Then I saw the garage from across the field. It looked familiar and I convinced Dory we should go check it out."

"That's right." Dory nodded her head. "And we found this guy out there skulking around."

"Just a minute." Ben looked back at Rob, standing patiently beside Mike Clifton. "Detective Fuller, why don't you take Clifton to the patrol car and put him in the back seat. You can wait in the car with him. I'll just be another minute." He turned to Mae once more. "So the garage looked familiar?"

"It's the one I came across when I got lost during the snowstorm. The visibility was so bad that day I never saw the house or the barn," she said with a little frown. "I thought it might be the same one when I saw the outside, but when we went inside I knew it was—same place, same pile of copper pipes near the door. Then we saw Mr. Clifton. We were both so mad about the treatment of those poor dogs, and we thought he was Jerrod. I guess we didn't give him a chance to say who he was …." she trailed off.

Dory chimed in. "He sure acted guilty when he saw us. And he looks a lot like the DMV photo of his brother. We thought we'd made a big collar." She looked abashed.

Ben closed his eyes briefly. "All right, Rizzoli and Isles. That was an honest mistake. But do both of you realize that what you did could have been dangerous?" They nodded, giving him big eyes and looks of sincere contrition. *What a pair.* "Detective Fuller and I will take it from here. I'll see both of you later." He gave Dory a sharp look, kissed Mae on the cheek, and went to the patrol car. Climbing in on the passenger side, he tried hard not to grin.

BEN WATCHED OUT the patrol car's back window as Mae and Dory walked across the field, climbed into Dory's red T-bird and drove off. "My apologies, Mr. Clifton," he said, looking into the back seat at Mike. They really had no grounds to hold him, let alone arrest him, and Mike Clifton had no reason to cooperate with them. Ben had to try, however. "Let's get those cuffs off, Detective." Rob got out and went around to the back, freeing the man's hands, then returned to the driver's seat. "I'm not going to detain you any further, but it's urgent that we get in touch with your brother."

"I'd like to get ahold of him too," Mike muttered, rubbing his wrists and frowning. "He told me to come up here—said he needed my help with something. I get here and he's not around."

"Would you be willing to come to the office and answer some questions?"

Mike's brown eyes were wary. He didn't answer right away.

"Do you know Jerrod's cellphone number?" Rob asked. "We need to speak with him about leaving his dogs without anyone to care for them, and we need his help with another matter as well."

"It's on my phone," Mike told him. "Along with my ID. I can get you the phone number if you'll let me out of the car. Maybe I'll come to your office tomorrow; maybe I won't. I'd like to wait and see if Jerrod turns up before then, all right?"

"Sure," Ben told him. "Drive back over to the barn, Rob, and we'll let Mr. Clifton get on with his day. Are you staying at your brother's house tonight?"

"Only if my brother shows up. I've got no way to get inside the house without him. Otherwise, I'll get a motel room."

Rob put the car in park and got out to open the back door for Mike, who stood up and inclined his head toward the old white Pontiac with South Carolina plates parked behind the barn. Rob and Ben followed him over to the rusty vehicle, and Mike grabbed his wallet and cellphone from out of the center console. He flipped the wallet open and presented his driver's license to Rob. The detective read it and nodded at Ben.

"So Mike, could you give me your brother's number? We need yours, too." Ben took a business card out of his breast pocket and handed it to Mike Clifton.

"Yeah, here's Jerrod's." He read the number off his phone and Rob entered it into his own cell. Mike gave his own mobile number to the detective.

"We'll be in touch, Mr. Clifton," the sheriff informed him. "Let us know if you hear from your brother. And don't leave the area."

Chapter Sixteen

———

January 13th
Sheriff Ben Bradley

BEN CALLED DETECTIVE Wayne Nichols on his way to the office. The chief detective was driving back to Tennessee from Michigan, and Ben told him the tale of Dory's first 'collar.' The two lawmen shared a laugh, then Ben said, "We called the number that Mike gave us for Jerrod, but he didn't answer."

"I'm thinking you could take this Mike Clifton to the morgue," Wayne replied. "He might be able to identify the floater. But even if he can't, it'll probably shake him up. You might learn something."

"That's a good idea. Thanks, Wayne. Will you be in tomorrow?"

"I will as long as the weather holds. These roads are pretty bad today—snowed a lot last night. If it starts snowing again it might slow me down a little bit."

"All right. Take it easy and we'll see you soon." Ben clicked the off button.

He decided to heed Wayne's advice and take Mike Clifton to the morgue, in case he could identify the stabbing victim.

When he got to the office, Rob Fuller was already at his desk.

"Call Mike Clifton back and tell him that I have some questions. We can question him in the car on the way to the morgue."

Rob's eyebrows shot up.

"You better get your Dramamine," the sheriff said.

Rob called Mike, who agreed to be picked up from his motel in half an hour. Ben drove his own truck, thinking the unofficial vehicle might put Mike at ease enough to answer questions without reservations. Rob knocked on the door of room number 17 at the Country Rose Motel, while Ben stayed in his F-150 with the motor running. Mike opened the door and peered out, then followed Rob to the truck after locking the flimsy door. Rob waved him to the passenger side and climbed into the back seat.

"Good morning. Thanks for agreeing to talk to us."

Mike Clifton gave Ben a small nod, looking around the leather swathed interior. "Yeah. Nice truck. Didn't know sheriffs made this kind of money."

"The bank owns it, not me." Ben backed out of the parking space and pulled onto the road. "Your brother didn't answer his phone when we called. Have you heard from him since yesterday, Mike?" Mike shook his head and looked away. Ben caught Rob's eye in his rearview mirror. They would check his cellphone later to see if he had lied about talking with his brother.

"You said your brother Jerrod asked you to come back to town?" Rob leaned forward.

"Yeah. He said he had a chance to make some big money and wanted me in." Mike scowled. "Said he could use my help and to get here right away."

"Had he found a different way to make money off the pit bulls? Dog fighting, maybe?" Ben asked, clenching his jaw.

"No. He said he was going to shut down the dog operation.

Wasn't making enough money on it and he needed the barn for storage."

"What would he have been storing?" Rob's voice was casual; just a friendly conversation.

"Didn't say. What the hell's this all about, anyway? Should I be worried about my brother? Is he okay?"

"It's about a murder." The sheriff gave Mike a flat stare. "We need you to ID a body for us." Mike's face went white.

"Is the dead guy my brother?" he asked.

"No, it isn't Jerrod."

Their passenger pursed his lips and looked out the window. They rode the rest of the way to the morgue in silence.

THEY ARRIVED AT the hospital and Ben drove around and parked in an underground loading dock with a double door that opened into the morgue. He got out, keyed in the code, and the doors slid open. Ben waited in the doorway while Rob and Mike walked in ahead of him. Even the strong, mingled odors of bleach and disinfectant could not cover the odious smell of death.

"Ever been in a morgue before?" Sheriff Bradley asked Mike.

Mike Clifton shook his head. Rob had already called and made an appointment with the ME while they were driving to the motel. Dr. Estes and his assistant—a young white guy wearing a name tag identifying him as "Charles Dep, Diener"— were waiting for them when the large cargo bay slid open.

"Dr. Estes, this is Mike Clifton. We think he may be able to identify the John Doe we brought in a few days ago from the river. Hello, Dep."

Dr. Estes nodded at his Diener, giving him permission to show the sheriff the dead man. Ben had recently learned that the word 'Diener' was German for 'corpse servant,' an ancient occupation—the person who transported the dead and cleaned the morgues. Some, like Mr. Dep, even did the dissections prior to autopsy. Dep walked over to the bank of refrigerated drawers and pulled one open. A white sheet lay over the corpse.

"Can we make this snappy? I have other work to do," Dr. Estes asked, exhibiting his trademark irritation.

"Yes, sir," Sheriff Bradley said. "Go closer, Mike." The sheriff prodded Mike in the shoulder. Charles Dep pulled the sheet off the man's face. "Pull it down farther, Dep. I want him to see his wounds. Do you know this guy, Mr. Clifton?"

Mike grimaced, stepping back. "It could be this guy I saw once at my brother's place. Maybe a year ago. I think Jerrod called him Web." He looked at the dead man's face once more. "I'm not sure, though. And you better get me out of here before I puke."

The three men left together. After dropping Mike Clifton off back at the motel, Ben turned to Rob.

"Did you find our John Doe's fingerprints in AFIS?" The Automated Fingerprint Identification System was the largest biometric database in the world. It was maintained by the FBI and housed the criminal histories and fingerprints of seventy million subjects in the master file.

"No luck, boss." Rob sounded as discouraged as Ben felt. An uncertain ID of a first name wasn't going to be much help and it had been almost a week since Mae found the body. Time was bearing down on him.

Chapter Seventeen

—

January 13th
Mae December

WHEN MAE WALKED into her kitchen, Thoreau—the grizzled old Rottweiler she had inherited from Noah—was standing on the rug in the middle of the room. She patted her pocket where she kept her treat stash.

"Come here, Thoreau." The big black and tan took a step toward her and stopped, swaying where he stood. Mae went over to him. "Are you okay?" She patted his head. He leaned into her leg and fell to the floor, twitching. The big dog was having another seizure—his third in as many weeks. Mae sat down on the rug beside him, stroking his flank until he stilled. His side heaved when he took in a deep breath. Thoreau struggled to sit up, looking at Mae with eyes clouded by cataracts.

"It's all right, my sweet boy. You stay here. I'm going to call Dr. LaBelle."

Mae called the vet's office and got an appointment for 11:00 the next morning. "I think it'll be okay to wait until then," she told the receptionist. "He just stood up. He's walking around like he feels fine now."

"That seems to be the way with our older patients," Amy, the receptionist, said. "I pulled his chart. He'll be fifteen in two more months."

Fifteen? How could that be? "I guess Noah got him when he was in high school. Thanks, Amy. See you tomorrow."

Mae had known Thoreau was getting old, but he had outlived the average lifespan for his breed by almost three years.

Ben was coming to pick her up at six for dinner at her parents'. Earlier this morning, Ben had begged off, pleading his work load with the unsolved murder and the copper pipe theft. "Did you hear me say that there was a pile of copper pipes in that garage on the Clifton property?" Mae asked, just before he got off the phone. There was a brief pause. "Thanks, I forgot about that." Ben said a quick goodbye. Later on, he had called back to tell her that he was taking an evening off. Apparently Mike Clifton had only been able to give them a first name for the stabbing victim.

Using one hand, she picked up the Tater—her adorable young strawberry-blond corgi—put her in her crate in the kitchen and made sure her three older dogs had fresh water in their bowls. Then she went upstairs to change into her new jeans and a hip-length ivory sweater with loose sleeves. Mae checked her reflection in the bathroom mirror. She'd recently lost five pounds (hence the new jeans) and was happy with the slight reduction in hip size. Her hair was another story. The cold, dry air, atypical for a Tennessee winter, seemed to have added flyaways to her list of unruly hair issues. Blonde, thick and curling to her shoulders, her hair had a mind of its own. Several wisps stuck straight up.

Mae leaned closer to the mirror. "Clearly, Thoreau's not the only one who's getting old," she told her brown-eyed, rueful reflection. Three of the upright hairs were gray.

"Who're you talking to up there?" she heard Ben call from the bottom of the stairs.

"Myself." *Because that's what gray-haired old people do.* A wry expression crossed her face and she realized she was being ridiculous. "I'll be right down."

She combed on some mascara and slapped on a quick coat of lip gloss, plucked out the offending hairs and hurried downstairs. Ben was standing at the bottom of the stairs, and Mae kissed him. He was taller than she, with dark hair and vivid blue eyes. With her blonde hair and dark eyes, she thought they made a handsome couple. And he didn't seem to be holding a grudge over the Rizzoli and Isles episode, thank goodness. Ben had agreed not to mention the 'collar' of Mike Clifton to her parents. In Mae's opinion, it would be better for everyone if they didn't know. They had freaked out enough when Mae told them about breaking her wrist after finding the body by the river.

"Hi, baby girl, how's the wrist doing?" Mae's father, Don December, gave her a hug when she and Ben walked into her parents' house. Mae was the Decembers' youngest child and in her father's mind, had never really grown up.

"It's better, Daddy. I'm just tired all the time. Everything's more of an effort when you only have one working hand."

Mae's dad made a sympathetic noise and then shook Ben's hand. "Sheriff, glad you could make it. Come in."

"I didn't see July's car. Are she and Fred coming tonight?" Mae asked her mother, Suzanne, who had walked out of the kitchen. Usually family dinners included Mae's older sister, July, along with her husband Fred and their three children, twins Nathan and Parker and their youngest, Olivia.

"No, they couldn't make it. Too much going on with the kids, apparently." Suzanne hugged her daughter and rose up on tiptoe to kiss Ben's cheek.

"I'm kind of glad it's just the four of us tonight. Your daddy's got a surprise for you, Mae. It's in the dining room."

They followed Suzanne's petite frame to the formal dining room, which overlooked a creek that rippled through the backyard. Mae exchanged a smile with her father.

"I hope you took some pictures of that when we had all the snow, Daddy. I bet it was just beautiful."

"I did." Her father nodded. "Such a rarity to get this much snow here. I wanted to record it."

"Oh, that reminds me." Ben turned back from the window. "I took some pictures on my phone from up on the ridge right after the snowstorm."

"I'd like to see them. Maybe I can do a winter painting for you—for your birthday." Mae smiled at her boyfriend.

"I was hoping you'd say that," Ben answered with a little grin.

Mae looked at her father. "So, Mama said you had a surprise for me?"

Don December gestured at a large coffee table-sized book that lay on the gleaming walnut of the table. "I do. It's right there."

Mae went to the table and touched the cover, a photograph of a microphone standing on an empty stage. "*Offstage*. Good title."

"Open it, honey," Don December said.

She flipped the cover to the dedication page. "To my youngest daughter, Mae—none more brave or lovely in my sight," she read aloud. She looked up, tears stinging her eyes.

"Thank you, Daddy." She cleared her throat. "Are you happy with the way this book turned out?"

Over the course of his thirty-five-year career as a photographer, Don December had put together three other books; all collections of his work. He'd photographed many of the legends of the country music world, but his latest book featured the hardworking but not-so-famous songwriters, sound engineers, and session musicians. Mae knew there would be several pictures of her fiancé, Noah, who had just started to make a name for himself as a songwriter before he was killed in a tragic car accident, only months before they were to be married.

Ben put a hand on her shoulder and looked down at the book. "Any pictures of you in there, Mae?"

Her father came over and opened the book to a page near the middle and began pointing out pictures to Ben.

"Here she is, with Noah. And there, with my brother Phil."

"I don't think I've met your brother yet," Ben said. "Is he a musician?"

"Yes, he's a songwriter. Usually co-writes with John Ayers, although they haven't done much lately."

Mae closed her eyes for a second. "Excuse me," she murmured and escaped to the powder room in the hall. Ever since she had learned that Tammy and Patrick were getting married, Noah had been on her mind. Her current awareness of Thoreau's advanced age was making the memories even more poignant. She didn't want to look at pictures of Noah now. She was Ben's girlfriend and happy to be with him. However, the pictures of Noah and those early years still saddened her, considering his untimely death.

MAE AND BEN arrived back at her house after ten that night. She went into the kitchen to get the Tater out of her crate and heard whining in the dark room. When she flipped the light switch on, Titan, her older male corgi and Tallulah, her black pug, looked up at her. The black pug, whimpering, sat beside Thoreau, who was sprawled across the rug. Titan sat on his other side.

"Oh, no! He must've had another seizure. Ben, can you come help me?"

He came in, running, and knelt beside the fallen Rottweiler. Ben laid his hand on Thoreau's neck and looked up at Mae.

"Honey, I'm so sorry. He's gone. There's no pulse." Ben stood up. "Do you have an old blanket I can wrap him in?"

"You're not going to bury him tonight!" Mae burst into tears. "I haven't said goodbye to him, and it's cold and dark out there."

Ben wrapped his arms around her and held her for a few

minutes, while she sobbed. He loosened his grip and stepped back.

"If you want to wait, I'll bury him tomorrow. Let me wrap him in something. I'll take him out to the garage to keep the other dogs from getting more upset."

Still unable to speak, Mae nodded and went to get a blanket. Tomorrow she would have to watch as a dog she loved—her last remaining tie to the life she'd shared with Noah—was buried in the cold ground. Bidding farewell to the big Rottweiler would be the final scene of her life with her former fiancé. Up till now she had always kept a small part of herself for him, but it was time to stop looking back. Now she could give her whole heart to Ben.

Chapter Eighteen

—

January 14th
Sheriff Ben Bradley

Ben had a hard time digging a hole big enough for Thoreau's grave in the almost frozen ground of Mae's backyard. He had let the three house dogs out into the frosty morning, ushered them back into the kitchen after they took care of business, and gone out to the barn for a shovel. Mae had three boarders in the kennel—the Boston terrier pair and Lulu. All were sleeping peacefully. The three pit bull pups she was fostering were also sound asleep in their accustomed pile.

He grabbed a shovel and a pair of work gloves and went out to the very back of Mae's property. After fifteen minutes of serious digging he had removed his coat and was starting to sweat, despite the atypically cold weather. He pulled out several large rocks, finally got a decent-sized grave dug, and then went back in the house. He knew Mae would want to say goodbye to Thoreau before he buried the big Rottweiler.

Mae was dressed in jeans and an oversized sweater, sitting at her kitchen table and staring at the steam rising from her coffee cup. "Thank you for doing that," she said quietly. "I guess it's time." Mae closed her large dark eyes for a moment. When she opened them, tears starred her lashes. "I'm not sure I can do this, Ben. I know he was old, but it's hard to say goodbye ...." Her voice trailed off into sobs.

"I know it's hard, sweetheart. When I lost my old basset hound, Buttercup, I cried like a baby. I was a twenty-eight-year-old police officer and still I cried. I didn't shed a tear when Katie left me, but losing that dog was rough." Mae looked at him and sniffled as he went on, "I'm going to tell you what my mom told me then. She said, when you lose a dog, they take all the bad things in your life away with them when they go. That's how you know it's time to move on to a new phase of your life. You have a lot of memories tied to Thoreau, but we'll be making new memories together."

He held his hand out to Mae. She took it and got out of her chair, giving him a trace of a smile. "I guess today is the first of many three-dog days around here."

Ben gave her a smile in return. "Have you ever heard the expression, 'three dog night'?"

"No, I haven't." Mae shook her head.

"It's an Alaskan night that's so cold you need to sleep with three of your sled dogs just to survive. So I guess it's a three dog day all right. But by my count you actually have nine dogs on the premises—three sets of three."

"You're right, I do. And at least Titan, Tallulah, and the Tater are all young enough that they'll be around for years to come." She took a deep breath. "Let me get my coat, and I'll come with you to say goodbye."

Mae was quiet after they laid Thoreau to rest. Ben helped her with kennel chores and scrambled some eggs for both of them. When breakfast was over, he gave her a hug and she clung to him, her face turned into his shoulder.

"You need to go to work. As you know, I've usually jumped in to getting information about your cases, and we've had our differences of opinion about it. But this time, when I really could help, I'm just so worn out from my wrist, and things keep happening to stop me. But I don't want you to worry about me. I'll be fine." Her voice was muffled by his shirt.

"I probably can't put it off much longer," he agreed. "But I will be thinking about you. It takes a lot of energy to heal a broken bone, you know. And you're right; my cases have come between us. Wayne's taking some time off, though, so it's a little different working on this one. I'll call you later." Ben brushed Mae's hair off her face, kissed her gently, and walked out to his truck in the frosty morning light.

ON HIS WAY to the office, Ben called Detective Fuller's cellphone. "Good morning, Rob. Have you uncovered anything new on the copper pipe case?"

"I've been checking out contractors and flippers, and there are several of them that have had copper pipe go missing. There's this one flipper I talked to named Cliff Newcomb. According to Cliff, he isn't making as much money as he did."

"Why is that?" Ben asked. A wintry mix of sleet and rain had begun to fall, and sheets of it skidded nearly horizontally across the road in front of him. It was taking Rob a while to get to the point, but Ben forced himself to be patient. Rob was new to this detective business.

"This all happened right around Christmas time. The thefts happen just after the auctions and before the keys are handed over the next day. Cliff would purchase a house at auction, but he wouldn't get the keys until the following day. When he got inside the house, he often found a lot of copper pipe and antique fireplace surrounds that were visible in the photographs of the interiors, had gone missing. Replacing the plumbing was expensive and added to the total cost of the renovation. That ate into the profits for the flippers. So Cliff decided to get permission from the auction firms to put video cameras in the houses. When the cameras detect motion, they're wired to call the Mont Blanc cops. I went over to Captain John Granger's shop and looked at the footage. It's two guys. They always run like hell as soon as they hear the sirens, and nobody's been caught so far."

"Good work, Rob. So nothing has happened since then? No thefts since the first of the year? We got the first call from Logan Yancey on January fifth, but he didn't know how long his materials, including the pipes, had been missing."

"Right, which makes me think it could be Jerrod Clifton who's doing this."

"It's strong circumstantial evidence, for sure. I've been looking into how copper pipe is fenced," Ben told him. "It's usually sold for drug money, cocaine or meth. The drug dealers who buy the copper pipe sell it to exporters. Ultimately the pipe ends up in India or China, where they're doing an enormous amount of building."

"What would you think about a stakeout?" Rob asked. "There's a historic home auction coming up."

"Good idea. I'm wondering if Jerrod Clifton is involved in the pipe theft, because Mae found copper pipes in his garage. Whether he's involved or not, we've got to crack this case. I'll talk to John Granger over at Mont Blanc, see if he's willing to let you take the lead on this. If I can get John's agreement, who would you like to do the stakeout with you, George or Cam?"

"What do you think I'd like better, Sheriff?" Rob laughed. "A stakeout in the company of the divine Miss Gomez or the farting George Phelps?"

"Okay, but watch yourself, man. No putting the moves on Deputy Gomez. Remember the no-fraternizing rule? I'll get the necessary permissions going."

Ben called Captain Granger. After summarizing Detective Rob Fuller's information to date, Ben asked about a stakeout using his people.

"Normally, I'd tell you to butt out, Ben," John Granger said. "However, since Rob Fuller is now a detective, he actually works for both of us, just as Wayne Nichols does." He was referring to the practice of sharing detectives in the case of serious crimes. "I can assign him this stakeout without pissing off any of my other officers."

"Thanks, John."

"No problem. How are you coming on that floater your girlfriend found in the Little Harpeth River?"

Ben sighed heavily. "We finally got a probable on a first name. Mike Clifton thinks his name is Web, but we're still looking for a last name. We found the body near Jerrod Clifton's place. We think Jerrod did it, but we haven't found him yet. We're sort of at a standstill."

They said goodbye, and Ben drove the rest of the way to the office, deep in thought. The murder had to be connected to the puppy mill. *I hope Wayne makes it in this morning. We could sure use his help.*

Chapter Nineteen

—

January 14th
Detective Wayne Nichols

DETECTIVE WAYNE NICHOLS sat in his car for a moment before going into the office. He had arrived back home from Michigan late on the evening before. Lights were on in the reception area of the sheriff's office, but the staff offices were still dark. He felt anxiety rise in his gut as he thought about the questions he was going to face. He twisted his neck and tapped a curled knuckle against his mouth. His immediate reaction was to clamp down on giving the staff any information, but on the drive he had made a decision to be more open about his life with people he cared about. He got out of the car and walked up to the office door, stomach churning.

Cam Gomez, the good-looking young Hispanic woman Ben had recently hired as his new deputy, was sitting at the desk. She looked up alertly as he came in.

"Good morning," Wayne smiled at her. "Anyone else around?"

"Not yet, sir, but Sheriff Bradley will be in soon and so will Detective Fuller."

"Right, it's Detective Fuller now." He would have to negotiate a new relationship with Rob now that there were two detectives in the office.

"Yes, sir. Sheriff Bradley left some papers for you on your desk. Could I get you some coffee? Just put on a fresh pot."

Such solicitude. He was more accustomed to Dory's steel hand in a velvet glove approach. "Thank you, Deputy Gomez."

"Just Cam is fine, sir." She gave him a bright smile. "How do you take your coffee?"

"Black. Thanks."

Wayne took the coffee she handed him and walked down the hallway to his office. Quite a stack of papers awaited him in his in-basket. He opened the window a crack and felt a welcome cold breeze. Sitting down at his desk, he sipped his surprisingly excellent coffee and started to go through the backlog.

Detective Rob Fuller had collared Jacko in a seedy bar and poured coffee into him until he sobered up. Jacko thought some of the copper pipes might be stored in a barn in Rose County. He wouldn't say anything more without money. It was common practice to pay snitches. Usually it was only a couple of twenties, but this time Jacko held out for five hundred dollars, which Rob had negotiated down to two-fifty. Wayne frowned. It didn't seem like Jacko had given Rob enough information to justify such a big payment. Some things never changed in the criminal world. Snitches always wanted more for their info than it was really worth.

Then he picked up Ben's report, labeled "John Doe." Their new murder case. Ben had called him several times about Mae's finding the body and the lack of an ID. His blood quickened. It would be the perfect thing to move the focus of the staff away from him and onto the job at hand. He felt a quick jab of shame that he had no pity for the dead man, only considered him a puzzle to solve and a way to divert attention from his own story.

He settled down to a careful perusal of Dr. Estes' report on the victim. He noticed, as Ben had mentioned earlier, that the window in which the murder could have occurred was fairly large. The ME had listed the time of death as somewhere between January first and January sixth. That was going to make it more difficult to solve this murder, although finding the body dumped near the Clifton property, combined with Jerrod Clifton being in the wind, made it look like a slam dunk. He assumed Ben had asked Dr. Estes for further studies that might pin the date down tighter. He saw that the BOLO hadn't turned anything up. He wondered whether they had gotten a search warrant for the Clifton house.

After nine, Wayne heard the noises of people entering the office—Ben's voice, Dory's throaty, amused contralto, and George's sulky tone. He heard Rob say, "So the great investigator, Eudora Clarkson, is actually sitting at her desk this morning." He didn't hear Dory's response, but Wayne could tell from the sound of her voice that she was not pleased. He heard Ben say that the staff meeting would start in fifteen minutes.

"Hey, Wayne." Ben stood in the doorway of Wayne's office a few minutes later. "Cam just told me you were back." His boss was pale, with dark circles under his eyes.

"Are you all right, Ben? You look a little peaked this morning."

Sheriff Bradley ran a hand through his curly, light brown hair. "Yeah, I'm okay. It was kind of a rough morning. Thoreau—that sweet old Rottweiler of Mae's—died last night while we were over at her parents' for dinner. We found him on the kitchen floor when we got home, and I buried him in her backyard before I came in this morning."

"I'm sorry to hear that."

"Thanks. Glad you made it back from Michigan in one piece. How'd it go?"

"I'll tell you in the meeting. I'd rather say it once than tell everyone separately."

Ben gave him a half-smile. "Sure, I understand. Did you read the reports I put on your desk yet?"

Wayne nodded. "I did. I'm ready for the staff meeting."

Ben led the way to the conference room and he and Wayne took their usual places. When everyone else was seated and the donut box had been passed, Ben turned to Wayne. "Do you want to lead off this morning, tell us what happened on your trip to the Huron Valley Prison?"

Taking a deep breath, Wayne looked around the table at the faces of his work family. "I'm not sure everyone knew why I went there," he began, trying to find the words. "I was in the foster care system as a kid." Wayne paused and Cam Gomez leaned forward, concern etched on her sweet features.

"My foster mother murdered my foster father after years of abuse. I located her in Huron Valley Prison in Michigan, serving life for his murder," Wayne looked around at everyone's unblinking attention. It was pin-drop quiet. He cleared his throat. "I started looking for her after we closed the Tom Ferris case at the end of last summer, but it took me a while to find her since she was serving time under her Native American name. Anyway, once I located her, I went to see her. She's elderly now and very sick. Since the murder was committed in self-defense, there's a possibility she could get her sentence commuted by the governor. An attorney at the capitol in Lansing is working on it."

"That's it?" Dory asked, frowning. "No more to that story? Sounds like there must be. Were you living with her when she killed her husband?"

Wayne raised his hands, feeling ripped open like a gutted fish. "No. I ran away when I was seventeen. I went back to my foster family's house when I was twenty, shortly after she killed him. I tried to get my foster mother to turn herself in. She wouldn't go to the authorities that night, but later on she did."

"So," Rob's voice was quiet and intent, "didn't that make you an accomplice to murder?" His intensity was unsettling. "Abetting a murderer, obstruction of justice?"

"Yeah. Mr. Big Detective here wants a con ... fess ... ion," Dory drawled out the word. "Not likely," she added, and Rob glowered.

The sheriff intervened. "How about we let Detective Nichols off the hook for the moment, Detective Fuller? We have a copper pipe case and a murder to solve. And it just occurred to me that Wayne Nichols is now truly chief detective, since your promotion." Wayne had always been referred to as "chief detective," due to his years of seniority.

Wayne gave Ben a grateful look. "Before we start on the murder, I have a question. Miss Dory, what's going on with you? Have you lost your appetite for blueberry donuts?" He had noticed her surreptitiously pushing the box away.

"Mr. Pretentious, our uppity new detective, is just trying to make me fat," Dory said. "I have been suggesting celery sticks, peeled carrots, and granola bars for staff meetings. So far, despite George's pudginess, I have no takers." The rest of the staff avoided her eyes.

"I'll take you up on it, Dory," Wayne told her. "I'm trying to lose a few more pounds."

"Okay, people." Ben redirected once more. "Besides Mike Clifton saying he might have seen the victim at his brother's place, what else has anyone found on our floater?"

"Not much, boss," Rob said. "He's not in the system, as you know. George and Cam haven't come across any missing persons reports, and the hospitals haven't treated anyone with stab wounds within the time frame."

Ben sighed. "I'm going to call Dr. Estes later and reiterate my request to narrow down the window on when this guy died. Did you turn up anything, George?"

"I did," George said, looking rather pleased with himself. "At Meeker's—the hunting and fishing supply store closest to where the body was dumped—I found out that Jerrod Clifton purchased a new deer rifle and hunting knife last fall. They don't keep legal records on knives, but he bought the knife the same day. Both items were on the receipt. The knife was the same model we were looking for, the six-inch ceramic blade Boker."

"George, that's just excellent." Ben shook his head. "Exceptional work. You've linked the murder weapon to Jerrod Clifton. Now, if we could just find him, we could wrap this one up."

"Nice going, George," Dory said. Rob patted George on the shoulder and Cam shook his hand.

"Okay, turning to our other big case …. Rob and I talked this over on my way in. He and I have agreed that we'll do a stakeout at a big historic house that's about to go to auction. The copper pipe thieves have been very active in removing copper pipe from foreclosures and auctioned properties as well as new builds."

"Since we talked earlier, Sheriff, I spoke with Captain Paula at the East Nashville post. They've had half a dozen reports and already have two detectives on it. She'd like us to butt out of the case and turn our reports over to her men. They're putting security cameras on a dozen different warehouses in the city where they think the pipes might be stored. I told her I'd check with you."

"Wayne, what do you think?" Ben asked.

"Hell, no," Wayne said. "The Yancey theft occurred in Rose County. That's our jurisdiction. If they'd found a cache in any of the Nashville warehouses, they would have said so. They don't have a primary location yet. It could even be in Rose County. I'd go ahead with the stakeout."

"Right. I'll call Captain Paula and tell her we're proceeding to follow the leads here in Rose County."

Ben turned to Deputy Gomez. "Cam, how are you coming on that search warrant for the Clifton property? Did I tell you that Mae found some copper pipes in the garage at the Clifton place? It was also the site of the puppy mill where Dory found the knife. I'd like a look inside that house. The side door to the garage was open when Dory and Mae were out there so we can do a careful search now, including fingerprints. As soon as we get the search warrant, we can go through the house. Our cases might just be coming together."

"When the search warrant comes through, who do you want to take the lead on that?" Rob asked.

"You and George can go out there and have a look as soon as we get a warrant. Let's try to find any paperwork about who buys his pit bull puppies and for what purposes. I'm thinking Clifton must have had a regular buyer, and it wasn't an individual looking for a pet. He had too many pups there to rely on the pet trade. You could also start checking with local veterinarians."

"I agree with the sheriff," Wayne said. "We need to pursue the puppy angle. There had to be a reason our victim was on the property. It probably has to do with the dogs. Find out if the local veterinarian practices know anything."

"Wayne, do you want to start checking out those leads?"

"No. I think I'll just stay here today. I have a conference call with the attorney for my foster mother this morning. I want to work this case with you guys, but I still have things left to do."

"Anything on the BOLO we have out for Jerrod Clifton?" Ben asked.

"Nada, boss," Dory said.

"Let's get an APB out on him, too. And Dory, can you get Ray Fenton and his mother to come into the office? I'd like him to look at some mug shots. Cam, pull anybody who's been convicted of animal trafficking in the last few years for the kid to see. Dory, tell the others about your feeling about the kid who turned in the puppy mill."

"Okay. The day of the ASPCA raid, when the rag and knife turned up, Ray wouldn't look at the material. It might have just been squeamishness, but I got a funny feeling. Ray Fenton had been going over there every day to feed the dogs. He might have seen something."

"Okay, let's bring him in. What turned up on the house to house, George?" Ben asked.

"No luck, Sheriff. It's all big farms in that area. Everyone's all spread out. We left a second citation on the front door for Jerrod. Want me to go back out there and see if anyone's turned up yet?"

"Okay," Ben said. "In fact, I'll go with you. I'll get Hadley from the lab to go with us to do prints from the garage. Just hang on a minute." Ben left the room with Wayne and followed the big man to his office.

"What's up with not wanting to investigate? That conference call sounded like an excuse," Ben said as soon as they were alone.

"It's not over yet, Ben." Wayne's voice was bleak. His shoulders were hunched and he rubbed his nose. He tried to control his voice by clearing his throat. "The problem is that the attorney for the Abused Women's Commutation Project says that lifers aren't usually eligible for parole. The parole board takes no action on their applications, even when there is a case for compassionate release. There's something else. My little brother Kurt was murdered by my foster father. As it stands, his death is listed as murder by 'person or persons unknown.' I have the evidence that Aarne killed him, but if I turn it over, I'll have to serve time."

Ben didn't say anything for a moment. Then he rubbed his forehead and said, "God, Wayne, you can't serve time. Gen pop would be a nightmare with you being in law enforcement." Wayne didn't respond. "Plus, your career would be over."

There was a long awkward silence before Sheriff Bradley said, "As your boss, I have no say in it, but if you'd like to talk to me about that evidence, I'm here as a friend."

The men stared at each other in silence. Wayne looked away, cleared his throat, and then glanced back. Taking a shaky breath, he said, "I appreciate that, Ben. I've always known that there are no clear victories in law enforcement, just battles. But having a friend"—he hesitated—"a friend who has your back in this battle we keep waging … it's the only victory there is in our business."

Ben shuffled his feet. His lips twitched into a lopsided grin. He turned quickly and left the room.

Wayne was breathing hard. If it was the only way to nail Aarne Outinen as Kurt's killer, he might have to ask their lab people test the gun for fingerprints. If he did, he would be violating every police rule governing the handling of evidence. But unless he could get Aarne listed as his brother's killer, and free Jocelyn, the guilt would never leave him. He walked on the edge of a razor.

Chapter Twenty

———

January 14th
Dory Clarkson

GRABBING A COFFEE while assiduously averting her eyes from the siren lure of the gleaming donut box on the conference room table, Dory went back to her desk. She felt quite proud of herself. She had nailed Mr. Presumptuous Fuller, who thought he was so high and mighty, and raised the dietary standards of the office to boot. Ben had asked her to get an All-Points Bulletin out on Clifton and make an appointment with Ray and his mother to come into the office for an interview. However, she decided to call the ASPCA first.

"ASPCA," the bored teenaged voice answered.

"May I speak to Mr. Gunderson? This is Dory Clarkson."

"Hang on."

Dory inspected a nail that was chipping and kicked her heels off under her desk until the man picked up.

"Gunderson."

"Good morning, Mr. Gunderson. It's Dory Clarkson. I'm calling to find out whether Mr. Clifton has contacted you?"

"No such luck. As I told you the other day, we obtained a

court order to put all of the dogs into fostering—all of them but Big Daddy. We couldn't get anyone to take him, so we're keeping him here for the moment. Going to run him through the database."

Dory wondered what sort of database there was for dogs. "Can you hold a hearing if the owner doesn't show up?"

"No. We have to wait three days for him to show. If the owner doesn't appear in that time, and the animals have been abandoned, we can seize them. Did the sheriff issue a citation?"

"Yes, he did, and a second one yesterday, but Mr. Clifton hasn't contacted our office yet. We've had a BOLO out for several days. This morning the sheriff asked me to get an APB out too."

"We presented the ASPCA case to the prosecutor's office for further evaluation. I argued for prosecution on the basis that the animals were abandoned. They agreed."

"If Jerrod Clifton shows up, I'll let you know. Please let me know if he contacts the ASPCA."

"Will do. And … Miss Clarkson? You know I wish the press would just keep their noses out of our business, but our attorney said I had to turn over the names of the people who are fostering the puppies. They'll be contacting Miss December. I thought I'd let you know so you can warn her."

They said goodbye. Dory sent Mae a quick text to let her know she'd be contacted by the press; then she called Ray's home phone number. When the shaky voice of his mother answered, she said, "Mrs. Fenton?"

"This is she."

"This is Eudora Clarkson from the sheriff's office. I'm calling to schedule you and your son to come into the office."

"Oh dear." The woman's voice was so soft Dory could hardly hear what she was saying. "I don't drive anymore and Ray doesn't have his license yet."

"That's no problem. We can come and pick you up. I'm just trying to get a time when you both could come in. Would tomorrow morning work for you? Around ten?"

"Why do you want to talk to me? I don't know anything. I have multiple sclerosis, and I'm in a wheelchair."

"I'm sorry Mrs. Fenton, but Ray is a minor, so a parent has to be with him when we talk to him."

Dory heard the woman catch her breath.

"What do you want to talk to him about?"

Dory had a niggling feeling that Ray Fenton hadn't even told his mother about the knife discovered on the Clifton property. She lowered her voice and spoke slowly, "Mrs. Fenton, did Ray tell you that we found a knife buried on the Clifton property?" There was a long pause. She heard the woman coughing.

"No. I didn't know," she whispered.

"Yes, and a body was found nearby in the river. There was no identification on the dead man and we're hoping that Ray can tell us who he is. We just want him to look at some photographs."

"Do you really need me?" She sounded frightened. "It's okay with me if he comes in alone. I'll sign something giving you permission if necessary."

"In that case, we'd like to talk with him today. Could I have one of the deputies come by your house and get your signed permission? Once we have that document, would it be okay with you if we go by the high school and pick him up?"

Ray's mother agreed and Dory clicked off the phone. She was going to ask Wayne Nichols, their chief detective, to use some of his finely tuned skills to get the kid to tell them everything he knew. And Dory was determined to be in the interview room with them.

THE PHONE RANG a few minutes later and Dory picked it up, absently saying, "Sheriff's Office."

"Dory, its Evangeline," her friend said, breathlessly.

"Good morning, Evangeline. Always good to hear from you."

"Have you got a TV in your office?"

"We do. What's up?"

"Turn on Channel Three right now. The news is on. They've got a story about the raid at the puppy mill. You're on television, girl."

"OMG," Dory said. She quickly hung up the phone, dashed down the hall to the break room, turned the TV on and flipped to Channel Three. Wayne, who was in the room getting coffee, stayed to watch.

The reporter, Carrie Allen, was saying, "All of Rosedale was shocked recently to find that a puppy mill has been operating in Rose County." She looked angrily into the camera. "The breeding facility was discovered on property belonging to a Mr. Jerrod Clifton." Her voice faded as video of the rescue day came on. Dory was pleased to see herself looking quite slim. Not quite as slim as she wanted to be, but less curvy than before. Black jeans and celery sticks could do that for a person.

The reporter continued. "All the rescued dogs are presently being fostered, but Channel Three is asking all our viewers to step up to the plate and give these beautiful baby pit bulls 'Forever Homes.' We will be continuing to follow this story and interviewing the temporary foster parents. More information concerning a grisly discovery made at the site will be reported on Crime Beat, coming up right after the station break."

After a half dozen commercials, the program switched to the crime reporter, Ellis Knox, a seriously handsome black guy with tightly curled hair and a goatee. He was interviewing the young girl who had been working with Ray the day of the raid.

"I'm talking today with Miss Allison Ware, who was present the day of the puppy mill raid. Miss Allie, can you tell us what else was discovered that day?"

A terrible sinking feeling hit Dory's stomach. This was going to be bad.

"Yes, sir. There was an investigator from the sheriff's office there. Her name was Clarkson. She found a bloody rag and a knife buried on the property." Dory swallowed, feeling sick. Ben was going to kill her.

"Did you speak directly with Investigator Clarkson about the discovery?"

"Yes, I did, and she also talked with Miss Carrie Adams about what the dog dug up."

Ellis Knox turned back to face the viewers, saying, "Rumors have been circulating that a dead body was recently found in the Little Harpeth river. However, the sheriff's office has continued to say 'no comment' when called by this station. The amount of blood on the rag found at the Clifton property implies a probable murder scene." Dory's heart was beating hard, as video of the dark hole, the bloody rag, and the knife was shown. The camera switched to Dory, standing beside Carrie Adams, who was asking whether the blood came from a person or an animal.

Dory watched herself start to blurt out something about the body that Mae found and then saying, "This interview is over." Seeing the footage recording her stupidity, Dory felt light headed. She pulled out a chair and fell into it.

The camera returned to Ellis Knox. "I'm only speculating here, but one wonders, when puppy mills are not against the law, why an investigator from the sheriff's office was on site for an ASPCA raid? Did Sheriff Bradley place Investigator Clarkson on the case knowing in advance a murder weapon might turn up? Does the sheriff already know where the bodies are? We have also heard an unsubstantiated rumor that Sheriff Bradley's girlfriend—local dog breeder and boarder, Mae December—found the body. If so, that's the second body she's found in less than a year." He paused for dramatic effect and Dory snuck a quick look at Wayne, whose eyes were glued to the screen.

"As we all know, this is an election year. Will the good citizens of Rosedale reelect a sheriff who employs investigators who leak sensitive information to underage girls working for the

ASPCA? And even worse, a sheriff who is likely investigating a third murder in Rose County in less than a year? Can Sheriff Ben Bradley really keep the people of Rose County safe?"

Dory flicked off the television, horrified and full of guilt. *I'm doomed. Ben Bradley is going to fire me or kill me or both.*

She had asked Deputy Cam to get Mrs. Fenton's signed permission paper and pick Ray Fenton up from high school before Evangeline called and she made her mad dash to the break room. Knowing they would be back soon, Dory asked Wayne if he would interview the boy.

"Sure, I'll talk to him," Wayne said. "Have you told Ben about talking to that reporter?"

"No," Dory said, pinning her arms against her sides. She could feel her stomach roiling. "I was hoping they'd never use that footage."

"You better call him. If you don't, the sheriff's going to hear about it some other way. If you can get the police artist drawing of the victim, I can show it to the kid and have him look at the mug shots Cam pulled of animal traffickers."

"I'll tell him when he gets back to the office, don't worry. Can I be in the room when you talk to Ray?" Dory asked. Wayne shrugged. "Please? He knows me, and he's kind of timid. He might feel more comfortable with me there."

"Okay, if you think it would help, you can be in there." Wayne walked out of the room.

Dory went back to her desk and located the police artist sketch of John Doe. While she was in the interview room with Ray and Detective Nichols, she hoped to extract an identification of the victim. Without getting an ID for their John Doe, Dory was afraid she would find herself out of a job—as soon as her boss learned about her on-air blunder.

WHEN DEPUTY CAM brought the teenager into the office, Dory buzzed Wayne. Detective Nichols walked into the reception area.

"Detective Nichols, I'd like to introduce you to Ray Fenton," Dory said. "This is the young man who risked losing his job when he turned Jerrod Clifton in for neglect and cruelty to animals. And he was with me when we found the knife."

"Pleased to meet you, Mr. Fenton," the Detective said. Ray's shoulders straightened at being addressed as "Mr."

"Pleased to meet you too, sir," Ray's voice squeaked.

"Come down to the conference room, Ray," Dory said and led the way. She opened the door and got Ray seated at the table.

Detective Nichols rested a hand on the drawing of John Doe. Taking his hand away, he said, "This is the man who was found dead in the Little Harpeth River that runs behind the Clifton property. Do you recognize him?"

Ray looked at the drawing for a long time. He shook his head, but Dory could practically hear him trying to decide what to say. He might not have been prepared to outright lie to the police, but he was definitely holding back.

"Are you sure?" Detective Nichols asked quietly. "Take your time, Ray. I need you to be honest with me. I'm going to ask you again. Do you recognize this man?"

"No. I mean, yes," he said, his voice very quiet. Ray took a deep breath. There was the faintest sheen of sweat on his forehead. He rubbed the back of his neck.

"Just tell us what you know about him," Wayne said. He used his calmest tone of voice, which had an almost loving quality. Dory could see it had an effect on the boy.

"Um … yes. I do recognize the person," Ray said in a wavering voice. He dragged his hands through his hair. He looked furtive; his Adam's apple bobbed. "Mr. Jerrod had him come out sometimes, usually when I wasn't there. But the next time I came to work, some of the puppies would be missing. I only saw him once or twice. I'm pretty sure his name was Johns or something like that." He blinked and Dory thought he was fighting tears.

"You must've hated his guts," Dory said. "Smart as you are, you probably figured that he was doing something bad with those puppies."

Ray's lips were moving, as if he was struggling to find the right thing to say. He bit his lower lip. "See … this one day, he tried to take my puppy. My own Pearl Jam …." The words seemed to burst from him.

"Okay, let's step back here a minute," Wayne said. "I wasn't informed that you had a pup of your own. Did it come from Clifton's puppy mill?"

"Yes, Mr. Jerrod said I could have a puppy. She was the last in the litter and he wanted to breed the female again. That's how I got Pearl Jam. I named her that because of the color of her fur. She's almost all white."

"And where was Pearl Jam the day of the raid?" Dory asked, keeping her voice soft and sweet. She smiled at Ray.

"I hid her in a crate under some old rugs behind the barn. I couldn't have her at home because my mom is too sick. So I'd keep her at Clifton's. But the day the ASPCA came, she got loose somehow and *Mr. Gunderson took her.*" As Ray told his story, the timbre of his voice became higher and more strident until it was nearly a wail. He struggled for composure. At last he took a deep breath and said, "It's going to be okay, though, because that awful man is dead now and Miss December is taking good care of my puppy."

There was a quick rap on the conference room door and Dory went to open it. Cam was standing in the hall.

"Miss Dory, I'm so sorry to interrupt," she whispered, "but Sheriff Bradley just called in. He and Deputy George are on their way back here. You said you wanted to know when he got back."

Dory thanked Ray and asked Cam to take him back to school. She turned back to Detective Nichols, who was giving her a strange look. "Ben said to have Ray look at mug shots of known animal traffickers," he said quietly. "I'll finish up here before Cam takes him back to school."

"We better not. The sheriff's on his way back. He's going to be mad as hell that I talked with the press and that I was in the interview room with you. I should be at my desk."

"Indeed," Wayne said and Dory quivered.

Sheriff Bradley and Deputy George came through the office door minutes later. Dory was sitting meekly at her post.

"The APB paid off and the state troopers picked up Jerrod Clifton. When he gets here, get Detective Fuller to book him on suspicion of murder," the sheriff told Deputy Phelps over his shoulder. "We're going to let him sit in a cell overnight and question him in the morning." He turned to face Dory. "Miss Clarkson, I want a word. In my office." Ben's expression was a study in barely controlled rage.

Investigator Clarkson, looking hangdog, presented herself at the door of the sheriff's office. Ben just looked at her for a moment or two. He waved her in but didn't invite her to be seated.

"What the hell, Dory? What the hell were you thinking leaking the discovery of the probable murder weapon to the press?" Ben stopped as Dory raised her hand. "Not to mention you almost slipped and told them about the body Mae found. Oh yes, I know all about the news coverage."

"Sir, I didn't tell them about the body, I only said—"

"Save it, Clarkson. Zip it. You're in so deep here, you better not say another word."

"Yes, sir," Dory said.

"Not even 'yes sir.' Nothing. I want *silence*, is that clear? Are you totally unaware of the office policy? As you should know, what we say to the press about any serious crime until we have a suspect in custody is 'no comment.' "

"I just didn't remember the policy until it was too late." Dory said plaintively.

He shook his head in disgust. "It's clear to me that you lack any vestige of common sense."

Tears formed in Dory's eyes.

"Detective Nichols, Detective Fuller, and I will obtain the vic's identity and find his killer with no further *help* from you."

"May I please say something, Sheriff?" Dory asked. Her voice was positively pitiful.

"It had better be good." Ben's expression was thunderous.

"Ray Fenton said John Doe's last name was Johns or something. That was good, wasn't it?"

Ben took a deep breath. "It's a help, but you shouldn't have been in there questioning him in the first place! I am normally a patient man—"

At the moment, Dory found this hard to believe.

"But my patience is at the breaking point here. Why the hell did you overstep your bounds this way? I swear to God, woman," Ben stared down at his desk.

The tears were streaming down Dory's cheeks now. "Am I fired, boss?"

Ben hesitated, shook his head and sighed. "I'll probably regret this, but no. I'm not going to fire you. But I am demoting you. You're no longer an investigator."

Dory bit her lip to stop herself from begging.

"You're back on your former duties, including *full time* on the phones. Now get out of here."

Chapter Twenty-One

———

January 14th
Mae December

M AE HAD RECEIVED a text from Dory saying that the press intended to speak with all the people in Rosedale who were fostering the dogs taken from the puppy mill, so Mae was not surprised when Carrie Allen's assistant called to schedule an interview. The assistant said that Carrie would like to come to Mae's house and tape the interview "as soon as possible, to help you find homes for the puppies." With a gulp, Mae agreed to a one o'clock taping. Miss Allen's assistant had asked Mae to have the puppies in the house so they could get some footage of them playing together.

Mae looked around her kitchen with a critical eye. It was messy, but what her grandmother had always called 'a quick flish' soon took care of that. Mae continued through her main floor with Tallulah and the Tater on her heels, picking up dog toys, books, and random bridal magazines Tammy had bestowed upon her. Finally, when order was restored, she dashed out to the barn to check on her boarding dogs. She brought her three foster puppies back into the house, after giving them a moment to play in the cold grass.

Titan, her male Welsh corgi, was dozing on his favorite rug in the kitchen. When she came in with three excited puppies, he gave a weary sigh and hauled himself to his feet. True, Guinness, and Pearl converged upon him with glee. Titan uttered a low growl and Mae gave him a stern look. "Stop that, Titan. Go to your room if you can't be nice." She pointed to the laundry room and he trotted off. Mae watched him go in and lie on the big dog bed where her other two dogs were already curled up. "Good boy," she told him and closed the laundry room door.

"C'mon, puppies." She walked down the hallway toward her studio, and all three of them ran after her. When she stopped at the doorway, they ran on into the mostly empty room where Mae worked on her landscapes if she ever got a free moment. There was a blank canvas on the easel at the moment—the painting she planned on starting before breaking her wrist.

Mae closed the bottom half of the Dutch door and watched the pups run around, chew on the legs of her wooden easel and sniff everything. They started to lose steam, slowing down until they eventually came to a stop, looking up at her and wagging their tails. "I'll be right back," she told their alert little faces and bright eyes. She got an old soft blanket out of the linen closet in the hall and dropped it over the half-door and onto the wooden floor of the studio. "Feel free to tussle or nap," she told them. "I'm going to go freshen up and then we're going to be interviewed and filmed."

Luckily, she had already taken some time with her crazy hair earlier that morning, so Mae only needed a change of clothes and a quick application of mascara and lip gloss to be camera ready. She inspected her teeth in her upstairs bathroom mirror. They were free of food particles, and she thought her off-white sweater was flattering and wouldn't show dog hair. She gave herself a nod of approval and went downstairs to await Carrie Allen, the Channel Three reporter.

Half an hour later, she looked up from one of the ubiquitous bridal magazines at the sound of her doorbell. She glanced at her cellphone; Carrie and her crew were a few minutes early. She got up and opened the door to the reporter and two men, presumably her cameraman and sound tech.

"Hi, c'mon in. I'm Mae." She opened the door wide, gesturing them inside.

"So good of you to let us come on short notice!" the attractive brunette gushed. "I'm Carrie. Oh, you hurt your arm. Are you all right?" Mae nodded as the woman rolled on. "What a wonderful house. Where should we set up?"

Mae stepped back to allow room for the two men and their equipment. Once everyone was inside, she quickly shut the door to keep out the cold. "Thank you. The house is a hundred years old. And the puppies are in my studio right now. You can set up in there if you want. Would you like to see them?"

"A studio? I thought you ran a kennel, Miss December," Carrie said, peering around with interest. "No one told me you were a musician."

Mae laughed, leading the way through the kitchen and toward the puppies. "I do run a kennel, and I'm also a breeder. But it's not a music studio. I'm a painter." She stopped at the Dutch door. "And those are the little cuties I'm fostering."

True and Guinness were play fighting on the blanket. Pearl finished piddling in the corner and came running to the door. She sat down and looked up at them with a little yip.

"How precious," Carrie cooed. She looked at the cameraman. "Get some footage of them, Doug. Then we'll set up for the interview back in the living room." The cameraman got to work.

"Seth, let's start the interview, and you can dub it to run during the puppy footage." The sound tech nodded and followed Carrie and Mae back to the living room. "Let's you and I sit on the couch, Miss December."

Mae sat down. "Please call me Mae." She patted the cushion beside her. "Have a seat."

Carrie sat down and Seth hooked a small microphone to her collar then stepped back. "I'm here in the lovely, historic home of local dog boarder and breeder Mae December, who, despite her wrist being in a cast, is currently fostering three of the pit bull puppies rescued during an ASPCA raid on a Rosedale puppy mill."

The cameraman came in and he and Seth moved Mae's coffee table out of the way. Doug began setting up his tripod as Carrie went on, "I know you want to find permanent homes for these puppies, Mae."

"Yes, I do. I'm taking care of them until we find them 'forever' homes." Mae smiled into the camera that was now in place on the tripod. "They're very sweet, healthy puppies who deserve loving homes. If you're interested, you can contact the ASPCA in Nashville."

"That's right," the reporter said, "and there's no reason to be concerned about the pit bull breed, is there?"

"Well, these puppies weren't taken from a dog-fighting operation, so they weren't bred to fight." Mae bit her lip. "But the ASPCA has taken the extra precaution of having all the dogs tested for the so-called 'warrior-gene.' It's a genetic marker for severe dog aggression. The Vet school helped by doing the blood work for them, and we should know the results soon. All the dogs and puppies that don't carry the gene will be available to go to new homes."

Carrie Allen glanced at the copy of *Today's Bride* that Mae had left on the coffee table. "I see. That's very interesting. And are congratulations in order for you and Sheriff Bradley?"

"Not for us." Mae shook her head, looking at the camera. "I'm hosting the wedding for two dear friends of mine. Just looking for some ideas."

"I'm sorry, Mae." Carrie Allen didn't look sorry. "Just being a reporter. Speaking of that," Carrie leaned in closer, staring intently at Mae, "is it true you found another body?"

Mae straightened up and leaned away. She gave the nosy woman her brightest smile. "Well, Carrie, all I can say about that is … 'no comment.' "

Carrie Allen's eyebrows went up and she gave a tiny smirk. "Thank you for your time this afternoon, Miss December." She pulled the microphone off her collar and rose gracefully to her feet, handing it to Seth. "That's a wrap."

Chapter Twenty-Two

January 15th
Detective Wayne Nichols

THE STATE COPS had spotted Jerrod Clifton in Knoxville and transported him to Rosedale. It was around eleven p.m. when they got him in the cell. So far he hadn't asked for an attorney. When the sheriff arrived the following morning, everyone clustered around, wanting to know who was going to participate in the interview and who was going to observe.

"Wayne and I will do this one," Ben said. Detective Rob Fuller frowned, but Dory gave a little smirk. Wayne had noticed several sniping interactions between the two of them recently, and he guessed that Dory felt Rob was getting too big for his britches. She was probably pleased he would be relegated to observation for this important interview.

"George, bring Jerrod Clifton into interrogation please."

George Phelps walked off to get the probable murderer of the floater Mae had found in the river. He came back shortly, leading a big guy with dark eyes and a clenched jaw. His light brown hair was cut very short, and in build and features he strongly resembled his brother. George had handcuffed Mr.

Clifton with his arms behind his body before bringing him in. The previous night, Wayne and Ben had discussed how they were going to conduct the interview. Wayne was going to be bad cop; Ben would be good cop, taking off the handcuffs, getting Clifton coffee and generally lowering his stress level.

"Deputy, I thought I told you to bring Mr. Clifton in without handcuffs. I'm sorry, Jerrod. Get those off him right now, George," Ben said, frowning. "Mr. Clifton, can I have my deputy get you come coffee?"

Clifton nodded and George left to get Clifton's coffee. After delivering the coffee, he departed, flipping on the audio capture as he left.

"Let's start, shall we?" Ben said, pleasantly. "You were read your Miranda rights yesterday, correct?" Jerrod nodded. "Sorry, Mr. Clifton, you need to say aloud that you were read your rights. It's necessary for the audiotape."

"I was read my rights," Clifton said. He seemed calm.

Ben quickly stated the date and time. He continued by saying, "This is Sheriff Ben Bradley and Chief Detective Wayne Nichols. We are interviewing Jerrod Clifton regarding the recent dead body found near his property."

Clifton's eyes widened.

"Hand Mr. Clifton the police artist sketch please, Detective."

Instead of sliding the police sketch down the table to Jerrod Clifton, Wayne produced the grisly ME photos, including some of the man's torso.

"What the hell?" Clifton said. Wayne watched his expression closely. He wasn't sure, but he thought the dead man could have been a surprise to Clifton. If Jerrod Clifton wasn't the perp, this case was going to be a lot harder to crack.

"Who is this guy?" Wayne said.

"It's Web Johnston," Clifton said. "He's the guy I hired to shut down the puppy mill when I left for Knoxville. He's dead?" Ben and Wayne looked at each other. The victim's ID had been confirmed.

"Murdered, actually. How long were you in Knoxville, Mr. Clifton?" Ben said pleasantly. "What were you doing there?"

"Visiting my cousin Jake."

"When did you leave town?" Wayne asked.

"I left January first. I was going to stay a few more days, but your officers brought me here last night." He sounded belligerent. "They put me in a cell with three other guys, took my shoelaces and all my personal stuff. I had to spend the rest of the night with three slime balls and an overflowing toilet. All I've had to eat was a bologna sandwich that I couldn't stomach because of the stench." He clenched his teeth.

"I'm sorry that was necessary, Mr. Clifton," Ben said soothingly. "But as you can see, this man was murdered and he was found near your property. Given the situation, we needed to talk with you promptly. We take murder extremely seriously. Tell us a bit more about Mr. Johnston and what he was doing for you."

Jerrod sniffed, rubbed his nose and shot an angry look at Wayne Nichols.

"Web Johnston worked for me the last two years. I raise pit bull puppies. He sells them for me. He was supposed to get rid of all the dogs before I got back."

"How would you describe your relationship with Mr. Johnston?" Ben asked, still calm and composed.

"We worked together, that's all," Jerrod said, defensively. "I certainly had no reason to kill the guy."

"Let's cut the crap here, Clifton," Wayne interjected. "This guy was brutally murdered then put into the river, probably from your property. You left town right after you killed him and went to your cousin's place. And family members …." Wayne trailed off, shrugging his shoulders and looking at Clifton intently.

"What my colleague is implying here, Mr. Clifton, is that a family member is not usually considered rock solid alibi material. A guy's family might cover for him, you see," Ben

Bradley said with a friendly smile. "Does your cousin live alone?"

Wayne could see Jerrod got the point.

"He's single, yeah. But I had no reason to kill Web. I needed him to get rid of the dogs."

"We talked to your brother. He said you were going to shut down your operation. Why was that?" Wayne asked, with a penetrating stare. "If it was lucrative for you, why have Johnston dispose of your dogs?"

"I wasn't making as much money lately. And I've got a line on a new business."

"Copper sells pretty well these days, doesn't it?" Wayne said. Clifton grimaced, then sniffed again. Wayne made brief eye contact with Sheriff Bradley.

"Like that pile of copper pipe in your garage, that's probably worth quite a bit," Ben pointed out, with another pleasant smile.

"That's for some plumbing I'm doing—gonna put a bathroom in out there. And I didn't kill Web, damn it. I was out of town until last night."

"Where did you get those cuts on your arms?" Ben asked, indicating a pattern of scratches. "Did Web Johnston fight back?"

"Just one of the dogs. I'm telling you guys, I didn't kill him." Clifton was adamant.

"There was also a bloody rag and a hunting knife found buried on your property," Wayne said. "We're going to find your fingerprints on the knife and your DNA all over the rag. Soon as we get a trial scheduled, you're going to be somebody's bitch in Riverbend Maximum Security prison. It will be quite an education." Wayne smiled like a big cat hovering over its weakened prey.

"I want a lawyer," Clifton said.

"Certainly, Mr. Clifton. Give us the name and number and we'll get ahold of your lawyer," Ben said.

Clifton hesitated, frowning. "I don't actually have one. What about my phone call? I'm supposed to get a phone call. My brother's in town. He can get a lawyer for me."

"Interview concluded," Ben said for the audio capture. George opened the door and took Clifton's arm.

"Should I put him in the drunk tank?" George asked.

"No way. I want this guy put with the violent offenders," Wayne said and Clifton paled. They didn't actually have any violent offenders in their small jail, but Wayne thought it would shake Clifton up. "I think Butka will be interested in meeting you."

After George left with Clifton, Ben turned to Wayne. "We're going to go over that guy's alibi with a fine-toothed comb. Who do you think I should assign this to?"

"Dory usually does this stuff, but what about giving it to Cam and Dory together?"

"Good idea. I want to find out what Cam will do with a big assignment." Ben buzzed Deputy Gomez, who knocked on the door in only moments.

"Did you need me, sir?" she asked.

"Yes," Ben said. "Mr. Clifton *appears* to have an alibi for the time of the murder, but I doubt that it's water tight. I want everything checked. He said he was with his cousin Jake Clifton in Knoxville. So ask the cousin what dates Jerrod was there. The key time period during which the victim was killed is January first through the sixth. Jerrod says he was in Knoxville the whole time, but that's less than four hours from here, which doesn't rule him out as the killer. I want his financials checked down to the decimal point, particularly credit card transactions. See if he bought food in Knoxville every day. Jerrod and his cousin are both bachelors, so they probably ate out or bought prepared foods. And find out when he last had his oil changed on his truck. Maybe we'll get lucky and we can get the mileage. Have Dory check out his LUDs and give you a hand with this."

"LUDs, sir?"

"Local usage details for his cellphone."

"In Nashville they called them CDRs—call detail records."

"I want to know who Jerrod called, who called him, whatever you can get. I think he's lying about being in Knoxville the whole time. I think he came back here, did Johnston, and drove back to Knoxville the same day."

"When would you like this information?" Cam asked.

"It's going to take you several days. Do you have any questions?"

"No sir," Cam replied. She was turning toward the door when Wayne thought about how junior she was. In her previous job at the Nashville post, most of what she did was to check people in and out of the drunk tank and take evidence to the evidence locker.

"This is a big job the sheriff's given you," Wayne said. "Are you sure you're up to it, Cam? Would you like help from anyone besides Dory?"

"I'm good, Detective. I like a challenge. This is exactly the sort of thing I hoped I'd get by coming here," her face was flushed and her dark eyes sparkled.

Wayne looked at Ben, who nodded at her, "Good luck."

"I think she'll need it," Wayne said after Cam departed.

WHEN EVERYONE ELSE left the office around six, Wayne asked Ben if he would like to go out for a brew. "Or are you headed over to see Mae? I bet this puppy mill and animal cruelty stuff has her all riled up."

"It sure does. I wish I could grab a beer with you, but I'm taking Matthew over to my parents' house to spend the night. We'll have dinner there and I'll go to Mae's after he's in bed. She's got a broken wrist and she's really worn out—no energy. Besides fostering the puppies and doing a little investigating," his boss smiled and shook his head, "*very* little, for her, she's also got all this wedding stuff going on. I'm trying to help when

I can, but Matty hasn't seen my parents in a while. I've got to order the tuxes and help Mae with little stuff she wants repaired on the house before Tammy and Patrick West's wedding … if I can ever find the time. It's going to be at Mae's house on Valentine's Day."

Wayne was alarmed. "When's Valentine's Day this year? Lucy's probably expecting something from me."

His boss laughed. "It's February fourteenth, every year."

"Do you think I have to get her candy or flowers or something else?"

"Well, it's been my experience that lingerie goes down pretty well." Ben cracked a wise-ass grin. "Of course that means going into Victoria's Secret, a tough *undercover* assignment."

"No doubt it does," Wayne smiled back, "unless you know how to shop on the Internet."

THAT EVENING WAYNE called Lucy and invited her to go out to dinner. Afterward, sitting together in front of her fireplace with glasses of red wine, he told her he had seen Jocelyn.

"What was that like for you, Wayne?" she asked, tentatively. There were tiny frown lines on her forehead.

"Tough, really tough. She's down to skin and bones. She remembered the night she killed Outinen vividly, though. I'm working with an attorney who runs the Abused Women's Commutation Project in Lansing, Michigan. She's trying to get her released."

"That would be wonderful, for her and for you. You wouldn't need to feel guilt or responsibility any longer." She smiled at him.

"You know I want to set the record straight about Aarne Outinen killing my brother and get Kurt buried properly," Wayne said quietly. "Just can't figure out my next step yet."

"While you obsess about that some more, my next step is bed. Would you care to join me, Detective?" she asked, raising her eyebrows.

"If I *ever* say no to the question you just asked, you have my permission to shoot me."

They walked to the bedroom, hand in hand.

Chapter Twenty-Three

—

January 16th
Mae December

M AE'S BUSINESS PHONE rang at ten-thirty that morning. She was in her kitchen, playing with little Tater on the floor. She stood up and grabbed it on the third ring. "Mae's place, how can I help you?"

"Miss December, this is Larry Gunderson calling you from the ASPCA. Do you have a minute to talk?"

Her eyes flew to the calendar hanging on the pantry door. January sixteenth, today's date, was circled. Inside the circle, Mae had written; 'test results for W.G.' in red. "Yes, Mr. Gunderson, I can talk right now," she swallowed.

"Well, there's no good way to say this, I'm afraid. Several of the dogs and puppies tested positive for the Warrior Gene." He sighed. "The male puppy that you're fostering is one of them."

"Oh, no, not Guinness! He's a sweet puppy …." Mae leaned her forehead on the wall.

"I'm sorry, Miss December. I know its bad news, and I'm sure you're already attached to him, but knowing that he carries the gene, we can't in good conscience allow him to be adopted.

He'll have to be euthanized, unfortunately."

Mae didn't answer, and Mr. Gunderson was quiet for a moment too. "You hadn't already found a home for him, I hope?"

"No, I haven't found homes for any of them yet. I was waiting for the test results," she told him sadly. A horrible thought crossed her mind. "What about the females? Are they okay?"

"They have no more likelihood of becoming aggressive or dangerous than any other dog," Mr. Gunderson responded in a happier voice. "Both of them tested negative for the gene, and you can go ahead with finding homes for them. As I'm sure you know, if they're cared for and trained properly, they'll be fine pets."

"I'm glad they tested negative," she responded, trying to remain calm. "What do I need to do with Guinness, Mr. Gunderson? Do I take him to my vet, or bring him to you?"

"We're asking everyone who has dogs or pups that tested positive to bring them back to the ASPCA. The volunteers from the vet school who did the testing are going to euthanize the animals." He cleared his throat. "It's going to be a sad day here. If you could bring him in this afternoon, that would be best. And thank you for fostering. It really is a big help."

Mae agreed to bring Guinness back to the ASPCA and ended the call quickly. Crying, she sat down on the floor and the Tater climbed into her lap. The little dog licked her face and Mae let the tears fall until they slowed of their own accord. She hugged her little corgi to her chest, then got up to go into the hall bathroom and blow her nose. Tallulah, who was reclining on the big dog bed in the laundry room, lifted up her head as Mae went by. The black pug followed Mae into the bathroom.

"I'm okay, Tallulah." The pug tilted her head to one side, staring up at her with wide, lustrous eyes. Mae couldn't help but smile. "Really, I am." She blew her nose with a loud honk, splashed cold water on her face, and rolled her head from side to side. Her two corgis appeared in the bathroom and sat on either side of Tallulah, all three dogs regarding her solemnly. She bent down and petted them. When she stood back up they all followed her down the hall to the kitchen. *They must think I shouldn't be alone right now, and they're probably right.*

MAE GOT BACK from the ASPCA after three that afternoon, feeling sad and lonesome despite a house and barn full of dogs and puppies. Ray Fenton was in the barn when she went out to give True and Pearl Jam their afternoon meal.

"Oh, hi there—forgot you were coming today."

"Hi, Miss Mae," the skinny teenager said. "Where's Guinness?"

She told him about the test results and he stood looking down at his shoes for a minute, wordless.

"The girls are both fine though, don't worry." He looked up and glanced over at the female puppies. "I was just about to feed them. Do you want to take care of that?" He nodded. "Oh, and Domino and Maggie Pie can have their supper now too. If you could walk Lulu and then give everybody fresh water, they'll be all set. Come into the house when you're done and I'll find a snack for us both."

"Can I bring True and Pearl Jam inside?" he asked with a little squeak to his voice.

Mae smiled at him. "Of course."

She was on the phone with Tammy when Ray brought the two puppies into her kitchen twenty minutes later. "So, do you want to call that caterer back, or should I?" Tammy said that Grace, her mother, would take care of it. "I need to go, Tammy. Ray's here with the puppies and I'm going to fix us something to eat."

"Mae, I've been thinking, would your niece Olivia like to be my flower girl?"

She looked at Ray, standing patiently with two pups squirming against his chest. "Hang on just a second, Tammy."

"Do you want them in the studio?"

"Yes. Did you make sure they did their business outside first?"

Ray gave her a shy grin. "Yes Ma'am, they both did um, everything outside. I'll just put them in there and take your house dogs out in the yard for a little while."

"Perfect." She picked her phone back up off the counter. "Sorry, you still there?"

"I'm here. Who's Ray?"

"He's my new employee." She heard the scrabble of toenails and the click of the door as it closed behind Ray Fenton and her three dogs. "He's a nice kid. He's actually the one who turned Jerrod Clifton in for animal cruelty, but he lost his job out there. Dory talked me into hiring him." Mae looked out her kitchen window at the teenager, who was throwing a ball for the Tater to chase. She took a deep breath and told Tammy the heartbreaking news about Guinness.

"Oh, Mae. I'm so sorry."

Mae put her phone on speaker and set it on the counter, then painstakingly opened a can of tomato soup and dumped it into a saucepan to heat up. "Yeah, it's been a rough one. Anyway, I can ask July about Livy being your flower girl. Do you want Matty to be the ring bearer?" She got out some bread to toast for pimento cheese sandwiches to have with the soup.

"That's a great idea! The two of them would look really cute together."

Ray, the Tater, Titan, and Tallulah clattered back into the kitchen on a gust of cold, damp air. "I'll ask about both of them, then. Talk to you tomorrow." The two friends said their goodbyes and Mae put the sandwiches together, filled two soup bowls, and set everything on the kitchen table.

"Help yourself, Ray."

He sat down and wolfed his food in short order. Small and skinny though he was, the boy could eat like a champ. He wiped his mouth with a napkin when he was finished. "Thanks, Miss

Mae. That was good. Is there anything else you need me to do today?"

"I don't think so. I want to ask you something, though. Do you think any of Jerrod Clifton's dogs were being sold for uses than than pets?" Ray gave a little nod. "For dog-fighting, maybe?" Mae guessed.

"I really don't know." Ray looked down at his feet for a moment. "Just sometimes a lot of dogs would go at the same time, not just puppies. I'd come back to work and some of the full grown ones would be gone, too. I asked Mr. Jerrod about it once and he said to mind my own business."

Mae did not like the sound of that at all. "All right, Ray, thanks. You can go play with the puppies if you want, while I finish eating."

Ray took his dishes to the sink and disappeared down the hall toward her art studio/puppy holding area. Mae ate the rest of her food. For a voracious teen, soup and a sandwich was a snack, but this was an early dinner for her. Ben wouldn't be over until late tonight, but she planned to share her suspicions with him then. After she ate and took Ray home, she would be hashing out some more wedding details and taking a hot bath—with a nice glass of wine.

IT WAS ALMOST nine that night and Ben had yet to arrive at her house. Mae had already taken her bath and spoken with Tammy's mother, Grace. The catering decisions had been finalized. Mae's sister July had agreed to Olivia being the flower girl—apparently Olivia was already the proud owner of what July described as "the perfect dress"—and they had no family plans that conflicted with the February fourteenth event.

"I'll try and get a sitter for the boys, and Fred and I will come with Livy," her sister said. "Unless you want them for ring bearers or ushers or anything?"

"I think Matthew's going to be the ring bearer, but Nathan and Parker would be great ushers."

"As long as they behave themselves," her sister said doubtfully. "Ask Tammy. If she wants them to do it, I'll put the fear of God into them and we can have a family Valentine's Day celebration."

The Tater jumped off the couch where she'd been curled up beside Mae and ran to the door. She gave one sharp yap. "I've got to go, July. Ben must be here."

"Hello, girls." Ben came in dressed in jeans and a heavy coat. Slipping it off, he hung it on the stair post and plunked down on the couch beside Mae, giving her a quick kiss.

"Glad you've got the fire on. It feels great in here." He leaned back into the cushions with a sigh, turning to look at her. "Are you okay, babe? You seem quiet."

She told him about her day—test results and having to take Guinness in to be put down, dinner with Ray and her fears that Jerrod had been supplying dogs for illegal purposes, as well as her progress with wedding planning.

Ben listened, and when she was done talking, he moved Tatie from in between them and pulled Mae close. She lay against his chest and felt herself melt into him. The tightness in her throat that had been there ever since Mr. Gunderson's phone call finally eased and she took a deep breath. "Thank you." She sat up and gave him a smile. "How was your day?"

He frowned and shook his head. "Not great. Matty was a real chore at my parents' tonight. Just tired, maybe, but he was extra picky about dinner and cried about everything. And the DNA results came back from the rag and knife Dory found. It was the murder weapon, and there was DNA from two men— Web Johnston and someone else. We don't have the results on the comparison with Jerrod Clifton yet. If he isn't our guy, I'm at a loss as to where to go next, Mae. Maybe you can help figure out what Clifton was really doing with his dogs, though."

His blue eyes were dark in the subdued light of her living room and his brown curly hair was ruffled. As usual, he smelled great.

Mae stood up. "I'll look into it. And I know where you need to go next. Will you put Tatie in her crate, please?"

"Sure. You going to bed?"

She untied her robe and let it slip until it caught on her cast, showing her bare shoulders and chest. "I am. It might be cold up there, though."

Ben was on his feet and in the kitchen with the little corgi before she could blink. "Don't worry. I'll keep you warm," he called over his shoulder. "You aren't going to need that robe at all."

Chapter Twenty-Four

—————

January 17th
Dory Clarkson

As soon as he and Detective Nichols finished questioning Jerrod, Sheriff Bradley had asked Dory to let Mr. Gunderson of the ASPCA know that Mr. Clifton was in custody. He wanted the ASPCA to schedule the hearing on the Clifton puppy mill. Ben had told the staff he suspected Clifton of master-minding the copper theft ring and potentially the murder. If Jerrod were given jail time for animal cruelty, that might provide the sheriff with a chance to collect sufficient evidence for a felony indictment on the other two crimes.

Judge Garrett Sower, an animal lover who had made a specialty of hearing ASPCA cases, moved the case to the front of his calendar. A lucky cancellation on the court docket had given them a January seventeenth date. George and Rob were assigned to bring Jerrod Clifton to the court dressed in an orange suit and cuffs. Dory had arranged it as a nice theatrical touch.

Dory dressed carefully for the hearing, hoping the ASPCA attorney would call her as a witness. The ASPCA attorney,

Miss Marina Seng, and Dory had already had several meetings while waiting for Jerrod to turn up. Dory was bringing young Ray with her. The drive to the courtroom would give them a chance to talk. She was concerned about him, knowing it was going to be a tough day for the teenager.

Marina Seng met Dory and Ray Fenton on the courthouse steps and escorted them into a nearby conference room for a briefing. Marina was a young Asian woman with smooth dark hair cut in a bob and beautiful ivory skin. She was dressed in a silver gray suit and a black blouse. Dory looked at her reed-like slimness and compared it to her own, more curvaceous self. More celery sticks were in order.

Miss Seng asked Dory a few last-minute questions, reassured Ray Fenton that he would be safe from reprisals, and took them both into the courtroom. She said she would be leaving it up to Judge Sower to determine whether either of them would be called. When they entered the courtroom, the defendant, Jerrod Clifton, was sitting at a table in the front of the room beside his attorney.

"All rise," the bailiff said, and everyone stood.

"This is a hearing on animal cruelty. Mr. Clifton, how do you plead?" the judge said. Jerrod and his attorney, Jim Mitchell, approached the bench.

"My client pleads not guilty, Your Honor," Mitchell, a skinny guy with a military style haircut, stated.

"Given the exigencies of the situation and the need to get the animals placed in permanent care, we're hearing this case today. This is not a remand hearing. You may begin, Miss Seng."

"I have photographs to show Your Honor," she said and pulled photos from her briefcase. There was a mild ruckus in the back of the courtroom and the judge banged his gavel. Dory's heart sank. It was her nemesis, Carrie Adams, along with her crew and reporters from other local stations.

"Quiet in the courtroom, or I'll have the bailiff evict all

of you," Judge Sower said. His brow was deeply furrowed in obvious resentment at the interruption. "Go on, Miss Seng."

"On January eighth, the ASPCA conducted a raid of Mr. Clifton's premises and took custody of several female pit bulls, fifteen puppies, and three adult males. All the dogs were thin, some almost skeletal, and as you see from the photos, their cages were filthy. Only one cage had a filled water dispenser. All the food bowls were empty. This is clearly a case of neglect, verging on cruelty. The following witnesses are present and prepared to testify today—Mr. Gunderson of the ASPCA and his assistant Allison Ware, Ms. Dory Clarkson, an investigator from the sheriff's office, and Mr. Ray Fenton, who alerted the authorities to the matter. In addition, we have a veterinarian, Dr. Sheldon Weil, here as an expert witness."

"Very good, Miss Seng. You may call your first witness," the judge said.

"I call Mr. Lawrence Gunderson, Director of the Nashville ASPCA Office."

Gunderson came up, was sworn in and took his seat in the box next to the judge.

"Mr. Gunderson, how long have you worked for the Nashville ASPCA?" Marina asked.

"Twenty-three years."

"Do you consider yourself an expert on telling when an animal is in poor condition?"

"Certainly."

"How would you describe the condition of the dogs on Mr. Clifton's property?"

"They were weak from dehydration and lack of food, and one female was close to death."

"I understand that you went out to the property at the behest of Sheriff Ben Bradley of Rose County, prior to the actual raid. Is that correct?"

"Yes, the sheriff's office had received a tip about neglected dogs on the Clifton property. I sent two officers to the property the day we were notified. Unfortunately, the ASPCA is not able to take possession of any animals without notice to the owner. If we can't find the owner, we have to wait three days. In this case we couldn't locate him."

"When were the photos taken that I presented to the judge?"

"We took those the day of the raid, January eighth."

"Thank you, Mr. Gunderson."

"Are there any questions from the defense?" Judge Sower asked.

"No, sir," the defense attorney said, after a brief consultation with Clifton.

"Very well. You may call your next witness, Miss Seng."

"The court calls Mr. Ray Fenton," Miss Seng said, and Ray shuffled forward, looking pale. He glanced quickly at the defendant and then away.

After Ray was sworn in and took his seat, Miss Seng asked, "I understand you had been working for Mr. Clifton part time as an animal care assistant. Is that right?"

"Yes, ma'am," Ray said.

"How long had you worked for him?"

"For about six months."

"During that time, did you notice any occasions when the animals were out of food and water?"

"Yes, a couple times. I only worked three days a week, after school." His voice broke. "I felt bad when I couldn't be there because I was worried that the dogs would be out of food."

"I understand you were the 'whistle blower' who reported Mr. Clifton to the sheriff's office, which then contacted the ASPCA. Is that correct?"

"Yes, ma'am." Ray seemed to shrink, looking anywhere but at Jerrod Clifton.

"Thank you, Ray. That will be all for now." Miss Seng stepped away.

"Anything from the defense?" the judge asked. The defense

attorney said no. "Hearing none, you may return to your seat, young man."

Ray stepped down, the color returning to his face.

"I now call Dr. Sheldon Weil to the stand," Miss Seng said.

Dr. Weil, a tall skinny man with a benign face, rimless glasses, and long thinning hair was sworn in.

"Dr. Weil, I understand that you are a professor and academic researcher with the University College of Veterinary Medicine, right?"

"I have been with the vet school for seventeen years," Dr. Weil stated. "I hold the rank of full professor."

"And you have testified before on animal cruelty cases, is that correct?"

"Many times. Determining the cause, severity and duration of an animal's injuries—as well as the extent to which the animal suffered or experienced pain—are important legal elements of a cruelty case." He looked straight at Jerrod Clifton.

"And in your considered opinion was there cruelty in this case?" Attorney Seng asked.

"Without question. It's critical in these cases to look at the amount of time the animals were left unattended. In this instance, it was clear that no one had been feeding, watering, or cleaning cages for days prior to the ASPCA raid."

"So you would not consider this neglect?" Marina Seng probed.

"No, ma'am. I could tell that the animals had been in a constant state of neglect for quite some time. Being abandoned on top of that raises the situation to cruelty."

"Thank you, Dr. Weil," said the judge. "Anything from the defense?" The defense attorney said no. Dory wondered what he had up his sleeve. "Hearing none, you may step down," the judge said. "Any more witnesses, Miss Seng?"

"May it please the court, I'm prepared to call Miss Dory Clarkson from the sheriff's office to the stand."

"What will be the nature of Miss Clarkson's testimony?" Judge Sower asked.

"She was present the day of the raid and found a knife and a bloody rag buried on the premises. Both items are key to an ongoing felony case."

"I won't have her testify then. Miss Clarkson's expertise would be in the criminal area." Dory was peeved that her big moment wasn't going to happen but slightly tickled that the judge said her *expertise* was in the criminal area.

"Are you finished, Miss Seng?" the judge asked.

"Yes, Your Honor," the attorney nodded.

"Very well. I now call the defendant, Mr. Jerrod Clifton, to the stand."

Clifton spoke quietly with his attorney for a moment and then stood and was sworn in. He took his seat looking completely self-possessed. Dory wondered how he could possibly be acting so cool in light of the horrific condition of the dogs.

"Mr. Clifton, you're accused of leaving multiple dogs and young puppies with inadequate food and water for a lengthy period. What say you?"

"Judge, I left Rose County on New Year's Day to visit my cousin, Jake Clifton, in Knoxville. I put Mr. Webster Johnston in charge of the kennel while I was gone. I had paid him to take care of the dogs while I was away before and it was never a problem."

"May I speak, Judge?" Mr. Mitchell, Clifton's attorney asked.

When Judge Sower nodded, he said, "My client, Jerrod Clifton, cannot be held liable for neglect or animal cruelty when he was out of town and had appointed Mr. Webster Johnston to tend to the dogs in his absence."

The judge didn't respond for a moment. He took a breath, glaring at Mr. Mitchell in vexation. "I believe it is my job, and not yours, to decide whether or not Mr. Clifton is *liable*," the judge said coldly. "I'm tempted to cite you in contempt for that remark."

"I beg your pardon, Your Honor." The defense attorney looked suitably abashed.

"Very well. I understand that the person who was assigned to care for the dogs, Web Johnston, was brutally murdered and found near the defendant's property during the period in question." The judge looked at the spectators seated in the courtroom. "I have a final question for Dr. Weil. I remind you, sir, you are still under oath. Please stand."

"Yes, Judge." Dr. Weil got to his feet.

"At the vet school, when the chief caregiver for animals is away, how are the animals cared for?"

"The policy of the vet school is to have a second and third person appointed for animal care duty. Thus, even if the second person falls ill or is unable to fulfill his duties, the third person is automatically prepared to step in. In fact, we have a phone and text tree that's put in place so that if the first or second caregiver is unable to care for the animals, they are notified immediately so that a third person can take over. We take animal care extremely seriously at the vet school."

"Very well. You may be seated."

The judge turned back to Jerrod, still sitting in the witness box. "Now Mr. Clifton, are you asking to have the dogs returned to you?" the judge asked.

"No, Your Honor," Clifton said. "I'd already decided to close down the operation before I went to Knoxville. I left instructions with Mr. Johnston to remove all the dogs from my property."

Dory's stomach clenched; this bastard was so smooth, she was afraid he was going to get off with a slap on the wrist.

"You may resume your seat at the defendant's table, Mr. Clifton. I am now prepared to make a ruling on this case," the judge said. "All the confiscated dogs will remain the property of the ASPCA. Further, the defendant, Jerrod Clifton, will serve sixty days in jail for not having arranged adequate backup care for the animals. He will also pay a fine of four thousand dollars to the ASPCA to cover their costs. Finally, Mr. Clifton, you are prohibited by law," at this, Judge Sower lowered his bushy eyebrows in a fierce frown, "prohibited, I say, under penalty of a severe sentence, to ever own a dog again. This court is adjourned." He banged his gavel.

Dory and Ray Fenton walked out together. As they exited the courtroom, they were mobbed by the press. Carrie Adams, dressed in a red suit, walked quickly toward them, an intent look on her face. Dory was not going to be caught out again. She grabbed Ray by the arm and started to push her way through the gaggle of reporters.

"Miss Clarkson, what can you tell us about the dead body found on the Clifton property?" Carrie Adams asked, pushing her microphone in Dory's direction. All the reporters joined in a chorus of questions about the identification of the dead man. Dory continued to say, "No comment" over and over again, pushing her way through the crowd of reporters and virtually running until she and Ray were safely inside her car.

Once she locked the doors and took a deep breath, Dory pulled out of the parking lot and drove to the Donut Den. She knew she was taking a risk. Those donuts were awfully tempting. Remembering the slim Marina Seng, Dory ordered black coffee for herself and chocolate milk and a bear claw donut for Ray. They were seated at a window table looking out at a bright windy day. The snow had melted, but the parking lot was wet with near freezing rain.

"Ray, Detective Nichols and I didn't have enough time to talk with you the other day in the office. I have the feeling you know something more than you told us about Mr. Web Johnston." Dory tipped her head to one side.

Ray kept his eyes right on Dory's. He blinked several times but didn't speak.

"My guess is that you were on the Clifton property before

the big snowstorm and you saw Mr. Johnston there. I think Mr. Johnston struck you and you fought back. I noticed the bruise on your cheek the first time I met you. Is that what happened?"

"Yes," Ray said, looking uncomfortable with the conversation. He turned his eyes away and Dory waited, sipping her coffee.

"Tell me about that day, please," Dory said. "How did you get out there?"

"I have a dirt bike and I ride on a trail that gets me over there. You're not supposed to ride them on the road, but I'm only on a road a little bit of the way. I did go out to Clifton's property the day before we got all that snow. Mr. Jerrod gave me the week off, but I wanted to see Pearl Jam and feed and water the other dogs. I was worried about them. When I got there, Web Johnston was about to load some of the puppies into cages in the back of his truck. I screamed at him to stop. He pushed me away. I scratched him." Ray was breathing hard. "He pushed me again and I fell down. He stood over me and yelled, 'If you know what's good for you, you'll get out of here.' I tried to hurt him, but he was way bigger and stronger than me." He looked at Dory with shame in his eyes. "After that, I was scared and I just left on my bike."

"I know, son. I'm sure you were scared." Dory put her hand on Ray's bony arm. "Don't worry. Web Johnston's dead and we're going to get the guy who killed him. The sheriff thinks Jerrod Clifton did it. I know you're still worried that Mr. Clifton will come after you, but for the next sixty days, he's in jail. And before he gets out, the sheriff hopes to get him for Web's murder."

Chapter Twenty-Five

January 19th
Detective Wayne Nichols

THE STAFF MEETING was about to start. Wayne was tired and knew he wasn't functioning at his peak, having stayed out late to meet with Jacko the previous night. He and Rob Fuller had met at Sal's bar, a venerable gathering spot caught between a working class area and the gentrification of upscale infill development. The weekly Rosedale paper had been full of efforts by local citizens to shut down Sal's bar. A new middle school was being built in the area and parents feared that drug dealers might be seeking the next generation of buyers from their base at Sal's.

Sal's was an institution in Rose County. Past Mont Blanc on the county line near Nashville, the building had originally been a stone farmhouse. The farmland had been converted into a rougher area of blue collar neighborhoods and strip malls and now sat on only a quarter of an acre. Sal had purchased the property decades ago and enlarged it over the years. The main floor had tables and a fine old wooden bar with the requisite picture of a naked woman. Unlike most such works displayed in bars, this one was by the French artist, Edouard Manet. Called, 'Olympia,' the woman wore nothing but a black velvet ribbon around her neck. An African American woman in the background was bringing her mistress some paper-wrapped flowers. Wayne had known the owner, Salvatore Notariani, for years and asked him about it once.

"My wife said if I wanted to have a picture of a naked woman, I had to have a classy one. The original of this painting is in a museum in Paris, so that's classy, right?"

Sal's served mostly bar food and sandwiches; their Rueben was known to be the best in the area. His clientele were older men in their fifties and sixties. The antique slot machines in the basement were a draw, although most no longer worked. Videogames were slowly replacing them. The space also housed the occasional illegal poker game. Wayne gambled there from time to time, picking up bits of information relevant to cases. Two "waitresses" worked the place, both in their late forties. One of them, a buxom brunette named Marie, was one of Wayne's confidential informants. When he recruited her, she said she was getting too old for the sex game and wanted an easier way to make a living. She had switched to waitressing, but wasn't making enough money. Wayne had gently refused her offers of anything beyond food, liquor, and information.

WAYNE HAD PICKED Rob up at his apartment, having told him to dress casually. Rob came down the steps from the brick building in new jeans and a black leather jacket. It looked expensive to Wayne, and he fought down the impulse to ask Rob if he had anything older. Even in jeans, Rob looked like a cop.

"Where are we going tonight?" Rob asked as he slid into the front seat of the pickup.

"We're going to Sal's bar. Tell me about the stakeout you and Cam did," Wayne said.

"We spent the night in one of the old brownstones in

Rosedale. A family home converted into apartments, falling apart and in foreclosure. It was coming up for auction the next day."

"Did you get anything?"

"No. We sat there all night in the dark. Cam brought coffee and sandwiches for both of us. Luckily, the one bathroom was still working. She found two old chairs and we sat there until the sun came up, talking like we were in college. I like her."

Wayne gave Rob a glance.

"Yeah. You're right. I'm attracted to her, but I found out she's dating a cop in Nashville. Undercover, actually. Ben reminded me of the 'no fraternization' rule before the stakeout, but I was still hopeful, until she told me she's in a relationship. No way I'm going to mess with that." Rob looked out the car window.

"So, nobody tried to get into the house or steal anything?" Wayne asked.

"No. Ben's convinced that Jerrod Clifton's the ring leader of the copper theft operation, and he's in lockup. So, it was a long shot, but worth a try."

"Did you go to the auction the next day?"

"I did. It was interesting. There were five bidders there. They have to buy the houses sight unseen, although they can walk around the outside and look through the windows. Bidders put down cashier's checks for ten thousand dollars to enter the bidding. If they win the house and can't produce the purchase price, they forfeit the down payment. This one went to a young couple—flippers who specialize in fixing up these older homes."

"When I read your report, it occurred to me that somebody from the auction house might be guilty of taking architectural elements from the houses. I couldn't understand why the purchasers didn't get the keys to the house until the day after the auction," Wayne said.

"Yeah, I thought about that too. Apparently the auction house needs a day to be sure the payments clear the banks. But they're considering closing that loophole. The auction house makes the same amount of money whether the house being sold is looted or not, but a group of flippers went to the auction board recently to complain. Starting next month, the people who win the bids will get keys the same day."

"Have you checked out the auctioneers?" Wayne asked, pausing for a stoplight.

"I started looking into them, but it's taking me a while. So, why are we going to Sal's?"

"Jacko hangs out at Sal's, and I have another CI there—Marie. She's a working girl, or she used to be."

Rob's mouth quirked into a surprised grin. Wayne thought Rob was going to enjoy this field trip.

They pulled into a parking lot. It was early for serious drinkers, only about ten o'clock. They walked in and stood at the bar. Wayne ordered a Budweiser. Rob asked for a Sierra Nevada Pale Ale. The barkeep just looked at him, frowning.

"He'll have a Bud," Wayne said, gruffly. Three beers later, Jacko made an appearance. They left the bar and joined him at a table. Marie came over and asked what they wanted to eat. Wayne told Jacko to order something to eat, then cast a warning glance at Rob when he asked if they had quesadillas. Once the sandwiches and fries and Jacko's whiskey arrived, Wayne got down to business.

"You've met my friend Rob here, I understand," Wayne said. Jacko nodded.

"I noticed you managed to extract a fair bit of change out of him while giving him next to nothing," Wayne said. His voice was flat.

"Yeah, well, I didn't know much then."

"You better know a bit more now," Wayne said. "Or you could join Jerrod Clifton in jail if you'd rather." Jacko sipped his drink, considering.

"Come on, man," Rob said. "Give us something."

Wayne put a hand on Rob's arm. "This is what we think's

going on, Jacko. We think Jerrod Clifton's involved in the copper pipe operation."

"He isn't the boss," Jacko said. "There's a guy in East Nashville who's heading it up. It's a big operation."

"And Clifton's garage was convenient. I need a name," Wayne said. "A name, Jacko, unless you want us to let Clifton know that you ratted him out."

"Okay, okay. Yeah, Clifton's just small change. He's a coke head and stored pipe to pay for his habit. The head guy's name is Manny Torres. He started out as a pimp and has moved on to better things."

"And we're also suspicious that an auctioneer might be involved in diverting old millwork, fireplace surrounds, etc. Who would that be?"

"Honest, Wayne, I don't know." Jacko finished his whiskey and stood up.

"Okay," Wayne nodded. "But no money this time. You got overpaid for this information already." They paid the bill and were about to leave when Marie joined them by the coat check.

"Hi, big guy. Who's your cute young friend?"

"This is Rob. He's looking for a little action tonight." At Rob's horrified expression, Wayne added, "Just messing with you, Rob. But Marie, I do have a question for you. Do you know Jerrod Clifton?" She nodded. "Any idea where he and Manny Torres meet up?"

Marie looked around briefly to be sure nobody was watching. "I know something, but I need money. I have a mortgage, Wayne. My daughter and her kids have moved in with me."

"How much?" Wayne asked.

"I'm going to need two hundred."

"A hundred has to do it," Wayne said. "I'll have more for you next time."

Marie looked at him intently. "Camille's Bar and Grill. Usually on Wednesday nights," Wayne pulled a C-note from his roll and handed it to Marie.

Wayne and Rob walked out to the parking lot and got into his pickup.

"It bothers me that these criminals have to be paid to tell us anything."

Wayne thought Rob sounded prudish and naïve. "Grow up, Rob," he said. "Information has a street value. Marie doesn't usually ask for much, but now that she's a grandmother, she's trying to go straight, set a good example."

"So you actually care about that woman." Rob looked at him in confusion.

Wayne snorted, but Rob had hit the nail on the head. He did care about Marie. She had not had an easy life, but she had never hurt anyone. She was just trying to make it like everyone else.

He put his hand on Rob's shoulder. "It's not all black and white, Rob. I've known Marie for years and she has a good heart."

Rob was going to need a lot of education about life beyond simply having a detective's license, Wayne thought. It might be interesting to pair him with Dory. She certainly had the life experience. The combination might work well.

Chapter Twenty-Six

January 19th
Mae December

M AE HAD JUST gotten off the phone with Renee Glasgow, a high-school friend of hers and Tammy's. Renee was back in town visiting her parents. She had completed her combined degree in social work and theology and was an ordained minister who currently worked at a women's rescue mission in Memphis. Renee had agreed to meet with Tammy and Patrick, and to come back to Rosedale and officiate at their wedding in Mae's living room. Mae was relieved, since finding a church and minister who were available on short notice for Valentine's Day had proved impossible.

She heard a knock on her front door and the Tater barked. Mae opened her door to a woman she had never seen before. "Hello."

The woman wore a green jacket over a gray sweater, jeans and boots. Her eyes were hazel, and she had light brown hair that fell in smooth waves to her shoulders. Giving Mae a friendly smile, she said, "Hi, I'm Gretchen Wilkes. I saw your interview on TV and I want to give the three puppies a home."

"Come in." Mae stepped back, deftly avoiding Tallulah and the two corgis that had accompanied her to the door, and gestured for Gretchen to come inside. "I've got some hot coffee going in the kitchen, if you'd like some."

With a smile and a nod, Gretchen followed Mae into the kitchen. "Sit down and I'll get you a cup." Mae indicated a barstool at her island counter, ushered all three dogs into her laundry room and closed the door. She poured the coffee and set it down in front of Gretchen. Before refilling her own cup, she got out the sugar bowl, creamer, and spoons. Then she sat on the stool facing her visitor.

"Thank you for the coffee." Gretchen took a sip. "Very good."

"You're welcome. Was there a reason you especially wanted all three puppies?" Mae asked.

Gretchen looked away, then quickly back. "Not really. I just thought they were so cute."

"They are. Unfortunately, I only have the two females left. The male pup tested positive for the Warrior Gene and had to be euthanized."

"That's too bad. I would have taken him anyway." She set her cup down. "Where are the two females?"

Before answering Gretchen's question, Mae felt she had to explain. "The ASPCA agreed to euthanize all the dogs and puppies that tested positive. If they let those dogs go to new homes and something happened, I guess they'd be liable. And I know they're cute, but three puppies of any breed would be a *lot* of work. True and Pearl Jam are out in the barn if you'd like to take a look at them."

"I would." She stood up. "It's cold out there. You don't need to come with me unless it's locked. I saw the barn when I drove up."

"It isn't locked and I do need to make a phone call," Mae told her. "Go ahead and I'll be right out."

She quickly called Tammy with the good news about Renee. "I gave her your cell number, so she's going to call you about meeting with you and Patrick this week, before she goes back to Memphis."

"That's awesome. We can just do the ceremony and reception at your house and nobody has to drive anywhere else. Thank you so much."

"You're welcome. I need to go—I've got someone out in the barn looking at the puppies. Talk to you later."

"Bye, Mae-Mae."

Mae put on boots and her barn jacket and hurried out to the barn. She flipped the wall switch to turn on the overhead lights and saw Gretchen holding True and Pearl Jam.

"I'll take them both," she declared, squeezing them awkwardly against her chest. Pearl Jam wiggled vigorously and Gretchen almost dropped her.

There's something weird about her. "You can have True, the one with the patch over her eye. The other one's already spoken for." Mae wasn't sure how she was going to do it, but she wanted Pearl Jam to go to someone who knew Ray Fenton. At least he could visit his dog that way.

A sharp frown creased Gretchen's forehead. She squeezed True so tightly that the puppy gave a squeak. "That doesn't do me any good," the woman said. "I told Anthony I'd …." She stopped talking abruptly.

"You're hurting her. Put them back in the pen, please. If you decide you want her, you'll need to go to the ASPCA in Nashville and fill out some forms. There're other pups being fostered in the area, so if you really want more than one, they're available. But you don't seem to be very experienced with dogs, and I'm curious about why one isn't enough." Mae looked into Gretchen's eyes and the other woman blushed and looked down.

"You're right." She looked back up at Mae. "They're for my boyfriend, Anthony." Her entire demeanor changed when she said her boyfriend's name. She stood straighter and her forehead smoothed. "He said to get at least two."

Mae tipped her head toward the open barn door. "I think you and Anthony should go to the ASPCA together then, and they'll let me know if you're approved to take this puppy." She waited until Gretchen left the barn to shut off the light, and then Mae firmly closed the door. Gretchen walked toward her car and Mae watched her drive away before she hurried back to the house. She called the ASPCA and left a message for Mr. Gunderson to call her back, then she called Ben.

"Hi, babe."

"Hi, are you busy?"

"Nope, just wrapped up a staff meeting. What's up?"

"Remember when we were talking about the murder case and you said you were looking into animal traffickers—people who wanted dogs for other reasons besides having a pet?"

"Yeah." Ben's voice sharpened. "Do you have any ideas?"

She told him about Gretchen Wilkes' awkwardness with the pups and her interest in getting "at least two" puppies for her boyfriend Anthony. "I don't know if it helps, but she drove a dark gray car. I think it was an Altima."

"That's very interesting," Ben said. "I'll see if we can track her down and find out why this Anthony wants multiple puppies. I agree that it might not be for pets."

"Thanks, Ben. Oh, one other thing I forgot to ask you. Do you think Matty would want to be the ring bearer for the wedding?"

There was a short silence from Ben's end. "Sorry, I was writing down the details about Gretchen Wilkes." He cleared his throat. "I think so. I'll run it by Katie, but she'll probably be happy to have a babysitter for Valentine's Day. See you tonight, Mae. Bye." He was gone.

I'm so frustrated with this broken wrist and lack of energy. I haven't been able to help Ben very much this time. Hopefully he can find Gretchen and that will be a good lead.

* * *

AFTER BEN GOT to Mae's house at eight that night, they shared a late supper of pizza, salad, and a bottle of Chianti. They had just finished eating when his phone rang.

"It's Wayne," he said after glancing at the screen. "I need to take the call. Sorry."

He got up from the table and went into the living room. Using her one good hand, Mae slowly cleared the table, rinsed the dishes and loaded the dishwasher. She could hear that Ben was still on the phone when she turned the water off, so she took the dogs outside one last time. It was a little warmer tonight, in the upper forties, and the stars were bright in the sky above her old farmhouse. The moon was waning—just past full but still lighting up her backyard. She stood on the steps enjoying the fresh air and night sky while her three dogs scampered about for ten minutes or so. When she called them inside, she found Ben back in the kitchen, pouring the last of the wine into their glasses. He handed Mae her glass, then crated Tatie. Titan and Tallulah went to their beds without further ado and Mae and Ben took their wine into the living room to sit on the couch.

"What did Wayne need?"

"He was reporting in with some really good news." Ben smiled and took a sip of his Chianti. "The copper theft case is wrapped up, at least as far as we're concerned."

"That's great! What happened?"

Ben told her all about the sting they'd set up using Jerrod Clifton as bait. "We decided to send George along with Jerrod to drive the truck. Clifton called Manny Torres and set up a meeting to pick up the pipes—he said he'd store them at his garage until they were ready to ship them overseas." He leaned back and stretched his arms above his head.

"Why'd you send George instead of Rob Fuller or Cam? Or Wayne?"

Ben laughed. "Wayne's too well known in those circles, and Rob and Cam are both too pretty. Plus Rob looks like a cop no matter what he wears. Camille's Bar and Grill is kind of a rough place for either of them to look like they fit in. But out of uniform, George makes a very convincing redneck. And it sounds like he played the part well. Wayne waited out in the parking lot with Rob and Cam in case anything went wrong."

"So everything went as planned?" Mae loved watching Ben tell the story. His excitement over the drama was plain to see in his sparkling blue eyes and animated gestures. She sipped her wine and watched him as he continued.

"Almost everything. Cam called Captain Paula when George backed the truck up to the shed behind the bar. She and Rob snuck around and waited back there, and Wayne stayed in his truck to watch the front door. Good thing he did." Ben looked at her with eyebrows raised. "The Nashville cops rolled in with sirens blaring and everyone was looking at the area behind the bar. Jerrod Clifton strolled out the front door. Apparently Manny paid Jerrod in product, so he had cocaine on him when his brother pulled up. If Wayne hadn't been there to tackle Jerrod, he would've gotten away."

"So it's all over?" Mae set her empty glass down on the coffee table.

"Yes. Captain Paula's unit will take it from here. We handed Manny Torres to her on a silver platter and tomorrow I'll be able to call Mr. Yancey and tell him we found his pipes. Then we can concentrate on the murder investigation. Since Jerrod tried to flee and got caught holding the coke, he's not going anywhere. I'll have plenty of time to prove he killed Web Johnston."

"Good." Mae kissed the side of Ben's neck. "Did you by any chance talk to Katie about Matthew being in the wedding?"

Ben gave a little smirk. "Yeah. She jumped at the chance, said she'd been looking for a sitter anyway. I think she's got a new boyfriend."

Ben paused. After a moment he said, "Mae … how do you feel about Matthew?"

Mae smiled. "I love him, what do you think?"

"I mean, do you wish you had children yourself?"

Mae folded her hands in her lap, giving the matter some thought. "I have the dogs …." Her voice trailed off. "I suppose it's never far from your mind when you're my age. I do love children."

"With Tammy being pregnant and all—"

"I don't feel jealous, if that's what you mean," Mae said, giving his knee a pat.

"Well …."

Mae put a finger to his lips. "No more talk for now, all right? I appreciate that you're asking me these questions, and I do need to think about them at some point."

"Can I just say … I love you?"

Mae laughed. "Yes, you *always* can say that." She snuggled in closer. "And I love you too. Wanna go upstairs?"

"Why, Miss December, how very forward of you." Ben drained the rest of his wine in one long swallow and plunked the glass down on the table next to hers. He stood and held out his hand. "I thought you'd never ask."

Chapter Twenty-Seven

—

January 19th
Dory Clarkson

DORY HAD BEGUN her siege three days ago, arriving at six in the morning. She had it all planned with the military precision worthy of a four-star general, knowing she lacked the manpower for an all-out battle, and that a stealth attack would not achieve her aim. The objective was to have Sheriff Bradley surrender, abjectly apologize, and reinstate her privileges and title as an investigator. So, a siege it would be.

She had begun by clearing her desk of all the little tasks Ben had asked her to take care of. She was a bit embarrassed to see that some of them had sat on her desk for months. She sent out letters, took citations to people's houses, met with the drunk-tank inhabitants, called parole officers, and even managed to get some people to pay their tickets. She actually offered to take some of the paperwork off Ben's desk. He frowned in confusion but handed her a stack of paper that would keep her busy for days.

Today she would initiate stage two of her plan. She planned to stay at her desk until six that night, keeping her curvaceous bottom glued to her desk chair and never failing to answer so much as a single phone call that came in to the office. She could feel her fanny getting bigger. Plus it was bor...ing.

While Ben was out on a call, she attacked his office with multi-surface spray cleaners until the whole thing shone. She even washed his windows. As a final touch, she ordered red carnations from the local florist and arranged them in vases scattered throughout the office. Ben seemed pleased but said nary a word about reinstating her former rank. Blasted man.

Although her boss had told Dory after the Ferris case the previous summer that she could start attending staff meetings, she sanctimoniously remained at her desk while everyone else trooped in and then out of the conference room day after day. Instead, she began typing up little three by five cards listing Ben's appointments for the week. When he left in the evening, she handed him his card with the next day's appointments. She had purchased different-colored pouch folders, at her own expense, reserving one color for each day of the week. Inside the folders she planned to put the paperwork relevant to the meetings and case discussions for the day. And during all of this, despite her quite obvious perfection as office manager, Ben failed to get the point. *Was the man just dense?*

During today's particularly long staff meeting—no doubt devoted to the Web Johnston murder or the copper pipe case—Dory called Evangeline in despair.

"The man just doesn't get it," Dory whined.

"Hang in there, Dory. He's bound to cave eventually," Evangeline said. "I have something to ask you about. It might just cheer you up."

"Give it to me, girl."

"Remember me saying that several buddies of my husband's would like to date you?"

"Um hum."

"Well there's this one friend of his, a gentleman named Al Peckham. He was a very successful salesman who worked for the Buick dealership in town, ended up as part owner. He's retired now and has a condo in the Virgin Islands."

"Car salesman, huh? Those horn dogs are known for nailing every woman in the county. I trust he's not married, at least."

Evangeline made an exasperated noise. "Dory, I wouldn't fix you up with someone who was married. Al's never been married, so no baggage there. I want you to give him a chance. He's really nice, has gracious manners and he says you two used to know each other from the clubs where Elmer, your ex, played music."

"I do have a faint memory of this guy. He's tall, right?"

"Tall, dark, and fine looking." Evangeline laughed. "So, how about Saturday night? We can make an evening of it. You know that old theater in town, the Granada? It's been totally redone. It's fabulous, gaudy, and tarted up like a madam's boudoir. They serve dinner and then there's a live performance. And they have a dress code. Women wear long gowns and men wear tuxes."

They agreed that they would pick Dory up at her house at seven before Dory had to end the call quickly. She could hear that the staff meeting was breaking up. God forbid Ben would catch her indulging in a personal phone call when she was working so hard to get her investigator's job back.

SATURDAY EVENING ARRIVED and Dory checked herself in her floor-length mirror. She had decided on purple velvet with long black gloves. The gown had languished in her closet for years and it still fit, but it had taken her a while to obtain the requisite foundation garments. She had purchased a "hide and sleek" high top panty and a strapless black bra from the department store in Rosedale. Black stilettos with a fair amount of toe cleavage showing, long chandelier earrings, and a black and silver evening wrap completed her ensemble. After her shopping trip she had visited her favorite hair salon, the Baroness Hair Boutique, and told Kiki to do her damndest. A stunning reflection looked back at her.

Just before Evangeline, her husband Gerard, and Dory's date Al were supposed to arrive, the phone rang. Her caller ID said Mae December.

"Hi, Mae."

"Hi, Dory. I'm calling to see if you'll be home tomorrow morning. I want to stop by and bring you a present. Can I come over around ten?"

"Sure. I'm not on duty tomorrow. Why're you bringing me a present?"

There was a brief pause before Mae said, "Sorry, Dory, I have another call coming in. See you tomorrow."

Dory was thinking that when Mae came by she would use the opportunity to talk to her about what else she could do to get Ben to reinstate her in her investigator position. The doorbell rang, and when she answered, she saw a large tuxedoed man of color standing on her porch holding a bouquet of flowers.

"You must be Al. Now that I see you again, I definitely remember you from the old club days. Are those flowers for me?" He nodded. "Thank you. Come on in a moment while I get them into water."

Al followed Dory into her kitchen. She reached for a tall crystal vase, filled it with water, and installed the dozen white roses.

"You haven't said a word, Al. Can't you talk?"

Al swallowed, and in a strangled voice said, "I can't seem to say a word except … wow. You're so beautiful."

"Thank you," Dory said graciously. It was true, after all.

Hearing a beep from the car in the driveway, Dory took Al's arm.

He leaned close to whisper, "I always envied Elmer for being married to you. Lucky guy. But you might need to put on a little weight. I think you've gotten almost too thin."

"And you're almost too smooth, my lucky date." Dory put a hand on her hip and a slow smile spread across Al's dark face.

* * *

SUNDAY MORNING DAWNED crisp and clear. The sun came out and Dory, only slightly hung over, made some coffee and popped a tray of blueberry muffins in the oven. Al did mention her needing to gain some weight, she thought with a smile. Ten minutes later, the doorbell rang and Dory went to let Mae inside. She was standing on the front step. In her right hand was a small white puppy with a black spot over one eye that also covered part of an ear.

"Damn girl, what'd you bring me a white dog for? Haven't you figured it out yet? I'm black! That better not be my present. Return that little critter to your car and then you can come on in."

"Just hold her for a minute, Dory. I have something else for you." Mae handed the dog to her before going to her vehicle. Dory took the puppy in and got the muffins out of the oven. She was sitting in the kitchen with the pup in her lap when Mae returned with two stacked bowls, a bag of puppy food, and a small leash held against her chest.

"The supplies are your gift and her name is True," Mae smiled.

True was licking Dory's hand. She broke off a piece of muffin, blew on it, and fed it to the puppy before sighing in capitulation. Dory cast Mae an oblique glance. "Okay. You win. Good to have someone be true to me. Lord knows it hasn't happened often. I'll keep the mutt, but on one condition. You have to help me with a little problem I've been having."

"What is it?" Mae asked.

"Well, you know that Ben appointed me as an investigator when the puppy mill tip came in, right?"

"I know."

"I stupidly talked to the press the day of the raid and it was reported later on Channel Three news. They got footage of the knife and bloody rag I found, plus I almost blurted out about you finding the body."

Mae nodded her head emphatically, blonde curls bouncing on her shoulders. "Ben told me about that. He was furious."

"Did he tell you that he demoted me for it?"

"No," Mae frowned. "He didn't. That's too bad."

"I'm just trying to get my previous title back, that's all. I didn't pass the physical for my deputy exam, so until I take it again and pass I can't be a deputy," Dory heaved a sad sigh. "I've been doing everything I can think of to get reinstated, but he doesn't seem to have noticed. Do you have any ideas?"

"Like most men, my boyfriend doesn't exactly pick up on subtle clues."

Dory raised her eyebrows and nodded in concurrence, passing another bite of muffin to her new dog.

"So it's possible he doesn't even know you want the investigator job back. Plus, he's really been stressed about work. I think you need to wait it out, or maybe you should talk to my mom. Between the two of you, Ben wouldn't stand a chance. Or do you want me to talk to him about it?"

"No, honey, that won't be necessary. But I haven't spoken to Suzanne in quite some time and she might have some advice. Sit down, child. Have a muffin and tell me what I need to know about this little stray." True gave a little bark and both women laughed.

WHEN SHE REACHED Mae's mother by phone later that day and filled her in, Suzanne December didn't have any ideas either.

"I don't have to tell you how stubborn Ben can be, but don't let the situation get you down. You just need to be patient and he'll probably come around. I'll let you know if I think of any ideas, though." Suzanne paused. "I can't believe you kept the puppy Mae brought you without asking first. That is *not* how she was raised. Besides, we've been friends for a long time, and I've never known you to have so much as a goldfish."

Dory laughed. "It was a bold move, no doubt, but I do have a soft spot for that child of yours, especially when she shows up looking pitiful in a cast. You know it and she does too. And I can't believe it myself."

Chapter Twenty-Eight

—

January 20th
Detective Wayne Nichols

WAYNE NICHOLS DIDN'T pray often—he didn't really believe in divine intervention—but since the conclusion of the joint sting operation that led to the arrest of Manny Torres, he had been praying nonstop for Jocelyn. Enid had asked him to locate Becky Wilshire and if possible get a letter of support from her for Jocelyn's hearing before the parole board.

Wayne's fingers were shaking as he punched in the phone number he had found for Becky Wilshire. She was living in an assisted living facility in Escanaba called Northwoods Place. It had been tough to find her, but once he got a phone number and called the facility, the director, who had lived in the area for years and knew the Wilshire family, confirmed her presence.

"Northwoods Place," the receptionist said.

"Can you connect me to Mrs. Wilshire's room?" Wayne asked.

"Certainly, sir." Wayne heard the phone ring four times before someone answered.

"Hello? Is this Mrs. Wilshire?"

"Yes," it was the quivery voice of an elderly woman. "I'm Becky Wilshire."

"I don't know if you remember me, Mrs. Wilshire. I'm Wayne Nighthawk Nichols. I was Jocelyn Outinen's foster child. I came to your house after the Outinen family moved away. Do you remember that?"

"I think so." She sounded a bit uncertain but then her voice strengthened. "Yes, I do remember you. You ran away, didn't you? When you were about sixteen or seventeen?"

"I did. I came back about three years later."

"Why are you calling me?" The old woman's voice sharpened.

"I found Jocelyn Outinen. Did you know she's in prison?" Wayne heard Becky Wilshire take a quick breath. "She was convicted of killing Aarne. Jocelyn told me you found her sitting in the field, crying, before Aarne died. Is that right?"

"Yes, I was up on the ridge and heard a scream. I came down the hill and found her. She said Kurt was dead. She should have called the police, of course. I told her to, but she said she wanted to be alone for a while. We were threshing and I needed to get back to help my husband and the boys. When we went over there a few days later to check on her, the place was vacant."

Wayne was picking his words carefully now. "I'm trying to get Jocelyn released. She's already served over thirty years, and she killed Aarne in self-defense." He waited, not wanting to lead Mrs. Wilshire, hoping she would say something about the years of abuse Jocelyn endured or the way Kurt died.

"I knew Aarne beat her. I tried to get her to leave him several times, and then he killed little Kurt, did you know that?"

"Yes, that's what Jocelyn said, but there was no evidence. They even suspected Jocelyn might have done it."

"Idiots," Becky Wilshire said. "My husband witnessed what he later thought was the crime."

Wayne almost stopped breathing. A witness. Maybe there

was a God after all. "Is Mr. Wilshire still alive?" *Please, God, let him still be alive.*

"Alive and kicking." Becky Wilshire laughed. "He'll outlive us all. He's having coffee with his friends at the Sip 'n Snack, reminiscing about old times. Do you want to talk to him?"

"Yes, please." They arranged a time for the call. After a few more minutes, Wayne hung up the phone. His hand was sweating and he could hardly breathe. What Mr. Wilshire saw might not help Jocelyn at all, but it could help Wayne get the record corrected. Mr. Wilshire's testimony might mean that Kurt would no longer be listed as killed by 'person or persons unknown.'

IT WAS THE day of Jocelyn's hearing before the parole board. She had always been turned down before and Wayne felt it was unlikely that she would be paroled this time either, although according to Miss Lawton she had been eligible for parole after serving ten years of her sentence. The only thing that had changed for Jocelyn this time was that Enid helped her prepare her application letter and rehearsed her on what to say.

Ms. Lawton had emailed Jocelyn's letter to the parole board to Wayne late the previous day. In the letter, Jocelyn presented her side of the story and the reasons she thought she should be paroled. She included a description of the night she killed Aarne, mentioned the fact that she had no prior criminal history, and listed her accomplishments in the facility, including teaching inmates to read and interpreting for the deaf. She said she had family living on the Potawatomi reservation near Escanaba in Michigan's Upper Peninsula who would welcome her. Wayne thought it was a good letter and covered the important points. And Enid's editing had preserved Jocelyn's voice.

Enid called his cellphone right after Wayne got to the office on January twentieth.

"Detective?"

"Ms. Lawton, thank you for sending me Jocelyn's petition.

What do you think her chances are?" Wayne heard the attorney sigh.

"I'm afraid they're still not very good. Even if the board grants her parole, it doesn't end there. The governor can still reject the board's decision, although I believe we've covered that possibility by meeting with his staffer ahead of time."

"What does the parole board look at when they're making these decisions?"

"First, they determine whether the prisoner has observed the rules of the institution. There's no doubt Jocelyn has done so. Second, they ask whether her release would jeopardize the public welfare. Jocelyn is elderly and terminally ill, so she isn't going to re-offend. The third thing is tougher and more subjective. The parole board must be convinced that her release would not depreciate the seriousness of her crime or promote disrespect for the law."

Wayne sighed. "So they're worried that if they release Jocelyn, more women will kill their husbands thinking they can get away with murder? It's ridiculous. On average, more than three women a day are murdered by their husbands or boyfriends in this country. My girlfriend's an ER physician. She says over a third of women who come to the ER are there as a result of partner abuse. It's remarkable to me that more murders aren't committed by abused women."

"I agree, Wayne. The hearing's at three o'clock today. I can be in the room, but I can't speak. In fact, I'll be seated behind Jocelyn so I can't even make eye contact with her. After she makes her case, the board will adjourn to deliberate. When they return, they'll give their decision. One good thing is that the prison doctor is going to ask for her release, on the grounds of compassionate relief."

"All of that sounds good. I wanted you to know that I've set up a bank account in Jocelyn's name in Escanaba. All the Huron Valley prison is obliged to do is buy her a bus ticket to her home town and give her twenty dollars. The account has a balance of one thousand dollars right now, and I'll continue to put money into the account monthly for the rest of her life. I put a check in the mail for two hundred to your office the other day, for you to get some clothes for her to wear if they release her."

"Yes, it arrived yesterday. I cashed it and called and got her sizes. Our receptionist is going to shop for the clothing today."

"Thank you. Is there anything else I need to do?" Wayne asked.

"Not for the moment. We should have a decision around five today and I'll call you as soon as I know anything."

"Do you think I could speak to Jocelyn before the hearing? I want her to know I'm thinking of her and to wish her luck."

"I'll arrange a call for tomorrow, but she's exhausted right now. Chemo is taking every ounce of energy from her. And her fears that she won't be released are also taking their toll. I don't recommend that any of my clients talk to family the day of their hearing. They need to focus on doing the best job they can of convincing the panel of their sincerity and remorse."

"Remorse …." Wayne hesitated. "Do you honestly believe Jocelyn feels remorse for what she did to Aarne?"

"Actually, no." Enid's voice was dry. "She feels that Aarne deserved it. We've gone over this again and again. I've told her no matter what she *feels,* she needs to *say* she feels bad about what she's done. The ticklish thing here, of course, is the murder of your younger brother. The parole board's going to say that Jocelyn was in the grip of rage when she found her son's grave. Since she killed Aarne later that day, they're going to say it was premeditated."

"Guess we have to hope that doesn't even come up."

"One other thing," Enid said. "You told me when we spoke originally that you wanted to have a grave for your brother."

"Yes, that's right," Wayne said.

"Have you tried the Unclaimed Person's Database? It's part of the Department of Justice database and contains information about deceased persons who have been identified by name, but for whom no next of kin or family member was available to claim the body for burial. Only medical examiners and coroners may enter cases in the UCP database. However, the database is searchable by the public using a missing person's name and year of birth. I imagine that Jocelyn gave them Kurt's name when she was arrested."

"Thank you, Ms. Lawton. I'll do that today. I've been afraid that he was buried in an unmarked grave by now." Wayne took in a strangled breath.

"I obtained Kurt's death certificate and autopsy report. His autopsy said he was killed by gunshot wounds to the chest. I'm sure they still have the bullets in the evidence locker at the police station, since it was an unsolved case. I can't talk any more right now, Wayne, but I'll tell Jocelyn you're thinking of her."

"Tell her I'm praying for her," Wayne replied quietly. He knew if the bullets from Kurt's body came from the gun in an old shoe box on his closet shelf, it would constitute conclusive evidence that Aarne was Kurt's killer. But no amount of wracking his brain brought Wayne any closer to a way to get the gun to the Escanaba police without implicating himself.

At four-twenty Wayne's phone rang. "They turned us down," Enid Lawton said, and Wayne's hopes crashed around him.

"We'll try the judge next, and then the governor." At least Enid wasn't giving up. "But it's a long shot. Michigan is known as one of the states that's the most reluctant to release prisoners. And nobody cares about abused women prisoners, nobody," she said bitterly.

A short time later his phone rang again. The name on the display was Mark Schneider.

"Yes, Mark. What's up?"

There was a hesitation and then Mark said, "I'm sorry to tell you this, Detective. The day you came over here, the captain asked what I'd been doing to help you. I told her I was trying to help you find the fugitive you were chasing. When I told her I found Mrs. Outinen in prison, she said the fugitive you were hunting wasn't a fugitive any more. I think Captain Paula's going to talk to Sheriff Bradley and tell him to deny your leave."

Wayne saw the handwriting on the wall. He logged on to his computer and withdrew his request for a leave of absence. He would talk to Ben about it again after the murder was solved.

Chapter Twenty-Nine

—

January 24th
Dory Clarkson

DORY HAD BEEN looking at Jerrod's cellphone records until her eyes blurred. During the period between January first and seventh, Jerrod had made four phone calls to Web Johnston and several to his brother, Mike. Jerrod's parents lived in Mississippi. He had called them on January first and then again on the fifth. Dory approved of that. Jerrod had also called a low-level hood named Manny Torres several times. Because of the successful sting operation, they knew Manny was the head of the copper theft ring. Clifton had made calls each day during the target period, but Sheriff Bradley was still not buying Jerrod's alibi.

"He could have made those calls from Rosedale, Dory," Sheriff Bradley said. "Did you get the OPC codes?"

Dory looked blankly at the sheriff.

"Originating point codes. That will tell us where he was when he made those calls. Once you get those, I want you to go over to the lab; they aren't answering the phone. Check with Emma and Hadley to see whether there was a GPS on his truck. Maybe we can get into the history on that device." Ben's features tightened. "Even though the initial DNA wasn't a match, I just know Jerrod murdered Web Johnston."

"Not such a big loss," Dory said, under her breath.

"Are you being dismissive about murder?" Ben rose to his full height, a picture of righteous indignation. "I don't care what kind of man Web was, he didn't deserve to be killed. And Jerrod's a thief and a druggie who's already been convicted of animal cruelty. Not such a great guy either, you know."

"Sorry, sir," Dory said. "I'll go around to the lab and see what they found in the truck."

She rose from her desk, grabbed her coat, and went outside. Walking around the back of the building to the lab entrance, Dory pulled her coat more tightly around her. A cold rain was beating down, and Dory felt increasingly discouraged. She had hoped all this scut work might reinstate her in Ben's good graces, but it hadn't. There were days she wondered why she still bothered to work for the sheriff's office. She was old enough; she could retire.

In addition, now that Dory had True, she was finding it difficult to leave the house in the morning. The puppy was smart, and as soon as Dory put on her boots, she started to cry. Dory could hardly stand it. One evening she was late coming home and there were puddles all over the kitchen. She called Mae, who reviewed the basics of crate training for potty-training a puppy.

"It's a cinch, Dory. All you have to do is keep her in the crate until it's time for her to eat. Then take her out of the crate, feed her and take her immediately outside. If she goes potty, give her a tiny treat—I recommend Cheerios—and lots of praise. Then bring her back inside, hold her a while, play with her, and pop her back into the crate. After you've followed that schedule for a week or so, you can keep the crate door open, just close her in it at night. The crate becomes her bedroom."

"I still think she's going to be lonely."

"I worry about puppies feeling abandoned, too," Mae confessed.

Despite having True in her life, Dory was lonely too. Her date had said he would call, but she hadn't heard from him. True had helped, of course, but she still wished Al would call. A mid-winter break at his Caribbean condo would definitely be a spirit lifter.

"Can you come home from work at some point during the day?" Mae asked.

"I usually don't."

"Then you need to find someone to check in on her at least once while you're gone. Otherwise she'll develop some bad habits."

Dory had followed up on Mae's suggestion. One of her neighbors, Mrs. Lottie Powell, was home-schooling her lovely granddaughter who was living with her while her son and his wife continued to work out their convoluted relationship. The granddaughter was twelve, a slip of a girl named Nell who had been begging for a puppy of her own.

"Nell will be tickled to help you with the puppy," Lottie said. "I'll have her go over around ten and then again around three."

"I'll pay her five dollars a day," Dory offered.

"Not necessary. She'll do it for free." Lottie smiled. "But thanks, she can use a little spending money. They key word is *little*. I think ten a week is enough. No kid that age needs too much money."

The arrangement had worked well and Dory felt somewhat relieved of the guilt she felt hearing the puppy whimper when she put on her coat to leave for work. Knowing Nell would be at Dory's house by around ten a.m. was a comfort.

On her way to work this morning, she was congratulating herself on getting this 'puppy mothering' down, when Mae had called with another set of ideas.

"I've been looking into puppy obedience classes for True," Mae said. "She's almost four months old. It's time for puppy kindergarten. True needs to learn some basic commands—mostly sit, stay, and to come when she's called. And I'd get her chipped too."

"Goodness," Dory said. "She has to go to school and get chipped? What the heck is a chip?"

"It's a subcutaneous microchip that's embedded in the dog. A vet needs to do it, but then if she ever runs away, you can get her back. Anyone who finds her can take her to a vet, who can scan her. Your name and contact information will come up. Also, while you're at the vet, you need to see whether True needs more shots. And you'll want to get her spayed right after she has her first heat. It's like a girl's first period, signaling she's capable of reproduction."

"Good Lord! She's just a baby."

"I know, but a puppy ages one year for every month of life during their first year. At the end of twelve months, she's like a twelve-year-old girl. I'll get you the information about the puppy obedience class. Bye."

DORY OPENED THE back door of the sheriff's office building to the lab. The wind almost ripped it out of her grip. Hadley Johns, their lab technician, was working in the glass-walled space created for DNA analysis. The lab bench he was working at was covered with little glass tubes, racks, and a large silver box that looked like a computer on steroids. The office had recently purchased polymerase chain reaction (PCR) equipment for the lab and Hadley had been like a kid at Christmas.

Behind the glass partition, Hadley was virtually invisible. He was dressed in a white suit, hood, and booties. Dory was about to rap on the glass when Emma Peters appeared. She was a pleasant girl with a curvy figure that met with Dory's approval, having a similar shape herself. Emma had dark curls and bright blue eyes. She was wearing a lab coat over jeans and a T-shirt.

"Hi, Dory. What can I do for you?" she asked.

"I wondered if Jerrod Clifton's truck had been gone over. Sheriff Bradley's hoping Clifton had a GPS. We're trying to figure out if he was in Knoxville the whole time he says he was."

"Yes, there was a GPS. We just got that report back from wonder boy."

"Who?" Dory asked in confusion.

"Mark Schneider, the one who works for Captain Paula," Emma said with a little grin. "I'm going on my third date with him this weekend, so I might find out just how wonderful he is at something other than computers."

"Is that how long you girls make them wait these days? Three dates? When I was your age it was a lot longer than that." Dory shook her head. "Mark's report should be a big help. Could you forward it to me? And is Hadley working on the DNA from the knife and the rag I found?"

"Hadley's working on the rag now, checking everything again. I'll forward Mark's report to you and tell Hadley to let Sheriff Bradley know as soon as he's got the results."

"Thanks, Emma. Let me know how your date goes." With a little wave, Dory went out the door. Unfortunately, the one and only time the building had been remodeled, the addition that housed the lab had been slapped on without interior access to the sheriff's office. She trudged back around the building, avoiding puddles as she went. Opening the door, she saw Cam making a fresh pot of coffee and gave her a grateful smile. As soon as the coffee was ready, Dory helped herself to a steaming cup. She checked her email before buzzing Ben's office.

MAE CALLED LATER that afternoon to say there was a puppy obedience class in the Rosedale Middle school gymnasium. It was starting that evening at seven.

"I registered True and emailed proof of her shots to the instructor. You're all set to go, Dory. The woman who runs these classes is named Marcia Conklin. I think you'll like her. You have to bring plastic bags for puppy poo in case of an accident. The class is an hour long, but because it's a puppy class, they give the pups a break. You can walk True outside midway through the session. You need to bring your leash and put True's collar on for the class. "

Dory got home from work at six. By six-thirty she was climbing back into her car. She drove to the middle school with little True sound asleep on the front seat. She carried her sleepy puppy inside, wanting to get her out of the weather. Just inside the gymnasium she stopped to see who else was in the class. There were five other puppy owners and a range of puppies from thoroughbreds to rescues. Before she put True down on the floor, Dory cuddled her tight against her chest, smelling that wonderful puppy smell.

Marcia Conklin, the instructor, was a whip-thin girl with short straight hair. She introduced herself and the members of the class to each other. She didn't share the names of the dog owners, only the puppies, which Dory found amusing.

"We're going to start tonight with the command 'sit.' Please put your puppies on the floor in front of you and begin with them in a standing position."

When Dory put True on the floor, she puddled into a sleepy heap. Dory knelt down and lifted her hindquarters into a standing position. Almost as soon as she got True standing, the puppy lay down again. Dory tried twice more before the instructor spotted them.

"No, no, no," Marcia said. "Here, let me help." She grabbed True under her tummy and lifted her back legs up in the air before setting them down in a standing position. When the pup started to sit back down, Marcia said, "Stand!" in a commanding voice. Little True looked bewildered and lay back down. Dory feared her smart little puppy was going to be a kindergarten dropout.

"True, stand up," Marcia lifted her into a standing position again. This time it worked and Dory heaved a sigh of relief.

"Now, sit." The instructor pushed True's little bottom down in a sitting position.

The class progressed, with owners of slightly older retrievers and pointers who were already old pros at this obedience stuff walking on lead. Dory looked at the woman standing next to her. Her cuddly golden cocker puppy looked as clueless as True.

"My name's Dory. This is True," Dory said.

"I'm Bailey Cartwright and this little girl is Penny." Dory reached down and petted Penny's soft, curly fur. "I sell real estate if you happen to be in the market," the woman said, reaching for her card.

"No thanks," Dory said. "I live in the flower pot district and I love my house. I'm getting a fence put around the back yard for True." Struck by inspiration, Dory said, "Do you sell foreclosed properties by chance? I work for the sheriff's office and I was wondering if you had had any trouble recently with copper theft?"

"Yes. There was just an article in the weekly paper about that, wasn't there? I thought they said a copper pipe ring was busted," Bailey Cartwright said. She looked down and said, "Sit, Penny." Obviously surprised at seeing the pup sit, she bent down and gave Penny a brightly colored M&M for a treat. Dory wondered what Mae would think about that.

"Do you know anything about an auctioneer who might be unethical?" Dory knew Rob was checking into one guy he thought was suspicious but had gotten nothing to date.

"I sure do. His name's Junior Barnes. I'm friends with his wife. She already regrets getting married in such a hurry right after her divorce. He told her he made a lot of money, but his income seems to have come to a screeching halt. In fact, just yesterday he asked her for her engagement ring back. Said he might have to pawn it."

"One of our detectives would be interested in asking him some questions."

"If you want to get more on the guy, talk to his wife. Her name's Cindy. Rumor has it that some architectural elements went missing from the houses he auctioned off. She wanted to replace a fireplace surround at their house, but the installer asked a question about whether they had the right one. Turns out, on the back of the surround someone had written 'Pine Lodge Estates, main floor living room.' "

"What did she do about that?" Dory asked.

"She called her husband, who said there'd been a mistake made by the delivery people and to have the workmen put the surround in the garage. He would make sure it got back to the developer." Bailey winked. "But I doubt it ever did."

"Thank you for the info," Dory said just as Marcia called them to leash up their dogs. They were going outside for a potty break.

True was a star in the second half of the class. She got 'sit' and 'down' and even came when called from a distance of about four feet away. Dory emerged from the class into the wintry rain feeling quite satisfied with her evening's work. Her puppy was a natural at obedience, and retrieving Logan Yancey's fireplace surround might just get her reinstated as an investigator.

Chapter Thirty

———

January 25th
Detective Wayne Nichols

DETECTIVE WAYNE NICHOLS and Sheriff Ben Bradley were at their usual two-top in the Donut Den. It was cold and clear; the rains had stopped. They were discussing whether Jerrod Clifton should still be considered a suspect in the murder of Web Johnston. Jerrod was being held in their jail for the duration of his sixty-day sentence for the puppy mill offense and would be charged for his participation in the copper theft ring as well as attempting to flee and drug possession. Ben was stirring his coffee, looking discouraged.

"I think you need to drop the murder charge against Clifton, Ben. Of the three big markers for murder—means, motive, and opportunity—he hasn't got a one. Jerrod didn't have a motive to kill Web. The man was doing him a favor in getting rid of the dogs. We thought Jerrod had the means—the knife—but after we got the search warrant, we located the knife Jerrod bought from Meeker's inside his own house. It was a different knife from the one Dory found. Same model, but different, and none of the DNA on the murder weapon was Jerrod's. His DNA wasn't on the rag either."

"I know. Hadley finished retesting yesterday. And Mark Schneider got the records from Jerrod's GPS. His car was in Knoxville when he claims, so unless he used someone else's to come back, he didn't have the opportunity either."

"Then he didn't do it, Ben. He isn't our guy."

"Damn it. I wanted him to be the killer." Ben slapped the scarred Formica table with his hand. "We have nothing. It took us all that time to identify Web Johnston, and it led us nowhere."

"I wouldn't say we have nothing," Wayne said, after a pause. "What we know is that the supply of puppies was coming to an end. Web was selling off every last dog. So whoever needed those puppies had his pipeline cut. What's Rob gotten from the veterinarians in the area?"

"Nothing much. We're going over to the vet school later today, following up on a lead from Mae. But for the most part, researchers don't do studies on puppies. Dogs, yes, but puppies, no. I called the University office that handles approvals for doing animal research. There's an Animal Use committee that has to review every application from a scientist to work on animals. I had them go back several years in their files. They didn't have a single approved project using puppies."

"Okay, then we're down to *unapproved* projects—pilot studies and the like. I was talking with Lucy about this, and she said no grant applications are allowed to leave campus, headed for consideration by a funding agency, without the signature of the University Animal Use Committee. She said that when she was a medical student, they were just starting to require medical students to have their projects go through that committee. What about a student project at the vet school?"

"Don't Vet students have to operate under the mantle of a lead researcher? I didn't find anything listed under the faculty members."

"I think so, but I bet there are student projects that fall through the cracks."

Ben was starting to look more cheerful. "Do you want to come with me over to the vet school?" he asked.

"Depends on the time. When are you going? Did I tell you I found a possible witness to my brother's killing?"

"My God, that seems impossible after all these years."

"It does, but I have a time set up to talk with the guy this afternoon."

"Any progress on getting your foster mother out of jail?"

"Not yet, and even if this witness saw Aarne kill Kurt, it won't help get Jocelyn out."

"But it might mean that you don't have to turn in that evidence we never discussed," Ben said. His voice had dropped to a whisper. "You're walking a hard road, my friend."

"You've got that right." Wayne nodded.

"My appointment at the vet school's at three," Ben said.

"Can't go then. My conference call is at that time."

AT THREE O'CLOCK Wayne put the call through to Mr. James Wilshire. The voice of the receptionist at the Northwoods Place was already familiar.

"Could I speak with James Wilshire?"

"Certainly, sir. He said he was expecting an important call. I'll ring their apartment now."

"Hello?" The old man's voice was still strong.

"Mr. Wilshire, this is Detective Nichols from the Rosedale Sheriff's Department in Tennessee. I spoke with your wife a few days ago."

"Yes, we talked about it. She said you found Jocelyn. I was glad to hear she's still alive."

"I'm trying everything I can to get her out of prison." Wayne felt a rise of shame for having left her there so long.

"I hope you do. Becky and I always felt guilty we did so little to help that little gal. In those days, you know, the police wouldn't intervene in a fight between a man and his wife."

"Did Mrs. Wilshire tell you that I want to get Aarne listed at Kurt's killer?"

"She did. She told you I saw the killing, but actually I didn't see much." Wayne's heart sank. "I heard three shots, right in a row. Crack, crack, crack, and I was worried. It wasn't hunting season and those weren't the sounds of a rifle. I started running, like I had this premonition, right over to the Outinen's back field. I saw Aarne dragging something.

"I was at the top of a little rise about fifty yards away. As soon as he saw me, Aarne dropped whatever he was dragging. I yelled, asking him what was going on. He said he had shot a coyote, but it didn't look like fur by his feet. It looked like denim. I started walking toward him, and he raised a thirty-eight revolver, one of those with a six-inch barrel, like the cowboys used in the old West."

"Then what happened?" Wayne tried to keep his voice level.

"Well, to make a long story short, he brandished his gun and told me to get off his property. Truth is, I was afraid it was Jocelyn he'd shot. Never crossed my mind that it was the boy. I just turned and walked back home, but I couldn't stop thinking about it. That night after supper, Becky and I went over there. Aarne came to the door, and we insisted on seeing Jocelyn. She came up behind him. She was just a little mouse, that woman. Anyway, once we saw she was fine, we left. It was a couple days later that Becky found Jocelyn crying about Kurt."

"Didn't you inform the police?" Wayne asked, his voice strangled. He could hardly talk.

"I called them after Becky heard that Aarne had shot Kurt, but you see, Becky never saw the body. At the time, Jocelyn was such a confused mess that Becky wasn't completely sure she knew what she was saying. We called the sheriff's office and they said they would send someone. Then there was this big fire in Barrett's General Store and it was a day or two before the deputy came out. He asked Becky to show them where she and Jocelyn were sitting when they talked. They started to dig. Once they found Kurt's body, they found Aarne's too. With Jocelyn missing, they assumed she had done one or both of the killings. That was the last we ever heard of the matter."

"Thank you for the information, Mr. Wilshire," Wayne said, but his voice was defeated.

"I've felt bad all these years, Detective. I've looked at it from every direction, wondering what I should have done different. There was no bringing back Kurt, you see, and Jocelyn was missing. So, I had to put it out of my mind. Had nightmares for months, finally had to see a shrink. I took every antidepressant they had then. Took electroshock to get me straight again."

Wayne took a deep breath, wanting to spare this good man any more pain. Thinking of Mr. Wilshire's words—that he had to put the incident out of his mind—Wayne said, "You did just what I did, Mr. Wilshire. I put it out of my mind too. I regret that now."

"Well you were just a kid and what's done is done. We have to concentrate on the living. I hope you can get Jocelyn released. She paid a terrible price for her marriage to old Aarne."

"Indeed," Wayne said, and they said goodbye. He thought for a long time about what he had learned from Mr. Wilshire. Since he hadn't actually seen the killing, his report would probably not be enough to convict Aarne of the killing, at least without the gun. He might never be able to get Aarne listed as Kurt's killer. He might never be able to bury his brother. After all his years in law enforcement, he knew some questions never got answered. He would force himself to take Mr. Wilshire's advice. It was time to concentrate on the living and on forgiving himself.

Chapter Thirty-One

———

January 25th
Sheriff Ben Bradley

Sheriff Ben Bradley, at the wheel of his own truck and feeling somewhat optimistic about the murder case for the first time in weeks, held the passenger door open for Mae. Detective Rob Fuller was already in the backseat. The three of them were going to the vet school. Mae had given him the idea of looking into Gretchen Wilkes, who had tried to adopt both of her pit bull puppies. Ben had learned to trust his girlfriend's instincts and put Cam on it right away. As she had confirmed, Gretchen was employed by the vet school, but Cam hadn't found other details of her employment.

The College of Veterinary Medicine was administratively part of the University, although it was geographically separate. A complex of large individual buildings, it was set amid rolling hills and stock barns. The school owned flocks of sheep, a modern dairy facility, and a stable of blooded race horses with an oval track for trotters and an ice cream parlor. The ice cream parlor was a popular spot for students and faculty because the cream came fresh from the dairy herd and the cones were delicious.

The three of them walked up to the large granite building with imposing Ionic columns. "I'm going to introduce you as a consultant, so don't be surprised," he told Mae.

"Ooh, a consultant. That sounds official." She gave Rob Fuller a sideways glance and he grinned at her. Entering the enormous glass doorway, they found themselves in a marble-floored expanse with a single granite pedestal on which stood a full-sized horse carved in clear Lucite. The animal's mane had been so skillfully done, it almost looked as if it moved in the wind. A spotlight from the ceiling shone down on the magnificent sculpture. On the left side of the marble expanse, Ben saw a bank of elevators, and on the wall, a box listing the names of the faculty and their office numbers.

The dean's office on the fourth floor headed the list. They were waiting for the elevator, and when the doors opened they saw a tall young woman and a large Irish wolfhound. The dog's long toothy jaw opened and it made a feral sound. The men waited respectfully for the girl and the dog to exit before entering the elevator. Mae made a happy noise in her throat and held out her right hand. The huge beast sniffed her hand and then licked it as she smiled. Ben held the elevator for her, with a wink at Rob.

The elevator rose silently to the fourth floor. When they stepped out into a bright open area with large windows and plants at either end, Ben could smell lilies. In front of them were the glass-enclosed offices of the dean. Dory had made the appointment and forwarded the name and drawing of the dead man's face as an email attachment. She asked the dean's secretary to provide any information the college might have about the man to the sheriff. Ben introduced himself, Mae, and Rob to the receptionist who buzzed the dean's secretary.

"Ms. O'Connell will be right out," she said. Shortly thereafter, an attractive woman, her high heels clicking on the marble floor, appeared. She had long legs, russet hair arranged in a French twist, and wore a sage-green pantsuit. Her eyes were dark and long-lashed. Although she appeared to be in her late forties, she was very slender and her movements were still graceful.

"Sheriff Bradley, Miss December, and Detective Fuller?" she asked, and at their nods said, "I'm Ruth O'Connell. The dean will see you now."

Dean Emmitt Wolfe, DVM, was a long-legged stork of a man in his mid to late sixties with pepper and salt hair and an open countenance. Ben had expected him to be stuffy, but when they were introduced and shook hands, he seemed like a down to earth person.

"Please come in. Would you like coffee or tea?"

"Nothing for me," Mae said with a smile.

Both men wanted coffee, and Ms. O'Connell poured for them. The dean's desk was a huge slab of redwood topped with glass. It contained a built-in computer monitor that disappeared when the Dean pushed a button, and nothing else.

"You certainly keep a clean desk, Dean Wolfe," Ben said, gesturing to the open, shiny surface.

"Yes, the vet school has gone *paperless*," the dean said. "I'm not sure when the idea was first proposed, but it seems to be working out. I understand you're looking for a man named Web Johnston."

"What I'm about to show you now is a photograph," Ben said, holding out a photograph of the dead man's face.

Dean Wolfe winced. "Yes, that's Web Johnston. He's dead, I take it?"

"Yes, we found his body in the Little Harpeth River and we've been trying to find out more about him."

"I see. Well, I don't know every contract employee for the school, but there was a problem with this guy. He supplied animals for experiments and didn't show at the time he was expected, so we called the campus police. When did he die?"

"The first week in January," Detective Fuller said. "We were wondering if he worked for the vet school."

"He's not an actual employee of the school. He was paid as a vendor to deliver animals for research studies, specifically dogs for Dr. Weil's lab. They're doing some state of the art work on Canine Leukemia and Parkinson's. If you don't mind, Sheriff, how did Mr. Johnston die? Did he drown?"

"No. Unfortunately, he was murdered, and we think his death may have been connected to his work supplying pit bull puppies. We're trying to locate his killer."

Dr. Wolfe was quiet for a moment. "I hope that whoever killed Mr. Johnston had nothing to do with the vet school. I know Dr. Weil well, and he certainly would not have been involved in a violent crime. I would appreciate you calling me when you know more. If someone from the faculty or staff was involved in Mr. Johnston's death, it would reverberate through every department."

"I will," the sheriff said. "Please keep the information I just shared with you about the murder confidential. We need to meet with Dr. Weil as a first step. Could you direct us to that laboratory?" Despite the dean's disclaimer about Dr. Weil, Ben felt his optimism quicken. He caught Rob's eye. They were finally about to learn something about the place where Web Johnston worked. Ben hoped it would lead to his killer.

"Ms. O'Connell will take you down there. His lab is at the back of the building, near the loading zone. It's a maze down there. Goodbye." He gave Mae a twinkly smile. "Lady and gentlemen. I'm wanted in surgery. Good luck." Dean Wolfe shook hands with Ben again.

Ben thanked the dean and Mae and Rob, and he followed the Dean's secretary to the elevator area. One elevator was labeled "Large Animals," and when it opened, they saw a burly man holding a German shepherd puppy.

"Ruth, is the dean coming down?" he asked. "He's supposed to be in surgery to fix this guy's leg."

"As soon as I take them to Dr. Weil's lab, I'll make sure he appears," Ruth O'Connell said.

"Yes, ma'am," the man said. The elevator doors slid shut.

"It's interesting working here, I bet," Mae said.

"It sure is," Ruth said, smiling. "Last week we actually had a yak in the large animal elevator."

When they reached the first floor and began walking down the corridor toward the back of the building, Ben noticed that every wall had large framed photographs of people with their pets.

"Those are our staff," Ruth O'Connell said with pride. "Everyone who's worked here for a year gets a photographic portrait taken with their pet at the vet school's expense. We frame them and they're hung throughout the building."

"Let me know if you see Gretchen's picture," Ben said quietly to Mae, who had stopped to study one of the portraits.

"That's her." Mae angled her head toward a portrait at the end of the row. A young brunette woman with a long-haired white cat in her lap looked back at them from the wall.

Ben looked at the label on the bottom of the frame, which read 'Gretchen and Maia.' He nodded at Mae and tapped Rob on the shoulder. "Keep an eye out for her," he told the detective, who glanced back at the picture and raised his eyebrows.

They finally reached the lab with "Bill Weil, Principal Investigator," lettered on the door.

"Here you are," Ruth O'Connell said. Ben thanked her and held the door for Mae and Rob to enter the lab. A smell assailed him, but Ben couldn't quite identify it. It might have been ammonia. A girl—her long hair caught up in a ponytail, young enough to be an undergraduate—looked up from her desk.

"We're here to see Dr. Weil," Ben said. "This is Miss December, who's consulting on one of our cases. I'm Sheriff Bradley and this is Detective Fuller." The lawmen showed the girl their credentials.

"He slipped his leash," the girl said in an ironic tone and grinned at their perplexed expressions. Mae stifled a giggle. "I'm kidding. That's just what we say when someone's out of the office."

"When did he leave?" Ben asked. "Specifically, we need to know whether he was in town the first week in January."

"He and Mrs. Weil were in France then. It was their twenty-fifth anniversary or something," the girl said.

"Is he still out of the country?" Rob asked.

"Oh no, he got back on January tenth. He's just not here today, went to a meeting in Memphis. He'll be back tomorrow."

"Who's in charge of the lab in his absence?" Ben asked, thinking if Dr. Weil and his wife had been in France the first week in January, he wasn't their guy.

"That would be Gretchen. I'm Megan, by the way," the girl said cheerfully.

"Pleased to meet you." Rob gave the ponytailed girl an extra-bright smile.

"Gretchen Wilkes?" Ben asked. That would be a lucky break. All Cam had found online was that she was employed by the vet school.

"Yep. She's gone, too." Megan gave him a little grin. "Went with Dr. Weil to the conference. They never take student helpers along, what a surprise. We just stay here, handle the phones, take care of the mail, and call the students when their experiments need to be checked. What did you want to see Dr. Weil about?"

"Just need to ask him some questions. When did you say he would be back?"

"Tomorrow."

"We'd very much like to talk to him as soon as possible. Could you leave him a note to call our office?"

Just then a willowy young woman came through the lab door. Seeing the sheriff's uniform, she said, "Can I help you, sir?"

Ben and Rob again produced their credentials. Mae introduced herself as a consultant after a quick glance at Ben.

"They're looking for Dr. Weil," Megan offered.

"We're here to speak with him in connection with a crime. What's your name?" Ben asked.

"I'm sorry. Where are my manners? I'm Julia D'Amato. I'm a PhD student working on a project on Canine Parkinson's under Dr. Heisey's direction. Is there something I can help you with? I'm sort of in charge at the moment."

Rob Fuller was the first to speak up. "Do you use puppies for studies done in the lab? Pit bull puppies?"

"Yes, we do, for Canine Leukemia studies and Parkinson's. I do the Parkinson's work. As you probably know, Parkinson's is a progressive disorder of the nervous system that affects movement. It develops gradually, sometimes starting with a barely noticeable tremor, but it can progress rapidly in a dog."

"What do you use the puppies for?" Mae asked, giving Julia a serious look. "And what happens to them afterwards?"

"Dogs with Parkinson's are often anemic. We give them transfusions. Whole blood transfusions from young animals that helps them enormously, but the puppies aren't harmed. As soon as they recover, we find good homes for them, don't worry." Julia gave Mae a quick smile. "Once the older dogs' iron levels are stabilized they can have the deep brain stimulation surgery we've developed here. We're implanting what's called a brain pacemaker with quite good results."

"Who supplies your pups?" Rob glanced at Ben, who gave a slight nod.

"A man named Web Johnston brings them to the lab on a weekly basis, although I haven't seen him now in a couple of weeks. We've been trying to reach him with no luck. If you give me your office number, I'll have Dr. Weil call you tomorrow." Julia picked up a pen.

"No need to write it down. Here's my card," Rob said.

"One more question," Ben said. "You mentioned Dr. Heisey. Do you work in his lab also?"

"No, Dr. Heisey's my dissertation director, so I meet with him weekly to go over my results. The transfusions are all done here in Dr. Weil's lab."

"Does Dr. Heisey supervise any other faculty or students who work with the pit bull puppies?"

"Yes, there's one other student, Anthony Puglisi, but he already defended his dissertation and went home to see his parents just after the first of the year." At the name 'Anthony,' Mae stiffened beside him.

"Thank you, Miss D'Amato. We'd appreciate your asking Dr. Weil to come to our office first thing tomorrow morning. Could you help us find our way out?"

"I'll take them out, Julia," Megan said. "I can hear your blood monitor beeping."

They followed the helpful Megan through the lab complex until she opened two large metal double doors into a delivery bay.

"Just head to the exit door," she said. "It's to the right of this cargo bay. This is where Mr. Johnston delivers the puppies. You can see the parking lot from there. I'll put a note on Dr. Weil's calendar to come see you as soon as he gets back."

When Megan left, the three walked along the side of the large cargo bay to the door.

"Not much point staying around to talk to anyone else until we talk to Dr. Weil," Ben said. "Certainly the slender Miss D'Amato, who is right-handed as I noticed when she grabbed her pen, couldn't have overpowered Web Johnston."

"It could have been that Puglisi guy she mentioned," Rob said. "Depending on when he left campus after the first of the year."

Mae raised her hand as if she were in class. "Gretchen said something about a boyfriend named Anthony when she came to my house."

"Or this Dr. Heisey," Ben said. "If he supervised several students who were using pit bulls in their research, having the supply cut off could have led to a confrontation. But the first thing we need to do is talk to Dr. Weil. He couldn't have murdered Web if he was in France the first week in January. We'll need to check his passport. He probably knows whose studies would have been most impacted by the loss of the pit bull puppies."

"Just what I was thinking." Rob gave a slight nod. "He can probably give us contact information for this Puglisi guy, too. Our window began January first. Puglisi might still have been in town then."

Chapter Thirty-Two

January 26th
Sheriff Ben Bradley

Dory brought Dr. Weil into the conference room after buzzing Ben to say he had arrived. Ben walked into the conference room as Dory was getting Dr. Weil coffee.

"Dr. Weil, do you take sugar or cream in your coffee?" Dory asked.

"Cream, thank you," Dr. Weil said.

"I attended the Clifton puppy mill hearing, where I heard your testimony," Dory went on. "I was very impressed."

"Oh yes. I remember that the judge didn't call you to testify. Miss Seng was going to call you, but the judge declined your testimony."

"That's right. It was going to be my big moment." Dory shrugged and smiled. "You did a wonderful job describing the animal care tree that the vet school uses."

Detective Rob Fuller came into the room and said good morning to Dr. Weil. Dory caught Sheriff Bradley's glance, said goodbye to Dr. Weil, and departed.

"Good morning, Dr. Weil. Thank you for coming to the

office," the sheriff said. "This is my colleague, Detective Rob Fuller." The two men shook hands.

"Happy to help. What's this about?" Dr. Weil asked.

"It's about Web Johnston, the man who delivers puppies to your lab for experiments."

"He hasn't shown up since January first, when I left for France. I was surprised when I got back to find that several experiments had to be shut down because we hadn't heard from him. I had our lab manager call the campus cops to try to locate him."

"I'm afraid Mr. Johnston is dead," Ben said, watching Dr. Weil's face. His surprise was genuine and Ben felt a brief sense of discouragement. Weil didn't look like their guy.

"My goodness, and he was so young," Dr. Weil said. "What did he die of, if you don't mind me asking?"

"He was murdered," the sheriff said.

Dr. Weil was silent for a few moments as the information sank in. "Do you consider me a suspect in the crime, Sheriff?" he asked, frowning. "Is that why I'm here?"

"We need to talk to everyone who knew Mr. Johnston," Detective Fuller said. "That's the reason we asked you to come in. If you don't mind, we will be taping this interview." Dr. Weil nodded and Detective Fuller clicked on the audio capture, murmuring, "Sheriff Bradley and Detective Fuller interviewing Dr. Sheldon Weil, January twenty-second."

Dr. Weil got a sharp look in his eye and said, "When was Johnston killed, Sheriff?"

"During the first week in January when I understand you and Mrs. Weil were in Paris," Sheriff Bradley said.

"That's right. We celebrated our twenty-fifth anniversary in Paris. I can bring my passport to your office if you need to confirm the dates."

"We'll need to see it at some point. Once we confirm the dates, we'll be able to eliminate you," the sheriff said. "We hope you can tell us something about the researchers and other students who used the puppies Mr. Johnston supplied to your lab."

"There are only two students, and no other faculty beyond Dick Heisey and me, who work with transfusions. I understand you met Julia D'Amato already. She and Anthony Puglisi are the only students using transfusions of whole blood from young animals. Dr. Heisey and I supervise both of them."

"And do you or Dr. Heisey need puppies for your own work?" Detective Fuller asked.

"I don't. I'm not an active researcher now. I'm nearing retirement age and am in the enviable position of not having to write grants or teach any more. I just putter around the lab and keep an eye on the student research studies."

"And Dr. Heisey?" Sheriff Bradley asked.

"Dick's only part time now. He's the dissertation director for my two students, but doesn't do studies of his own."

"Was Dr. Heisey around during the first week in January?" Detective Fuller asked.

"Certainly. Both of us can't be gone at the same time," Dr. Weil frowned. "However, if you're considering Dr. Heisey as a suspect, you'll shortly be able to drop him from the list." His voice was dry. "He suffers from Parkinson's himself and is confined to a wheelchair. His muscle strength is minimal at this point. He doesn't own a gun and couldn't have shot Web."

"Actually, Mr. Johnston was killed in a knife fight," the sheriff said.

Dr. Weil gave a little half smile. "In that case, Dick Heisey certainly isn't your man. He can barely lift his arms. In fact, he's dying. He's been my best friend for fifty years." A shadow crossed the man's face.

"I'm sorry to hear that," Sheriff Bradley said. "We'll check Dr. Heisey's whereabouts as a matter of form, but it sounds like we'll eliminate him as well. We don't believe that Julia D'Amato is strong enough to have been the killer. However, I'd like to ask Mr. Puglisi some questions. Do you have his cellphone number, Dr. Weil? I understand he is visiting his parents."

"Yes, he was planning on leaving for his home town of Benton the day he passed his PhD defense."

"What was the date of that defense?" Detective Fuller asked. He had a small notebook and pen in his hand. "Did he pass?"

"January third, I believe," Dr. Weil said. "And yes, Heisey sent me a text saying Puglisi passed. I have Anthony's phone number in my phone. Let me get that for you." He pulled his cellphone from his pants pocket and gave the sheriff the number.

"I want to be sure I understand," Sheriff Bradley said. "Once a student has passed his PhD defense, that's it? He's done?"

"Well, he or she has to submit two copies of his completed and bound dissertation to the graduate school. One is for the library. But then, yes, the student is free to start looking for jobs. Anthony Puglisi is one of our stars, Sheriff. He has a bright future in front of him. I understand the University of Connecticut and several other schools are interviewing him for positions. Canine Leukemia is an important disease and Anthony's work had been ground breaking."

"So, he wouldn't have needed to do any further studies after the defense?" Ben's attention was focused and intense. "Nothing that would have required more puppies? We're going under the assumption that the person who murdered Web Johnston needed more dogs. Mr. Johnston was getting rid of all the dogs at the puppy mill at the request of the owner. So the supply of puppies would've been cut off."

"Well, I wouldn't want to say that Anthony had absolutely *no* reason to need more puppies," Dr. Weil said. "I was in France, as I said, and not present at Anthony's defense. You'll want to ask Dick Heisey that question. Is that all, Sheriff? I need to get back to the lab."

"Is your passport at the lab?"

"Yes, it is."

"Then, if you don't mind, Detective Fuller will follow you

back to the vet school and check your passport date stamps, so we can rule you out of this investigation."

"That would be fine," Dr. Weil said. "I hope you find Web Johnston's killer, Sheriff. I'm going to have to get busy finding another breeder who can supply us with pups."

"Could you wait in reception just a moment, Dr. Weil? I need to speak to my detective."

"Certainly," Dr. Weil answered and left for Dory's domain. Ben and Rob could hear them chatting.

Sheriff Bradley turned to Detective Fuller. "Rob, once you've seen the date stamps on Dr. Weil's passport—provided he alibis out—see if you can find the lab manager, Gretchen Wilkes. You saw her picture on the wall at the Vet School."

"On it, boss," Rob said. "I'll see what I can find out about why she tried to get Mae's puppies."

"And also get some contact information for Dr. Heisey. Since he's in a wheelchair, I don't want to ask him to come in. If you can locate him, see if you can find out anything about that dissertation defense. I have a feeling what happened in that room on January third is vital to finding Johnston's killer. We need Mr. and Mrs. Puglisi's home phone and address, too."

"Got it," Rob said.

SEVERAL HOURS LATER, Rob called the station.

"The sheriff's been waiting for your call," Dory said and buzzed him through.

"Hi Rob, what did you find out?"

"Okay. First things first. Dr. Weil was definitely in France the whole first week in January. He alibis out. Second, I found Dr. Heisey. It's like Dr. Weil said, the man's in a wheelchair. He couldn't even lift his hand to shake mine. He's not our man. I cornered Gretchen Wilkes for a minute. She seemed evasive and would only say that she wanted those two puppies to help Julia finish up one of her experiments. I think we should talk with her some more, but she's right handed, and not tall enough to meet Dr. Estes description of the killer."

"She said she wanted the puppies for Julia?"

"Yes, that's what she said, but I spoke briefly with Miss D'Amato and she said Gretchen must have been confused. She didn't need any more puppies at this time. She would need more in a month or two for another study, but she didn't need any in January."

"And Mae told me Gretchen said that the puppies were for Anthony," Ben said thoughtfully. "So what happened at that dissertation defense?"

"That's when things got real interesting," Rob Fuller's voice sharpened. "It seems that our Mr. Anthony Puglisi, star of the vet med school, didn't quite finish everything. One of his committee members reminded him that he had to submit an article to a professional journal before he could accept any job offers or positions."

"So, it's not just the defense, the candidates have to write an article based on their dissertation research, too?"

"Right. And here's the most interesting thing of all. Anthony's sample size for his study was too small for a professional journal article. For that, he needed two more puppies."

"Ah," Ben said as the pieces clicked into place.

"We have Anthony Puglisi's cellphone, but we don't want to do this by phone, do we?" Rob Fuller asked. "Will we be going on a little field trip, Sheriff?"

"Oh, we certainly will," Ben said. "Anthony Puglisi is in my gun sights."

Chapter Thirty-Three

January 26th
Dory Clarkson

DORY WAS COUNTING each dragging minute until Ben left the office on the day of what she was calling the "evidence retrieval mission." She had asked Mae to help out by luring the sheriff away from the office and was expecting Mae's call to come in soon.

"All I need is for you to get him to leave the office early," Dory told Mae, when she asked for her help. Mae told her it wasn't a problem.

"He's coming here tonight anyway," she had said. "I'm picking Matthew up from his mom's at five-thirty and Ben is meeting us for an early dinner so we can get to the tux shop before they close. Why do you need him gone anyway?"

"It's my idea for getting my investigator title back." Dory was enigmatic. "The less you know about it, the better."

"And you're sure Ben is going to be happy about this?" Mae asked. She told Dory she wouldn't aid and abet this venture if it didn't benefit her boyfriend.

"He'll be gleeful," Dory said. "Seriously. He'll be so pleased by the initiative of his team."

"Don't get yourself or me into trouble, Dory," Mae warned. "We've both been on the receiving end of Ben's disappointment in the past."

"Not this time, Miss December. We're good." What Dory planned would end up getting Ben the support of Mr. Logan Yancey in his next election, she told Mae. Anticipating Mae's next question, Dory said, "I don't want you to worry, Mae. Since I won't be home until really late tonight, I've already called Nell to take care of True."

"Good. Speaking of puppies, I got some great news about the person who's taking Pearl Jam, Ray's puppy."

"Who is it?"

"Ray's father. Apparently Ray's parents divorced when he was little, before Mrs. Fenton got sick. Ray's dad picked him up from my house the other day and we got to talking."

"I just bet you did," Dory replied with amusement. "You should've gone into sales, young lady. You're very persuasive." She heard Mae giggle. "So does the story end with Pearl Jam being adopted by Mr. Fenton?"

"Yep, he and Ray filled out the forms at the ASPCA yesterday, and next time Ray comes over here to work, his dad will pick both of them up. By tomorrow afternoon I'll be out of puppies."

AT FIVE THIRTY-FIVE, Ben walked out to the front area wearing his coat, issued some last minute instructions and walked out to his car. Dory had already enlisted the luckless Deputy George and the eager Miss Gomez in her mission. When the front office door slammed behind the sheriff, Cam and George both sidled over to her desk to see if it was time.

"Rob has a date with a young woman he's been pursuing, and Wayne left at four," Dory whispered. "The dispatcher in Mont Blanc is handling our night calls. All we have to do now is sit tight until Rob leaves." The deputies went back to their respective stations. Around six-thirty, Rob came out to the front reception area.

"Still working, Dory?" Rob asked.

"Double checking everything we have on Web Johnston," Dory said, not raising her eyes from her computer screen.

Rob said he was leaving for the night and departed. Dory waited another half hour, watching the minutes go by in what felt like hours before giving the nod to George and Cam.

"George, are you ready?" Dory asked.

"Yes, I am. Should I bring my gun?"

"Seriously, George, seriously? No way. Go get the patrol car, will you?"

She looked at Deputy Gomez in her uniform and said, "Cam, we're ready to go. You're coming with me." George was walking past Dory's desk when she told him, "Deputy Gomez and I have to stop at the drug store to pick something up, but we'll meet you at the corner of Willow and Red Oak Drive in half an hour."

"Okay." George grabbed his coat and went out into the cold rainy night. The street lights lit up the wet pavement of the parking lot when the two women left in Dory's T-bird. Dory stopped at a nearby Walgreens and purchased an enormous red bow she found in the gift-wrap section.

"Now what did you want this for?" Cam asked when Dory returned to the car, her pretty brow furrowed in perplexity.

"We're giving Sheriff Bradley a big fat present," Dory grinned. "I want to put a bow on it."

"You're not going to put it on the culprit, are you, Dory?"

"It would look pretty sweet on his dumb head, but no, it's for the property that I'm going to put in the sheriff's office."

They got to their destination at the corner of Willow and Red Oak right on time. George was sitting in the patrol car with the radio on. Dory parked her distinctive vehicle in a nearby cul-de-sac, and she and Cam walked at a fast clip along the rain-slick sidewalks to join George in the patrol car. Dory slid into the front seat, Cam in the back. The three conspirators looked at one another in barely suppressed delight.

"So, here's the plan, George," Dory said, looking intently into his eyes. "I'm just going to go over it one more time, okay?" George nodded. "These folks have a semi-circular driveway that comes up pretty close to their front door. We're going to drive the car into the driveway and leave it running with the red light on top flashing. Just as we get out of the car, you'll turn the siren on and then off quickly. Then you know where you're headed, right?"

"Around back, right?" George asked. "And you and Cam are going up to the front door?"

"You got it, George, and if the guy goes out the back door, you get to arrest him."

"What if he runs?"

"For pity's sake, George, say, 'Stop, sheriff's department' and run after him. Trip him if you need to, but don't let him get away. You have the cuffs, right?"

George gestured to the handcuffs attached to his belt loops.

"Ready, Cam?"

"Ready," she said and George drove into the semi-circular drive of the large stone house. He turned on the siren for just a moment and flipped the button for the red revolving light on top of the car. Dory watched the house and saw a shadow of a woman near the front drapes. The silhouette parted the drapes slightly to allow for a view of the police car.

"Go, George!" Dory said. George ran, bent over, around the side of the house. Cam got out of the car with Dory right behind her. They walked to the large front door and rang the bell. Holly bushes by the front door glistened with rain drops. The motion light came on and a large birch tree with a remnant of yellow leaves shone. They could hear footsteps approaching and a woman opened the door.

"Good evening. I'm Deputy Gomez from the Rose County Sheriff's Office," Cam said and produced her ID. "This is

Investigator Clarkson, also from our office. Are you Mrs. Junior Barnes?"

"Yes, I'm Cindy," she said but made no move to open the door any wider. "What'dya want?"

"We just need to talk to you for a few minutes." Cam inserted her foot into the door opening. "May we come in?"

"I guess." The woman reluctantly opened the door wider. "What's this about?" Cam and Dory walked into a two-story entryway. It was floored in shiny patterned Carrera marble. Dory remembered Rob's report on the Yancey theft; several pallets of marble had gone missing. *I wonder if the flooring in the Barnes entry was installed recently.* A curving staircase with white spindles and a black curving handrail rose into the dark upper story of the house.

"We've had a report that you and your husband have a fireplace surround in your possession that belongs to Mr. Logan Yancey," Cam said. "We're here to take custody of the item. We need to confirm that it's Mr. Yancey's property. Can we see it?"

"There was an error in delivery," Cindy Barnes told them. "They brought us the wrong surround by mistake. I better ask my husband what he did with it." Turning toward the staircase she called, "Junior, come down here! The sheriff's office wants that fireplace surround." There was a sudden clattering of feet descending a back staircase and the sound of a door at the rear of the house slamming. Dory crossed her fingers that George Phelps would be up to the task.

"What's going on here?" Cam said in a severe tone, frowning at Mrs. Barnes. "That fireplace surround is stolen property. Unless you want to be taken to the office as an accessory, Mrs. Barnes, we want to see it now."

Cindy paled, nodded and led the way through the kitchen with its gleaming black granite countertops and white cabinets and toward the back entry of the house. She opened the door from the kitchen to the garage. Then she started to move toward the French doors that led into the backyard. All the motion lights were on, and Dory caught a glimpse of George running. Cindy Barnes reached for the French door handles.

"I'll stay with Mrs. Barnes," Dory said, taking Cindy firmly by the upper arm and pulling her away from the French doors as Cam flipped on the garage lights to see a half dozen fireplace surrounds.

"Those belong to my husband," Cindy said. "He's an antiques auctioneer. You can't take those."

"Don't waste your breath, Mrs. Barnes." Dory gave her arm a little squeeze. "We know what he's been up to."

IT WAS PAST midnight before the operation came to its successful close. Cam and Dory had gone back to the sheriff's office in the T-bird and returned to the Barnes residence in the CSI van to load the fireplace surround, which was luckily not as heavy as it looked. Mr. Junior Barnes, swearing and demanding an attorney, had been cuffed, arrested, and put in a cell. George had told the tale of his 'capture' a dozen times. The man slipped on the wet grass and George managed to grab him by the foot. The fireplace surround belonging to Mr. Logan Yancey resided in Ben's office, appropriately decked out in a giant red bow, and Cam and Dory were about to leave.

"Excellent work, both of you." Dory smiled at her team. "This endeavor has been a complete success. I can't wait to see Sheriff Bradley's face in the morning. And the two of you are going to tell him to reinstate me as an investigator, right?"

"I will," Cam said. "This was fun tonight."

"I might have to go to the ER." George was rubbing his scraped hand. "I feel a bit dizzy. Might have hit my head when I pulled the guy down."

"George, that dizziness is the sweet sensation of success," Dory said. "Come back to the break room and I will get you a bandage." She and Cam exchanged amused glances.

"It's not funny," George said. "I've been injured in the line of duty."

"Yes, yes. You were the hero." Dory bit her lip.

"Well then." Mollified, he followed Dory back to the break room to have his injury attended to. Then he left, followed shortly by Cam.

On her way home to the flower pot district, Dory sang the old Dolly Parton favorite—"Workin' Nine to Five." She wouldn't be working nine to five much longer. Investigators had much more flexibility in their jobs. It had been an excellent day.

Chapter Thirty-Four

—

January 26th
Detective Wayne Nichols

COUNSELOR ENID LAWTON's late night call startled Wayne awake. He had been watching the eleven o'clock local news and had fallen asleep in his chair. The news, such as it was, helped him keep his finger on the pulse of crime in Nashville and what little illegal activity there was in nearby Rosedale. He thought of it as more gossip than news since most of the news stories on TV were scandalously overblown. In fact, Rose County, in spite of the latest rash of serious crimes, was still one of the safest places in the country.

Before he drifted off, Wayne had been smiling, remembering a staff meeting in December when George Phelps gave his weekly report on crime in the small, bucolic town of Rosedale.

"Go ahead, George. Let's hear about the weekly infractions of the good citizens of Rosedale." The sheriff pursed his lips, ineffectively stifling his amusement.

George cleared his throat and began, "Mr. Billings left the back door to his barber shop unlocked on Wednesday night. I discovered the unlocked door on my rounds and locked it.

I informed Mr. Billings. He apologized." George looked up. Hearing no rebuke, he continued, "I pulled over Evan Addison again for driving on an expired license, and this time I wrote him a ticket."

"Wow, George," Dory chimed in. "Pretty tense, pulling Evan over. Probably a high speed chase. What is he now, George, ninety or ninety-one?"

George cast Dory an irritated glance. "And I was on duty in the high school cafeteria on Friday when a food fight broke out. It was the last Friday before Christmas break. I managed to get control of the situation." Everyone was looking down, lips twitching, but Wayne noticed Rob poking Cam in the ribs. She put her hand over her mouth to keep from giggling.

George had in fact instituted "Lunch Room Patrol Duty," by asking the principal of the high school if he could be present during lunch period, because there was so little for him to do in Rosedale. Wayne could just imagine the principal's amusement. Most of the cafeteria women reduced obstreperous teenagers to silence with a single scorching glare.

When the phone rang, Wayne glanced at the clock and screen on his phone. It was just after midnight and the call was from Lansing, Michigan.

"Hello, Ms. Lawton." Wayne was instantly awake. "Any movement on Jocelyn's case?"

"I'm sorry to call so late, Wayne, and with bad news. We struck out again. The judge refused to hear my petition. Once he saw the report from the doctor stating that Jocelyn was in late stage lung cancer, he decided he wouldn't review the matter. He said there were more pressing cases on his docket."

"I see." It was yet another blow. "Is there anything else you can do?"

"Well, as I told you when we started, the governor sometimes pardons women in their final days, but I just had a brainstorm. I may have found a loophole." Wayne could hear the excitement in Enid's voice. She sounded like a kid. "There's this thing called Grounds for Relief from a Final Judgment Order or Proceeding. They call it a six-oh-five. It's just a form you fill out on behalf of the prisoner. If the powers that be agree to the argument written in the six-oh-five, the prisoner's immediately released. How about that?"

Immediately released. Wayne's breathing slowed. He felt his shoulders go down and his taut belly relax. *Immediately released.*

"What are the grounds?"

"There are six, but numbers two through five aren't applicable in this case. The first one is 'mistake, inadvertence, surprise, or excusable neglect.' I can easily argue that a mistake was made in not offering Jocelyn an attorney. I think this will do it, Wayne, I really do, but there's also a number six, which reads, 'any other reason that justifies relief.' I will add her lung cancer diagnosis to buttress my argument as number six on the form. I'm really optimistic about this."

"Ah." In Wayne's mind the ceiling of his apartment opened up to the night sky. For a moment, he could see the stars. After seconds of stars filling his mind, he realized Enid was still talking.

"I'm going to fill out the form tonight and submit it tomorrow. If granted, this will be quick, Wayne. If everything works, my guess is she'll be released by the middle of February. I've only handled one other appeal for the Women's Clemency Relief Project, but I should have known about this. I was just flailing around looking for some loophole and on a whim, I called my old law school professor. He told me that the federal government passed the Prisoner Litigation Reform Act, which shut down a lot of opportunities for filing appeals for prisoners. In Michigan, felons are only allowed one six-oh-five, but Jocelyn's never had one, so this just might work."

Warmth radiated through Wayne's body. His heart was racing, drumming in his chest. He was flooded with adrenaline. He revisited all the steps leading to this moment and felt an immense gratitude for Enid Lawton who knew enough to get help when she needed it. His eyes blinked back sudden tears.

"Wayne, did you hear me?"

"I sure did, Enid. I sure did," he managed to say. "Let me know, will you? Call me day or night."

"I'll email you a copy of the form so you can see everyone who has to sign it."

"Sleep well, Counselor," Wayne said. There was a grin on his face that could not be contained. He would probably never be able to bury his little brother or get Aarne posthumously convicted of his murder, but Enid Lawton might just have set Wayne Nichols' soul free.

Chapter Thirty-Five

———

January 27th
Mae December

B EFORE GOING TO bed the night before, Mae had gotten a
very interesting phone call from her young employee, Ray
Fenton. She had asked Ray to help her figure out what Web
Johnson planned to do with Jerrod Clifton's dogs. Apparently
young Ray had been asking around. He gave her a name—
Travis Pritchett.

"I can't say who told me about him. It's someone at my
school." Ray's voice was quiet, almost whispering on the phone.
"If you go looking for him you better be careful, Miss Mae. I
heard he runs a dog fight and makes moonshine. Maybe that's
who Web was selling Mr. Jerrod's dogs to."

"Do you have any idea where this is going on?" Mae asked.

Ray gave her specific instructions, which she wrote down
with care. "Please don't tell anyone you heard this from me,
though," he said. "Travis Pritchett's a bad man. I don't want
him coming after me or my mom."

She promised to keep his name out of it and to talk to Ben
before she did anything else, thanked Ray, and ended the call.

* * *

ON THE BRIGHT, cold morning of January 27th, she performed her round of dog-related chores in a distracted state. After her second cup of coffee, she tried Ben on his cell, but he didn't answer. She called the office and reached Dory.

"Sheriff's office, Investigator Dory Clarkson speaking."

"Dory, he reinstated you? That's great, congratulations!"

"He did. How are you today, Mae? Arm feeling better?"

"It's okay," Mae replied. "Just itchy under this cast, but I'm getting my energy back. Listen, I was trying to reach Ben on his cell. Did he leave already?"

There was a slight pause. "It's okay," Mae said. "I know about Anthony. His girlfriend came to my house to try and get the puppies for an experiment he was doing. And I went to the vet school with Ben and Rob, so you don't have to be discreet with me."

Dory confirmed that Ben, Wayne, and Detective Fuller were on their way to Benton. "Cell service is terrible out that way. If it's an emergency I can try them on the police radio. Do you want me to call them on the radio?"

"Oh, no. Don't do that." Mae thought for a moment. "Remember how Ben asked for my help on the puppy mill case?"

"Um hum," Dory murmured.

"Well, he also asked me to look into what Web Johnston might have been doing with all those dogs, since we know he wasn't selling them to the vet school, at least not at the time Jerrod said to close down the puppy mill."

"Right." Dory sounded more alert now. "You found something, didn't you?"

"I did, but I can't tell you who told me. I got a lead on a guy who may be running a dog-fighting ring. And making moonshine ... but that's beside the point, at least as far as I'm concerned. I have a name and directions to the place. It's way out in the southwest corner of the county." Mae stopped talking before she said too much.

"You aren't thinking about going out there by yourself, are you? Somebody like that probably has some kind of security, especially for a moonshine still. The ATF could be after them at any time. If it's a big operation, they've got guns. Promise me you won't go alone."

Mae sighed. "I was thinking about going to have a look around. I'm not very threatening, you know. And I couldn't care less about someone making 'shine. But dog fighting ...." She swallowed and took a deep breath. "It's disgusting. Do you know that they'd use a sweet little puppy like True as bait to get the fighters riled up?"

"That's horrible," Dory said. "But if I let you go there by yourself and something happens to you, your mother will never forgive me."

"I know. She and Daddy are so protective. Mama's still mad at me for agreeing to host Tammy's wedding with a broken wrist." Mae gave a little laugh. "She saw my interview with Carrie Adams and that's how she found out. But Ben did ask me to look into this. He can't be mad if I do."

"Not at you, maybe. But believe me, he wouldn't want you doing this alone, and he'll be plenty mad at me if I let you. Do you want to go with George or Cam?"

Mae was surprised by the question. "Not you? Now that you're back to being an investigator, can't you go with me?"

"Honey, one of the deputies needs to go with you. They're armed and I'm not." Dory lowered her voice. "Just between you and me, Cam would be my first choice. George might shoot you by accident."

"All right." Mae capitulated. "Let me talk to her."

DEPUTY CAM GOMEZ agreed to come to Mae's house and then follow her out to Travis Pritchett's. She had also, after consulting with Dory, reluctantly agreed that Mae could go to the door alone. "I'll give you ten minutes in there. If you're not back out by then I'm coming in. We don't want to spook anyone with the patrol car or my uniform, but Dory's right. Anybody with a still probably has guns around." She looked Mae over with a smile. "At least they won't think you're law enforcement. And the cast makes you look harmless. You could get in and out without a problem."

The two young women decided that Cam would park the patrol car at the small convenience store near Travis Pritchett's place, get in the back seat of Mae's Explorer and stay out of sight when Mae went to the door.

"What reason will you give for being there?" Cam asked from the back seat. When Mae looked in her rearview mirror, a little frown disturbed the smoothness of Cam's forehead.

"I think I'll just say I'm lost and my cellphone died. Maybe ask for directions or to use their phone."

Cam smiled in the mirror. "That works. And speaking of your cellphone, let me have it for a second. I'll call my phone from yours and we can put yours on speaker. Put yours in your coat pocket and I'll be able to hear what's going on when you're inside."

Mae glanced at Cam in the mirror once more. "Good idea. Hang on a minute and I'll pull over and get it out of my purse. I've gotten pretty good at one-handed driving, but hands-free is another story."

She pulled onto the side of the narrow, twisting lane and pulled the phone out of her purse. Mae handed it to Cam and gave her the code to unlock it. Cam quickly punched in the code and called her own phone, looking down in concentration. Mae watched her accept the call and put Mae's phone on speaker.

"There." She handed the phone to Mae, who carefully placed it in the front pocket of her red winter coat. Cam nodded her dark head in approval. "It's like you're wearing a wire."

Mae pulled back onto the road and drove through a grove of

cedar trees and down a hill. She glanced at the directions taped to her console. "You better lie down," she said. "We're almost there. And since you can hear me, can you wait longer than ten minutes?"

Cam disappeared from the rearview mirror. "Okay, how about this? You say 'It's snowing again' if you need my help."

THE MAN WHO answered the door had to weigh 300 pounds. He wore a blue and gray flannel shirt, overalls, and a greasy Braves ball cap on his stringy dark hair. When Mae looked in his pale, almost colorless eyes, she felt a twinge of fear.

"What'dya want?" The man spoke around a wad of chewing tobacco inside his lower lip. He gave Mae a slow, unsmiling inspection from her boots up to her face.

"I'm lost. And my cellphone died. Do you have a phone I could use?"

The huge man continued to stand so the bulk of his body blocked any view of the room. "I figured you was lost," he said, and spat into a plastic cup he held in his meaty hand. "Travis," he called over his shoulder. "Got a pretty lil' gal here. Don't nobody know where she is." He gave Mae a mean grin, showing a brown and crooked set of teeth.

"Let her in, Parnell." Mae heard another male voice from behind the oversized man. "It's cold out there."

Parnell stepped aside and Mae squeezed past him, trying not to breathe through her nose. Apparently Parnell was not a frequent taker of showers. It was a little too warm inside the house, and dimly lit. There was a woodstove in the corner and the window blinds were all down except for one.

"Need a drink?" Parnell indicated a half-empty bottle of Bud on the stained side table.

"Uh, no thanks," Mae said, taking in the squalor of dirty plates and empty cans and bottles. Now that she was there, she wasn't sure how to buy time.

"We don't get many visitors out here, do we, Parnell?"

The huge man laughed, wheezing and shaking his belly. "Not in the daytime we don't. Should I let 'er use the phone?"

Parnell was standing between her and the door. Travis, a smaller version of Parnell, shook his head. "I am lost." Mae gave him a pleading look. "Please, can I just use your phone?"

He put the footrest of the recliner down and got to his feet. "No. Phone lines are still down."

"Are there any gas stations in the area? If you could just direct me there—"

"Not much in this area, and that's a fact. Where did you say you were on the way to?"

"Rosedale."

"From where? Maybe you need to get one of them there GPS things."

Mae looked past him out the window into the backyard and saw dogs in stacked up cages around the muddy, trampled ground. She saw Cam dart around the side of a dilapidated shed.

"You really lost, or just nosy?" Travis walked over to stand right in front of Mae, who froze. He stared into Mae's eyes. "What are you really up to?"

She swallowed, willing herself not to show fear. "I'm just trying to get to Rosedale," she said loudly. "I got turned around on these winding roads and then I noticed that it's snowing again."

"Doesn't look like it's snowing to me," the man said. She turned away to avoid his foul breath.

Mae heard a loud knock at the door.

"Open up, police!"

"Grab her," Travis said to Parnell in a low, urgent voice. "Take her in the other room."

More banging on the door was followed by a raised male voice. "Open the door right now, Pritchett, or we're breaking it down."

She heard Travis saying, "Hang on, I'm coming," before

Parnell grabbed her hair and pulled her into a small bedroom. He closed and locked the door and swiveled his huge bulk to look at her.

"My friends are out there," Mae told him. "You better let me go."

The hulking man looked her up and down. "You better keep quiet or you and me're gonna have a little fun before your friends can save you." He reached toward her as she backed away, fighting down a surge of nausea.

"You sure are pretty." He trapped her against the wall and put his mouth next to her ear. Mae wriggled, frantically trying to escape his grasp. "That's good," Parnell's voice roughened. "You're lively too."

There was a crash and the bedroom door caved in, falling in splinters at the feet of a man in a Nashville police uniform. Parnell stepped away from her and Mae could breathe again. Cam came in on the heels of the officer, who was busy reading Parnell his rights.

"I'm sorry, Mae." Cam gave her a concerned look. "He shouldn't have had time to grab you. Are you hurt?"

"No, I'm fine." Her heart was pounding, but she was okay, she realized. "And don't apologize. I've never been gladder to see someone in my life than you and …." She trailed off, watching with interest as yet another Nashville officer helped the first man cuff Parnell and remove him from the room.

"That's Billy Cornell." Cam smiled. "He's a friend of mine— works narcotics in Nashville. His partner's Sam Baxter. I'm sorry I called in the cavalry. I was a little worried when you suggested we take on this mission by ourselves and alerted Billy and Sam earlier that there might be trouble. They said they'd be glad to drive this way on the chance that something went wrong. I found evidence of dog fighting and a still back there right away. Then I found a huge stash of marijuana. I was on the car radio when I heard your signal, which is why they could move in so quickly. I'm just glad that guy didn't hurt you."

"He didn't." Mae gave an involuntary shiver. "He was going to, though. I'd like to go home now and take a shower."

Chapter Thirty-Six

January 27th
Detective Wayne Nichols

WAYNE GOT TO the office still feeling cheered by the news Attorney Lawton had given him the night before. Not even Ben's text saying he needed to wear a suit and tie today brought down his spirits. He arrived to a chorus of congratulations for Dory, Cam, and George, who had located and brought in the auctioneer, Junior Barnes. He had been stealing architectural elements from homes in the area—a lucrative scam. All Barnes had to do was remove any identifying marks, distress or repaint and sell the item at one of his auctions. Logan Yancey's fireplace surround, clearly marked on the back as his property, was in Ben's office with a big red bow on it. Wayne chimed in with his own congratulations.

"We're going on a field trip this morning," Ben told the group. "I have the contact information for Anthony Puglisi's parents. They live in Benton, that's down in Polk County in the southeast corner of the state. It's about a three and a half hour drive. Wayne and Rob are going with me on this one." He asked George to bring the car around. While they were waiting, Ben turned to Wayne, saying, "You look different today. What's up?"

"Counselor Lawton has a strategy that could work for my foster mother's release. We'll know in a couple of days."

"That's great, man. Really great. Let's get Rob and go."

Wayne was wearing a new navy suit, a white shirt, and a striped tie. He had purchased several pieces of clothing recently, because none of his old things fit anymore. Rob met them in the front office, also wearing a suit and tie. It looked much more expensive than Wayne's. It was standard when a suspect in a serious crime might be arrested to dress the part. Deputies wore uniforms, but detectives were expected to look professional.

Cam came into reception and stood by Dory's desk to see them off. George left the sheriff's car running outside and came back into the office, shivering a bit from the cold.

"Any instructions while you're gone, Sheriff?" Cam asked.

"George, you're on prisoner duty today. If anyone has a visitor, have them meet with family members in interrogation, rather than in the jail cells. You may wear your sidearm," Ben said.

George made no attempt to disguise his amazed pleasure. "Thank you, Sheriff."

"He doesn't mean you can *use* it," Dory said. "Just carry it."

"Cam, I'd like you to write a report on the arrest last night, and you can respond to any routine complaints that come in."

"What about me, boss?" Dory asked.

"I'd like you to hold down the fort, Investigator Clarkson," the sheriff said with a smile that crinkled the corners of his eyes.

"I believe I can do that," Investigator Dory Clarkson replied. "Thank you, sir."

"And Dory?"

"Yes."

"Don't ever go off on your own like that again. I appreciate that you had good information and needed to act quickly, but there's no excuse for not notifying me in advance. Given the result, I'll let it pass this time, but I can't have any rogue investigators on my force. Understood?"

"Yes, sir," she said, looking at the floor.

THREE HOURS LATER, Rob drove the patrol car across the Polk County line. The town of Benton was situated at the confluence of the Ocoee and Hiwassee Rivers just at the base of the Unicoi Mountains. Wayne had looked up the population and details about local law enforcement on his iPhone. The small town of just over a thousand people had a sheriff's department that they would contact as a matter of courtesy. As is usual, the sheriff's office was responsible for keeping the peace in all of Polk County, not just the village of Benton. Wayne was surprised to see that it was a bigger operation than their own. Sheriff Jeremy Davis was assisted by two detectives and several deputies. In addition, they had a drug unit.

Ben punched the speaker button on his phone so Wayne and Rob could hear the conversation with the local lawman.

"Hello, Sheriff Davis? This is Ben Bradley, Sheriff of Rose County in Tennessee. We're here in Benton looking for Anthony Puglisi. We want to talk to him in connection with a murder in Rose County."

"What can I help you with, Sheriff?" Davis asked. Wayne had looked Sheriff Davis up on his iPhone and handed it to Ben. They saw a picture of a good-looking fifty-something man with white blond hair and a pleasant smile.

"We need to talk to Anthony, but since this is such a small town, I thought you might ask him to come into your office. We could meet you there."

"Certainly, I'll send Lewis to pick him up. Anything I should tell him?"

"No, let's keep this very low key. I'm sure you know him and his parents?"

"Yes, Mr. and Mrs. Puglisi have two married daughters in addition to Anthony. They're a fine family. Mr. Puglisi manages the Family Dollar grocery store. Mrs. Puglisi is head of the community library in town. With you coming all this way, I hope it doesn't mean Anthony's a suspect in this killing. We're all proud of Anthony. Very few of the local kids here even go on to college, so it's rare to have one of ours go on to graduate school."

Wayne met Ben's gaze. This arrest was going to be very hard on this community and the Puglisi family. Today's emotional toll would be high.

"We'll be at your office in about a half an hour," Ben said and punched the off button.

"How do you want to handle the interrogation, Sheriff?"

"Wayne, I'd like you to take the lead. Rob, I want you in the room, but only to observe."

THEY PULLED INTO the parking lot of the Polk County Courthouse half an hour later. It was a large granite building with square columns. The weather had deteriorated and the wind was sharp as the three men stepped out of the car. The sheriff's office was in the basement of the building. They walked in, stamped off the cold, and told the receptionist why they were there. She buzzed Sheriff Davis, who came out to shake hands with the men.

"I put Anthony in the conference room. His father wanted to come with him, and Lewis didn't see a way to politely refuse."

"Okay, thanks for bringing him in, Sheriff," Ben said and they walked down the hall. Opening the door to the conference room, Wayne saw Puglisi's father, a man of about fifty with thinning hair and a pleasant expression, sitting with his son. Anthony was a good-looking guy with dark, curly hair and brown eyes. Both men stood up when Sheriff Davis opened the door. After the introductions and offers of coffee, which were declined, Sheriff Davis left the room.

Wayne glanced at Mr. Puglisi senior with deep compassion, knowing that for the rest of his life, the memory of three lawmen in dark suits would haunt his waking days and shred his nights. They were about to destroy this man's life.

"We're here in connection with the death in Rose County of Web Johnston," Wayne said, keeping a sharp eye on Anthony. "He was stabbed to death on property belonging to Jerrod Clifton during the first week in January. His body was found in the Little Harpeth River on January seventh. We know that Mr. Johnston was the person who supplied the puppies for your PhD studies. The pups came from Jerrod Clifton's puppy mill. Clifton had decided to terminate the breeding program and gave Mr. Johnston instructions to sell or otherwise dispose of the dogs. We're talking to you today because we suspect you of Web Johnston's murder."

Anthony Puglisi placed his right hand over his left, but not before Wayne saw the deep cut on his index finger. *That's a defensive wound.* Wayne and Ben exchanged a glance. "So you're a lefty," Wayne guessed, gesturing at the injured hand.

His eyes widened slightly. "I am," Anthony answered quietly.

"What was your relationship with Web Johnston?" Wayne watched Anthony lick his lips and swallow before he rallied and answered in a calm voice.

"It was like you said, Detective. Web Johnston supplied puppies to Dr. Weil's lab. There were several of us who used the pups in our studies. I was working on Acute Lymphoid Canine Leukemia. The disease originates in the bone marrow and proliferates rapidly to the spleen, liver, and bloodstream. Aggressive treatment is necessary to restore the growth of blood cells because this type of Leukemia actually compresses the bone marrow, leading rapidly to death." He sounded like a young professor already, proud to present his discovery. "I came up with a promising new treatment for the disease."

"Tell the detective what happened to the pups after they gave their blood," Anthony's father said. "He probably thinks they were sacrificed. My son would never do that."

"We found homes for the puppies or the Humane Society took them. None of them were killed or even traumatized by the transfusions. We gave them a shot to put them to sleep during the procedure and never took their blood more than once." Anthony gave them a lopsided smile. "I'm an animal lover."

"We're aware that you successfully defended your PhD dissertation on January third and left town to visit your parents late that day or the next," Wayne continued.

"That's right, Detective. I wanted my folks to know right away that I was finished. There was a big family party planned."

"Anthony's mom and I are very proud of our son, Detective." Mr. Puglisi senior straightened his shoulders and lifted his chin slightly. "This disease that Anthony found a cure for mostly attacks German Shepherds. The U.S. Department of Defense is interested in Anthony's work. The DOD often uses shepherds to do mine detection, drug discovery, etcetera. They don't want to lose their highly trained canine workforce."

"After you completed your PhD dissertation you didn't need any more puppies, is that right?" Ben asked. It was his first question.

There was a pause so brief that Wayne doubted anyone else caught it before Anthony shook his head. Wayne locked eyes briefly with the sheriff; they were about to catch this guy in a lie. Before Puglisi said anything else, Wayne continued.

"See, we were confused when Gretchen Wilkes, the lab manager for Dr. Weil, tried to take two puppies from their fostering facility. She said you'd asked her to get more puppies. If you were done, why did you need them?"

"Anthony?" Mr. Puglisi turned to his son. "Answer the detective." Anthony Puglisi didn't say anything and Wayne continued.

"We also spoke with your dissertation director and discovered something very interesting. He told us that you were a contender for an assistant professorship at the University of Connecticut, but they required an article based on your PhD research to be submitted to a peer reviewed Journal before tendering you a job offer."

"I didn't need any more dogs. Gretchen was mistaken," Puglisi insisted, but the color had drained from his face.

"Don't lie to me, Anthony," Wayne said quietly and saw the young man sag. Sweat was breaking out on his forehead. The detective continued calmly, as if he hadn't heard Puglisi's denial. "This is what we think happened. You needed a couple more pups to finish up the study for this journal article. You went out to Jerrod Clifton's place to get the last few you needed. You found Web Johnston out there. You probably tried to take the puppies. He wouldn't give them to you. Web stood to make more money from selling them to another source. He pulled a knife and you fought back. Was that how it was, Anthony? Did he attack you? Was it self-defense? It's going to go a lot easier for you if you tell us the truth."

"No, I wasn't there. It must have been somebody else." Anthony's voice was shaking.

"Why don't we stop this game now, Anthony?" Wayne stared at the young suspect. "You were there. We found the rag and the knife, you see. As a scientist, I'm sure you know all about DNA evidence."

Puglisi took a deep breath. Then he exhaled, straightening his shoulders.

Through the years, Wayne had seen this happen more times than he could count. People reached a point, a brink beyond which they would not step. It always began with an obvious lie that was caught and shrugged off by the suspect. Depending on the character of the person, the struggle to surrender would be fast or slow. Anthony Puglisi was a middle class kid without a blot on his record. He would not be able to hold out much longer.

"Tell us what happened. Was Web about to destroy your

future?" Wayne asked quietly. The silence seemed to suck all the oxygen out of the room.

"Web was going to sell all the dogs to a man who runs a dog-fighting operation, even the puppies!" he exclaimed. "He said this guy would use the puppies as bait for the fighting dogs. I couldn't let him do that, so I grabbed him and …. Web never should have come after me with that knife." Anthony didn't sound angry now. All Wayne heard in his voice was defeat. "My research was going to do so much to help those dogs, but he said this other guy was giving him more money and I couldn't even take the puppies." His eyes were bright with unshed tears. Anthony's father's face drooped, aging twenty years in front of Wayne's eyes.

Wayne nodded to Ben. It was almost like a choreographed dance now. All of them, including the murder suspect, knew their roles.

"Please stand up, Mr. Puglisi," Rob said, gently. He cuffed the young man's hands behind his back. Rob's face was nearly as white as Puglisi's and Wayne realized they were almost the same age. This was going to be a hard one for Detective Rob Fuller. At the sound of the metallic click, Mr. Puglisi senior fell forward against the conference table and gave a low moan.

Ben shook his head before saying, "You have the right to remain silent …."

Chapter Thirty-Seven

———

February 10th
Detective Wayne Nichols

IT HAD BEEN nearly two weeks since the arrest and subsequent arraignment of Anthony Puglisi for the murder of Web Johnston. Mr. and Mrs. Puglisi had engaged a top-notch attorney for their son, but the DA told Sheriff Bradley that they had Anthony dead to rights. Although his self-defense plea would mitigate the length of his sentence, he would definitely serve time. Wayne felt a combination of satisfaction with the arrest and sadness over the young man's ruined future. The big case had been solved. Cam Gomez and Mae had uncovered a dog-fighting operation in the far corner of the county on the same day as Anthony's arrest. After that, the sheriff's office had gradually returned to the slow pace that was normal in Rosedale, Tennessee.

Wayne always felt at loose ends during down times. He loved the hunt for the killer and even more passionately sought the truth of what had led the perpetrator to kill. To pass the time, he wrote reports on his old cases, cleaned his desk of paperwork, helped out over in Mont Blanc, and spoke on the phone with his CIs and Enid Lawton. Enid either called or texted each day as the Form 6.05 crept its way through the bureaucracy of state offices receiving one after another of the signatures needed to set Jocelyn Outinen free.

He was awake early the morning of February tenth and heard the phone ring just as he stepped out of the shower.

"Nichols," he said, wrapping a towel around his waist and grabbing his phone from the bathroom countertop.

"Only one signature still to go, Wayne." Enid's voice practically crackled with excitement. "This is the biggie. Yesterday the Form six-oh-five reached the final office needed for approval. The administrator's in town and I have an appointment to see him today. I'm so close, I can taste it."

"You are a wonder." There was a lift in his voice. "If this last person signs the form, when will Jocelyn be released?"

"On or about February fourteenth, Valentine's Day. Once the paperwork is done, these people don't screw around. They'll just open the door and out she'll go. I'm only an hour and a half away, and they've promised to call me when the final signature is inked. I will be there with the parka, mittens, and boots you bought. It's still brutally cold here and the prison is miles from the bus stop in Ypsilanti. I'll drive her there. I talked with Jocelyn a few days ago and she wants to take a bus to Escanaba."

"The bus! Enid, no. I'll drive up. I want to take her home," Wayne insisted.

"I've already told her you would, but remember how sick she is, Wayne. After all those years in prison, and the chemo treatments, she wants some time without having to talk to anyone. She told me she needs to look outside while the bus drives north all the way through the mitten of the Lower Peninsula and across the frozen straits at the Mackinaw Bridge into the Upper Peninsula. She wants to see all of it—deep in snow. She says the snow will make her clean again."

"Please ask her once more. I want to do this for her. Tell her she can be quiet with me."

"Give the woman some time, Wayne. She needs room to breathe. It's a long bus ride, and she wants to look out the window and rest. She told me she feels like she hasn't really slept in thirty-five years. However, Jocelyn does want you to come to the Potawatomi Reservation. It's in Hannahville, in the UP. She has a cousin there named Bourcier who'll take care of her."

"I want you to hire a nurse to ride on the bus with her in case she needs medical attention."

"Will do. Fingers crossed," Enid was gone.

Wayne checked his phone for messages every hour. Driving home that evening, he finally saw Enid Lawton's number on his screen. He pushed the button but his sweaty finger slipped off the key. He tried again and heard Enid's triumphant voice.

"We won. We actually won! I know I sound like I just wrote the slogan for the Governor's re-election campaign but he went against his law and order stance and agreed that Joci should be released. I'm going to read you the first paragraph of the article that *yours truly* will be contributing to the local newspaper.

" 'In a profoundly moral move that transcended race, culture, and gender, the Governor of Michigan today stunned his liberal opponents by agreeing to release a woman from prison who served over thirty-five years of a life sentence for the death of her husband who abused her and killed her son. The Native American woman, who is dying of lung cancer, thanked the Abused Women's Commutation Project that does all its work on a shoestring budget. The legal work for the former prisoner was contributed *pro bono* by Attorney Enid Lawton.' "

"Enid, I can never thank you enough." Wayne's voice broke. "I'll call you soon."

He dropped the phone and pulled his truck over to the side of the road. Putting his head down on the steering wheel, he sobbed in relief. His shoulders shook and his body was racked with tears that poured from deep inside him. He took deep breaths, gulping at the air. His hand held the gear shift so tightly, the blood left his fingers. Then suddenly it was over. He felt a happiness so intense it seemed to radiate from deep in his chest to encompass every person who signed Jocelyn's release papers as well as sturdy little bull-headed Enid Lawton, who just didn't give up. It took a long time before he thought his voice would be steady enough to call Lucy. He picked up his phone and dialed the number that paged Lucy on duty at the hospital. He pulled out onto the road once more. Fifteen minutes later she called him back.

"This is Dr. Ingram." She used her professional voice. "I got a page from this number."

"Dr. Ingram," Wayne drawled, "this is Detective Nichols calling to invite you to go with him on a little trip."

"Are we going to an uninhabited island in the Caribbean where we can lie on the sand naked?" Lucy asked, rich amusement in her voice.

"No, we're going to drive twelve hours north into the Polar Vortex." There was a pause.

"My God, she's free! You actually got her released."

Wayne felt a shiver run down his spine.

"She's asked me to come to the reservation. Can you check to see if you could get a few days off?"

"I will, on one condition, Detective."

"Name it."

"Next time we take a trip in one of the coldest winters on record, we go south, not north," she laughed.

"You got it," Wayne said, happy that Lucy was already planning another trip with him. "I hope you'll like Jocelyn," he said. "You may not find her easy. She's bitter sometimes but she's the only mother I have."

"She has a right to be bitter. And I want to know her. She's your mother. Any mother is better than not having one. My mother died in awful circumstances when I was just a kid."

"We should talk about that sometime," Wayne said, but Lucy was already gone.

LUCY DIDN'T FINISH her shift until eleven that night. They left Rosedale at midnight and reached the southern border of Michigan as the sun was rising. They found a hotel and slept a few hours. Wayne roused Lucy around eight. He was pushing hard to be sure he would be in Hannahville before Jocelyn arrived.

"What's Jocelyn's tribal affiliation?" Lucy asked when they were on the road.

"She's Potawatomi. When I was young she told me a bit of their history. The tribe refused to leave Michigan during the Great Indian Removal in 1834. A brave man named Peter Marksman, a pastor of the Methodist church at the time, found some land for them and assisted the people in moving there. Peter's young wife was named Hannah, and in gratitude the people named their village after her. Hannahville was formally designated Potawatomi land in 1870."

Despite the icy conditions on the roads, they crossed the Mackinaw Bridge in early afternoon. As far as they could see looking east toward Lake Huron and west to Lake Michigan, the water was frozen hard. Only directly beneath the bridge in the cobalt blue waters of the straits did they see crashing waves. They turned west toward Escanaba, the city on the edge of the Bay de Noc, and followed the road signs to Hannahville.

Reaching the tiny reservation town, Wayne stopped the car to ask one old man wearing a heavy parka for the house where Jocelyn's cousin lived. He pointed down the small gravel road to the right.

"Third house," he said.

They knocked on the door of a little white ranch with sagging front steps and peeling paint. An old car stood on cement blocks in the yard. An overflowing trash bin sat beside the front door. Wayne knew that in the old days, the Potawatomi built their houses out of tree branches that were supple enough to be tied in arches and filled in the open spaces with reeds. Wayne found himself thinking the snug natural domes were far superior to how the tribe lived currently. Clearly this band didn't have a casino; the miasma of poverty hung over the settlement.

They had reached the address of Waseta Bourcier, one of two women who had initially contacted the authorities to report Jocelyn missing. The woman's French last name told Nichols she probably had a French father or grandfather and would be considered a *metis*, a half breed. A young girl answered the door, and her dark blade of hair and arrogant tilt of the head brought to mind Tiani, the stunning Native American girl who had betrayed his trust as a teenager.

"We're looking for Waseta Bourcier," he said.

Looking over her shoulder, the girl called out, "*Koye*."

Her voice was high and clear. Wayne wondered if the word was a woman's name or a perhaps the word "aunt" or "elder." Wayne hadn't been taken into foster care until he was six. Some Potawatomi words had stayed in his memory, but he didn't know the word *koye*'.

A tall woman with thin, angular cheeks and black hair streaked with silver appeared in the doorway. Her eyes were dark and shiny. She wore long, silver and turquoise earrings.

"*Bozho Nikan*," he said. The words meant, *hello, friend.* Switching to English he said, "I am Joci Kemerovo's foster son, Wayne Nighthawk Nichols. This is Lucy Ingram. I thank you for taking Joci in. She will arrive soon."

The woman turned away from the door and held it open. She gestured for them to come in. They entered and she pointed to a broken-down brown couch. Despite the obvious poverty in which the women lived, Wayne felt comfortable in their home. He had few memories from the days before foster care, but this place was familiar. They had a pot-bellied stove, and a small window in the black iron door was golden red from the fire inside.

When a tiny elf of a woman stepped off the Greyhound bus in late afternoon, Wayne Nichols and Lucy Ingram were standing bundled up on the porch of a general store in Hannahville. A large group of Potawatomi well-wishers were waiting— laughing, crying, and shouting. Some held small flags; others were in full Native American dress. The sound of the Native drums rang in the frozen air. Joci looked bewildered when she exited the bus. The nurse who had ridden with her hugged her gently and wished her good luck before getting back on the bus. Wayne and Lucy came forward and took her by the hands.

AFTER AN EVENING meal of baked beans, beef stew, and cornbread—served to the din of excited conversation in the crowded home of Waseta Bourcier—Jocelyn asked Wayne to help her into bed. She was white with exhaustion. He supported her into the bedroom, pulled down the coverlet and lifted her into bed. She sighed and closed her eyes. Just as Wayne was about to leave, she said, "Stay."

Wayne pulled a chair up beside her bed and waited. Joci's eyes were still closed. This moment wouldn't come again. They were alone together, maybe for the last time. He needed to ask for her forgiveness. He spoke softly.

"Little mother, I feel such deep remorse for leaving you so long ago. I should have saved you. The weight of the abuse you suffered and the horror of Kurt's death lie on my shoulders. I am so terribly sorry I left." He waited. For a long time she didn't speak and Wayne wondered if she was sleeping, if she had even heard his plea for forgiveness.

"We are blood," she whispered, so quietly that Wayne hardly heard.

"No, we are not. I was only your foster child." Wayne heard the self-pity in his voice and blinked away tears.

"You are the son of my brother, Wabaunsee. There was a

half-white, half-Odawa girl, her last name was Nichols. He got her pregnant. She left to follow the Jesus road and brought you to your father. When you were six, he enlisted in the army and asked me to keep you. He died long ago, fighting in a white man's war. You remind me of him."

"You waited a long time to tell me this," Wayne murmured. It was a gift, knowing his origins.

"Wanted to be sure you deserved to know," she said, with a little quirk of her mouth. "One more thing, son of my brother. Bury Kurt in the cemetery of our people. Put a headstone on his grave. I would not have him forgotten."

WAYNE AND LUCY left Hannahville the next morning. He had lain awake all night thinking about how to honor his aunt's wish. When the old bedsprings creaked as Lucy slipped out of bed, he knew what he could do. It wasn't everything he wanted to do, but it would suffice. Wayne and Lucy kissed Jocelyn goodbye, thanked Waseta for her hospitality, and said they would come again in the spring. Then they drove to the town's grave office. It was a small stone building across the street from a large cemetery. They walked in and rang a bell at the front desk.

"Can I help you?" a cheerful, heavyset woman with ringlet curls asked when she emerged from the back. Her name tag read Constance.

"I want to order a gravestone," Wayne said.

"Is the stone for an adult or a child?" she asked. She was smiling. Wayne found her cheerfulness disconcerting, out of place.

"A boy," he said. "He was fourteen when he died."

"Oh, that's too bad," she said. Her eyes were kind. "Take a look at this book. There are a lot of designs to choose from." She handed him a three-ring binder with laminated pages showing the available headstones, designs artfully carved in their granite surfaces.

Wayne took his time, at last settling on one of a cluster of pine trees near a stream. He glanced at Lucy, who nodded. "I'll take this one," he said.

"That will be seven hundred and fifty dollars," Constance said. "It'll take about six weeks to carve. Make the check out to Heather Moon. She does the carvings for the stones. Write down the boy's full name and his date of birth and death on the form. Where do you want the stone sent?"

"Is there a cemetery for the Potawatomi tribe?" he asked.

"Certainly. It's on Maple Street, just behind the school. If you want the boy buried there, you'll need to buy a cemetery plot. That will be five hundred dollars. That check needs to be made out to Citizen Potawatomi Bank. "

Wayne pulled his checkbook out of his coat and wrote out the two amounts. He gazed at the woman who had managed to find pleasure in her grisly job. She looked at him questioningly as if to ask him something else, but he was almost done here. Already he felt distanced from this place. Something about the final steps in this process felt inevitable, as if he walked in footprints made by ancestors many decades earlier.

"Where's the body now?" Constance asked.

"It's not really a body anymore. He's been dead for thirty-plus years. There's only bones." Wayne cleared his throat and looked away. "I don't know if any of his remains can be located, but I want to do this anyway. If any trace of him can be recovered, I will have the remains sent here."

"That's fine. Do you want him cremated?"

"No," Wayne said, stirred by a fierce insistence. His little brother had been violated enough. He would not consign what little was left of him to the fires.

"Besides his name and dates, what message do you want to have carved on his stone?"

Wayne thought for a moment, remembering his shame at his own cowardice in abandoning his brother.

"His was the valor of the lion," Wayne said. He looked

down at the floor, afraid Constance or Lucy might see his eyes watering. His dauntless little brother had stayed to face Aarne Outinen and had paid the ultimate price.

"That's lovely," Constance said and held out her hand, but Wayne didn't take it. He wanted no more contact with attendants of the dead. She withdrew her hand and said with a pleasant smile, "Will you be here for a funeral?"

"No, I'm finished here." He turned around, reached for Lucy's hand and walked back to his truck. In his mind he was already miles away. It began to snow, and the pure white wind of the North Country stirred his soul. They drove east and then turned south toward the Mackinaw Bridge. Holding Lucy's hand in the warm truck, driving in snow so fine it was almost mist, Wayne felt absolved, innocent and free.

Chapter Thirty-Eight

—

February 14th
Mae December

SNOW WAS ONCE more falling in Rosedale, Tennessee, on the afternoon of Valentine's Day. Tammy was fretting, worried that the roads would be too bad and her wedding guests wouldn't show.

"Don't worry," Mae reassured her best friend again. "Everything's going to be perfect. And think how amazing your pictures will be in the snow!"

"If your dad can even get up your driveway to take them," Tammy muttered.

"He'll be here any minute. Mama called me and said they were done with the photos of the guys and they'd be here with Olivia by three to do our pictures. I hope Mrs. West gets here soon. Where's your mom?"

"Upstairs fussing with her hair, I'd guess," Tammy smiled. She looked around at Mae's transformed house. "At least they took your cast off in time, and they got the tent set up before the snow started."

Mae and Tammy had decided that Renee would perform

the ceremony in the living room, where rows of silver folding chairs formed an aisle. Ben and Patrick had moved the living room furniture out to the barn yesterday. This morning at eight the party rental company had set up the chairs for the ceremony as well as the huge white reception tent in Mae's front yard—complete with a stage for the band, a dance floor surrounded by small tables with red and pink linens, and more silver chairs. They'd also brought several large space heaters for the tent, as well as dishes and glassware for the caterer to use.

"I think Rhonda's outdone herself," Mae looked around at the abundant displays of flowers in shades of red, pink, and white. Tall branches spray-painted in white and silver formed a breathtaking tableau at the front of the room where Tammy and Patrick would take their vows.

"Yeah, she really came through for us. She said Valentine's Day is like the Super Bowl for florists, so I guess it's lucky she and my mom are such good friends. I think Rhonda must have been up all night working on this."

"She was here by eight-thirty this morning. As soon as the party rental guys were done setting up, she told me to get out of her way." Mae laughed. "She had a team of assistants and they decked this place out in no time. I love all the twinkly white lights they put up, too." Mae heard her parents and Olivia coming in the front door. "Go find your mom, Tammy. I'll get our bouquets and we can get these pictures done."

AT TEN O'CLOCK Mae and Ben were sitting at one of the little tables close to the dance floor. Ben had carried Matthew upstairs and put him to bed a few minutes ago, and July and Fred had taken their three kids home, but other than that the party was in full swing. Mae watched Tammy, radiant in her red gown, dancing with her new husband. Mae thought the vows, which they had written themselves, had been beautiful in their simplicity. The naked emotion on Patrick's face when he said "for now and forever, as long as I live, I'm yours," had been the ruination of Mae's mascara. And Tammy's reply of "Patrick, you may not be perfect, but you're perfect for me," had brought out the smiles and tears of everyone in the room.

"She looks so beautiful, doesn't she?" Mae turned toward Ben, who had removed his tuxedo jacket and bowtie and was leaning back in his chair.

"She does," Ben smiled. "It's too bad her flower girl and ring bearer stole the show."

Mae's niece, Olivia, had looked enchanting in her red dress with tiny white hearts embroidered around the neckline and a white silk sash. With her blonde hair in a French braid and huge blue eyes shining with excitement, she had indeed stolen the show. When she and Matthew, solemn as only a four-year-old could be in his tux, walked down the aisle, they were as adorable as anything Mae had ever seen.

"They did," Mae agreed. "July said they looked like a miniature version of us."

"You're wonderful." Ben's blue eyes darkened to navy as he stared at her. "I can't believe you did all this for Patrick and Tammy. You fostered those puppies and helped me solve another case while you planned this wedding. Not to mention busting a dog-fighting ring, an illegal still, and a marijuana farm … all with a broken wrist. And you're the most beautiful woman here, by the way." He stood up and waved at Jill Chapman, who nodded and turned to say something to her band members. They played the opening strains of "Miss December," the song Noah West had written right after he and Mae first met, but quickly segued into Eric Clapton's "Wonderful Tonight."

Ben took something from the pocket of the tuxedo jacket hanging on the back of his chair and walked around to her side of the table. He got down on one knee in front of Mae.

"I know we've been together less than a year, but I've never been more certain of anything." He opened his hand to show her a gold ring set with a glowing ruby. She held her breath.

"Mae December, I want to spend the rest of my life with you. Will you marry me?"

Everyone had stopped dancing and moved to stand in a half circle behind Ben. She looked from her mother's tearful face to her best friend's smile and her father's encouraging nod. The song faded away, and even Jill and her band were hanging on Mae's answer.

"Yes, I will," her voice rang out in the sudden silence. Ben slipped the ring on her finger with a broad smile. "As long as we can have a longer engagement than Tammy and Patrick did. I need a little time to recover before I start planning another wedding."

Ben got to his feet, holding out his hand. "Dance with me." The music started again and he held her close. As they swayed in time, he whispered in her ear, "We could elope. I know a judge who would marry us next weekend, if you'd like."

"I'm getting married in a church." Mae pulled away slightly, looking up into Ben's smiling face. He winked.

"Well, Mae December, I guess that means I am too."

Lyn Farquhar

Lisa Fitzsimmons

Lia Farrell is actually two people: the mother and daughter writing team of Lyn Farquhar and Lisa Fitzsimmons.

Lyn Farquhar taught herself to read when she was four years old and honed her storytelling abilities by reading to her little sister, Susan. Ultimately, her mother ended the reading sessions because Susan decided she preferred being read to rather than learning to read herself.

Lyn fell in love with library books when a Bookmobile came to her one-room rural school. The day the Bookmobile came, Lyn decided she would rather live in the bookmobile than at home and was only ousted following sustained efforts by her teacher and the bookmobile driver.

She graduated from Okemos High school and earned her undergraduate and graduate degrees from Michigan State University. She has a master's degree in English literature and a PhD in Education, but has always maintained that she remained a student for such a long time only because it gave her an excuse to read.

Lyn is a Professor of Medical Education at Michigan State University and has authored many journal articles, abstracts and research grants. Since her retirement from MSU to become a full-time writer, she has completed a young-adult fantasy trilogy called *Tales of the Skygrass Kingdom. Volumes I and II (Journey to Maidenstone and Songs of Skygrass).* Lyn has two daughters and six step children, nine granddaughters and three grandsons. She also has two extremely spoiled Welsh corgis. Her hobby is interior design and she claims she has the equivalent of a master's degree in Interior Design from watching way too many decorating shows.

Lisa Fitzsimmons grew up in Michigan and was always encouraged to read, write, and express herself artistically. She was read to frequently. Throughout her childhood and teenage years, she was seldom seen without a book in hand. After becoming a mom at a young age, she attended Michigan State University in a tri-emphasis program with concentrations in

Fine Art, Art History and Interior Design.

Lisa, with her husband and their two children, moved to North Carolina for three exciting years and then on to Tennessee, which she now calls home. She has enjoyed an eighteen-year career as a Muralist and Interior Designer in middle Tennessee, but has always been interested in writing. Almost five years ago, Lisa and her mom, Lyn, began working on a writing project inspired by local events. The Mae December Mystery series was born.

Lisa, her husband and their three dogs currently divide their time between beautiful Northern Michigan in the summertime and middle Tennessee the rest of the year. She and her husband feel blessed that their "empty nest" in Tennessee is just a short distance from their oldest, who has a beautiful family of her own. Their youngest child has settled in Northern Michigan, close to their cabin there. Life is good.

You can find Lyn and Lisa online at www.liafarrell.net.

CPSIA information can be obtained
at www.ICGtesting.com
Printed in the USA
BVHW031300010420
576583BV00001B/59

9 781603 819718